The Jewel of Veenah

Connie Peck

Dedication

This is dedicated to anyone who has ever been inspired by ordinary objects. The energy behind THE JEWEL OF VEENAH celebrates imagination no matter how wild, no matter how big, no matter how small. Be it fact or fiction, release your mind, throw wide the gates of your heart and let your muse teach the unbelievable.

And know, if it can be thought, it can be done.

Contents

Acknowledgments

This story would never have been conceived if it wasn't for my friend's flair – and her bling. Beautiful inside and out, Kathleen Ruth loves her jewelry. And one day, working hard in our critique group, her giant pearl ring spoke to me. Just like Elizabeth Gilbert's BIG MAGIC, this entire story flowed into my mind. It was like remembering a favorite movie that I'd watched a dozen times.

I sat down and wrote the outline as soon as I got home that day.

With the challenge of NaNoWriMo (National Novel Writers Month), I worked from my outline and pounded out the first, very rough, draft, way back in 2012. Then over the next four years I scratched and dug and pulled and prodded to revise the draft into something readable.

Finally, after the dedication of my critique group, Kathleen Ruth, and Shirley Amadore, the story began to make sense to someone other than myself.

And lastly, the most awesome online critique community ever, The Next Big Writer, helped me polish this to a sheen.

Thank you Lord Jesus Christ for providing, guiding, and giving me eternal life through your own sacrifice.

Thank you my darling patient husband who had to endure the endless hours of my absorption in this work.

Thank you one and all.

i

The Daughters of Veenah

A fem (female), having reached her fifteenth season, (three hands of five years) is considered old enough to form her own family, which is made up of five <u>fems</u> who live <u>together</u> in a femtog. This has been the way of the people as long as anyone remembers, because many fems cannot bear children, (they are sterile) and because so very few mems (males) are born in a village. Each member of a femtog has a skill to lend and in turn depends upon the rest of her family to help her run the household and raise the children. But not all fems can live together happily.

For this reason, the five fems who have chosen each other will go into the wilderness for the turning of the moon (one month) with nothing but each other, a long-knife which they forged by hand, and a woolen blanket. Everything else they must make – together – to prove that they can live and work together.

Mems in this society are, and have always been, born without arms and legs. No one remembers a time this wasn't so. He is honored and protected by his hearth sisters and mothers as a babe. Then, when his first tooth falls, he will go to the mem's lodge for training and is protected by a matron who is chosen to care for him. In the training lodge, he will learn the history and prophecies of his world until such time as he is chosen by a femtog.

When the five fems, now bond sisters, return from their quest in the wilderness, they will build a home, and eventually choose their husband. Often they must wait until a mem grows into adulthood. They will court him, showering him with gifts and even bringing meat to his family, until he consents to a union with them. Only after the uniting of the family, will the fems will be allowed to have physical contact with him. Then they will share the honor of carrying him.

It takes more than just love to unite a femtog. They must truly have trust and enjoy each other's company to share a home and a husband as well as their children.

Kia is the daughter of Trog. Her blood mother is Iva.

Stix and Kia have been best friends since birth. They always planned to become sisters.

Vee is Kia's hearth sister. She is a bit younger, but has been allowed to join the femtog anyway. She's always wanted to be sisters with Kia for life.

Song and Vee have been best friends since birth and always knew they'd become sisters.

Rok is older. She hasn't been courted because of her temper and her hearth mothers are 'scary'. Blood mother, Lona, Warrior leader, Aga.

Ch`e is the daughter of a family of healers, so she is also a healer.

Moon was born with physical deformities which nearly cost him his life at birth, but his mother Eve, Fem'ma couldn't return him to Veenah.

Stone from below
Light from above
Created by pain
Reflection of love

1 The Bonding

Kia stepped up to the precipice with her pledge sisters, two on either side of her. Her heart beat faster, pounding with the love she had for these fems.

As the day came to its end, Warmsun settled closer to the Forbidden Mountains that towered at the edge of the world. Shadows flowed across the badlands like honey on a cold day.

A sudden chill shot through Kia. She'd spent a night, sometimes two, in that rocky wilderness, but always in the company of her hearth mothers and other hunters. This time would be different. She would spend an entire mooncycle with only the help and protection of her soon-to-be bond sisters.

Could she do it?

A breeze rippled her stag-skin tunic. She shivered and glanced over her shoulder. *I should have worn my leggings.*

Huts, large and small, spread across the narrow valley behind her. The next time she saw this village, she and her new sisters would be given a place to build their own home. Would it be near the center, where the elders lived? Or at the far edge where the warriors stood guard? Maybe her home would stand closer to the cultivated fields where their food was grown. It all depended on the success of her quest. The elders would decide when the time came. She quivered in anticipation. No matter the area, Kia knew that love would live within the walls.

Her five hearth mothers stood near the front of the crowd, the place of honor. Iva, Kia's blood mother, carried her father, Syr Trog. Armless and legless, as all mems in the world were born, Syr Trog enjoyed riding in the arms of all of his wives, but this was a special occasion and he'd chosen her mother. He smiled broadly and nodded to her. One day, soon, Kia hoped, she and her sisters would choose their husband and she prayed they would all share the honor of carrying him.

The drums stopped. Everyone in the village pressed close to watch the first bonding ceremony in two seasons. The fever had taken so many fems and even some mems, and now they had hope. Kia felt their energy. Maybe this would be the season of the prophecy.

Kia didn't give much thought to the old legends, or what a mystical jewel had to do with fems bonding, though she'd listened to the stories of hope since childhood. No, this season would be just like any other, except she would be forever united with the fems she loved. Kia took a quick breath. Forever. Today, five would become one. Forever. Her head spun.

Why don't they hurry?

Three elderfems dressed in white, woven robes approached carrying their mems, the chiefs of the village. Following the elders came Loresinger, the spiritual leader, carried by his fem. His long red robe matched the one his elderfem wore and it brushed the stones of the pathway making him look as if walked. She thought it strange.

Mems have no legs. Why would Loresinger dress like that?

The priest sang the song of the prophecy. Kia tried to listen, but grew impatient. We all know the story.

Her face flushed. Such disrespectful thoughts could bring bad luck. But, so would looking at Warmsun as she traveled across Veenah, or watching Moonlight slip behind clouds to hide from Terah. It was also bad luck to look at a young mem, and she was doing that more and more these days.

And I haven't had any bad luck. I killed my biggest stag today. There is no luck or omens, only skill – and love.

"Kia, daughter of Trog." The priest's mousy voice nearly made her jump.

"I am here." Kia stepped forward.

"You have asked the council to approve your bonding. Do your pledges enter this union willingly and with love?"

"Yes, Loresinger." It was mostly true. Certainly, her best friend, Stix. She loved Stix with all her heart. And she loved Rok. But Rok loved no one and only consented to keep from being cast out because of her age and bad temper. Kia loved her hearth-sister Vee, but only because they grew up together. They mostly fought – about everything – except their plans to become bond sisters. And she loved Song, mostly because the tiny fem was beautiful – and because she was Vee's beloved.

"Pledges," the spiritual leader directed. "Form a circle and behold your sisters."

Kia faced the fems who would soon be part of her and the five of them entwined the fingers of their right hands. It felt right. She felt complete. And at the end of this trial they would stand here again and recite the bonding promise. Her eyes met Rok's and a shiver of happiness traveled up her spine. Yes, she loves me.

"The circle you have created has no beginning or end. It has no high points or low points, but the entire circle is equal and every point is exactly the same distance from the center. The circle simply goes on forever, equal and perfect in every way. From this day, you will be like this circle."

A lump formed in Kia's throat and tears of happiness tingled behind her eyes.

"Look to your hands, Daughters of Terah." The priest continued. Kia and her new sisters held their left hands toward the orange sky. Without looking, Kia knew that every fem of the village, save those who carried their precious mems, did the same. She, herself, had done this with every bonding ceremony she'd attended since she was a small child at her blood-mother's knee.

She tried to keep her eyes on her own hand, stretched toward Veenah, but her gaze followed the circle of fingers to her left and to her right. Five fems, ten hands, ten fingers each, the promise of an entire village. A tear fell down her cheek. She was ready to fulfil her destiny with the fems she loved most. She asked Veenah to bless this union.

The priest went on. "The fingers you see represent the perfect femtog. Five fems together. The perfect unit of Terians bound by blood and sinew, working together, helping each other, supporting each other. In your hands, you see a tall member. She is leader, but only if the rest follow. You see your first finger. She points the way and only finds

3

strength in unity. On the other side of your tall finger you find the member closest to your heart, but she only has love if she has sisters with whom she can share. And beside love stands beauty. She is not weak for she is the one who is able to close the hand and hold what is within. Finally, you see the powerful thumb. Without this member, the hand is clumsy, unable to work efficiently, but without the other fingers, the thumb is useless. Together, you are strong."

Kia trembled, smiling with joy, and listened to the Loresinger.

"Remember that each of you in a femtog is important, but dependent upon the others. And yet, you are not complete, you have no root or foundation without the palm. By this blessed symbol, we know our place and our family. One mem, five fems. When you prove to yourselves that you are indeed a unit truly bound and you have taken your place in the village, you will take unto yourselves your palm. Join hands with love and dedication. Go into the wild and learn to be a strong unit as the Prophecy has instructed."

The Loresinger again chanted the prophecy in a melody which belied his squeaky voice.

"Working together
The many unite
To search for the truth
And bring us the light.

Hand of the innocent,
Symbol of might,
Defender of honor,
Promise of life.

Light hidden by evil
Yearns for a hero.
Go! Take up your anvil
And banish our sorrow.

Jewel of the Covenant,
Gift of the soul,
Waiting in secret
Until life is made whole."

Now the village elder, wrapped in white leather, was lifted high by his elderfem. He proclaimed the quest in a rich voice. "Strive to fulfil the prophecy, daughters of Terah, search for this symbol of our freedom for one cycle of Moonlight. As you search you will work together as a single unit. You will support each other, depend on each other, and learn to love each other. When the time is fulfilled then you will return enlightened, and take to yourselves your palm, your husband, forever bound by love, blood, and sinew."

Kia tried to calm her breathing. Sure, she would strive – to lead her new family to safety in the wilderness. She would strive to keep them together and protect them from the Nightbird, Slither beast, and other predators. She would strive to fight off the Zid, rulers of Terah, giant reptiles who fed upon stray Terians, and dug deep into Terah with giant machines. Kia mouthed a prayer. Then she touched her fingers to the haft of her long-knife, safe in its sheath and strapped to her waist along with her woolen blanket.

Yes, I can do this.

The priest in his long, red robe continued. "Daughters of Terah do you pledge yourselves to be bonded?"

"We do," chorused the five fems. Kia felt the tremor in her hand blending with the surge of energy in the hands of her new sisters. As one, their fingers tightened, drawing them closer together.

"Repeat your vows," he commanded.

In chorus, Kia and her pledges said with boldness, "I pledge myself to you in love and loyalty."

Kia waited as her sisters spoke their life's promise. "I bond myself to you, Kia."

Her heart nearly burst from her ribs. She joined the vow as they all faced Stix, "I bond myself to you, Stix." And she repeated the promise to Rok then to Vee, and finally to Song. Behind her, she could hear sniffles and emotion filled sighs of the village fems. Somewhere a child clapped her hands and a hearth-mother shushed her. Kia could not slow the tide of emotion flowing down her cheeks.

"Prepare for your journey," the priest commanded.

The pledge sisters broke the circle and faced the wilderness, hand in hand. Kia stole a last glance at the village as she gripped the hands of Vee and Stix. They pressed together, ready to leap from the ridge to the trail, and race to the safety of faraway trees. At the exact moment when Moonlight pressed himself through the horizon at the edge of Terah and Warmsun touched the mountain they would run.

Kia held her breath. Would this be a night of a Darkening, when Moonlight would disappear out of the night sky as if being eaten by a worm? Would Moonlight turn to blood or fire? Kia's knees quaked remembering such a Darkening during a bonding when she was younger. The entire group of sisters had died in their quest. Such bad omens could not be foretold, even by the wisest mems of the clan. She prayed to Veenah this would not be such a night.

Vee whispered, "Is it time yet?"

Kia squeezed and shook her sister's hand, chastising her. "Shh, bad luck to speak," Kia breathed. Her heart froze Yes, I believe. I do believe in luck and the blessings of Veenah. She prayed harder.

Now the mems of the village, young and elder, began the songs of blessing. Kia listened for the voice of the young mem she and her new sisters hoped to court. He had the brightest golden eyes and thick yellow hair, and his voice rang out, richer than any other in the village. She'd not laid eyes on Kine since he had entered his training with the other unmarried mems, a full hand's summers ago, but she knew his voice and already loved him, as did Stix.

The last thing she'd said to Kine before it became forbidden to speak to him was, "Please don't forget me." Even though the fems were never allowed contact with a mem, the mems all knew about the village fems. What if Kine was waiting for the sisters of the Glen hearth, who were all likely fertile? She refused to think of it.

The song grew louder, the sun settled lower. A breath, maybe two. Kia tore her eyes from the red sunsetting to scan the trail she planned to use. She had to lead her sisters into the Woods of the Valley before Sun and Moon exchanged places in the sky – and they couldn't break their handholds until they were out of sight. Would little Song have the strength to keep up? Rok, the strongest of their group, would undoubtedly set the pace for a fast run.

Kia's legs trembled and barely held her as she leaned toward the trail. They dare not start before the song ended. Until Warmsun and her mate, Moonlight, were both at the edge of Terah.

Finally! The voices of the mems went silent!

6

Now!

As one, the bond sisters leaped for the narrow trail.

In the same instant, the world lit up in a blinding light, and the blast of an explosion pushed her from the precipice. Kia heard the unmistakable grind of a Zid rock harvester only a second before the ground turned on end and she fell into darkness. Only a moment to experience the terror of death before the breath was drawn from her body. A heartbeat of time for one last plea to Veenah for protection before her world went black.

Born out of darkness
Child of light
From the white breast of power
Drink strength for the fight

2 The Grief Of A Warrior

Rok gasped in shock at the violent shove on her back. Her hand was ripped from Stix's firm grip. She knew she would miss the trail and very likely slide to her death down the cliff. A war cry boiled from her as rage toward whoever did this filled her heart. She was sure it was Aga, leader of their femtog and the hardest of all the warrior class. Aga had done this to her so many times, she'd come to expect such a thing. But why now?

I will come back and kill you for this, Aga.

Twisting her body, Rok struggled for balance on the steep embankment. She screamed as she saw her family disappear in the flying dirt. Did her precious sisters make it to the trail?

A searing-hot blast wave. A dust cloud. Crashing stone. Terror replaced anger. This couldn't be Aga's doing.

What in Perg?

Jagged stone ripped into her tough, leather breeches. Outcropping boulders pummeled her sides. Debris in the air blinded her. The precipice dropped away. She fell with the rubble, landing hard.

Her body resisted movement, but the pain let her know she still lived and she lunged to her feet. Another war cry erupted from her, along with a prayer that her sisters would hear, if they were still alive. Stones rained from the sky and she scrambled from the chaos, ducking under her arms. The pounding reminded her of the blows she often received from Aga. Rok knew that if she didn't save herself, she could in no way save her sisters. She dashed into the night, away from the falling stones, without looking back.

Terror built in her as she ran. Visions of horrible creatures ready to pounce from every shadow spurred her to greater speed until her breath finally failed. She could barely hear the crashing of stone behind her.

A painful stab of guilt slowly replaced the terror. She bent double, sobbing, gasping for breath. She had run away, not to save her sisters, but to save herself. She ran because of fear. How could she do that, not caring what happened to the only fems in the world who had ever shown her love? Veenah would never forgive her. She'd never forgive herself.

Rok slowly caught her breath and her mind began to clear. Yes, she ran, but now she must think. What had happened? Why? What should she do right now? What would Aga do?

"How do I solve this?" She shouted and beat her fists into the darkness.

Moonlight began to shed light into the badlands and Rok oriented herself. Lumps rose on her head, causing a painful thumping. Her hands stung from the scrapes and cuts she'd received on her wild slide. She picked slivers of rock from her palms then brushed off her hands on her stagskin tunic.

I'll live. I've had worse falls than this, but those rocks hit harder than Aga ever did.

She flexed her back, letting her long, heavy braids fall behind her shoulders. The bruises would hurt for a few days, but nothing was broken. She thought of her blood mother.

Lona always said I have a hard head.

Scanning the horizon, now visible against the moonlit sky, her heart squeezed almost to a halt. A bluish dome of light covered the village. The vessel greater than the biggest lodge, settled into the ground. A second joined it, then another, clanking into place, creating a monstrosity which could reduce a mountain to ruin in days.

A sob escaped her and she sank to her knees.

The Zid rock harvester came to life and rumbled just over the ridge tearing chunks from Terah.

Zid.

At least that's what Terians called the greasy, gray, lizard beings. Lords of the world.

Not even the elders knew what they called themselves because no one understood their language of whistles, croaks, and grunts. But she understood their eyes, cold and cruel. Their only interest in Terians was for food – or slaves. She alone had survived the blast, but only because she shoved herself away from her beloved sisters.

Her remaining spirit failed and she fell to the ground thrashing in the pain of loss. If she'd held tight to Stix, her sisters would be here with her now. The training she'd received as a warrior had failed her. Leaving in order to save herself had cost her everything. How could she ever live with herself, knowing she'd committed this great crime? The ground shook under her and shards of her homeland flew into the air. The beings who ruled Terah were merciless.

Rok had no doubt that not one Terian was left alive.

Why hadn't her hearth mothers seen the attack coming? At least one warrior fem should have been standing watch. But the elders insisted the entire village attend the bonding. Rok heaved to her back, writhing in grief, kicking her heels into the ground.

"Why? Why? Why?" She cried out until her throat burned and she choked.

Her hearth mothers had always taught her, where there is life there is hope. She was alive, but in her heart, she knew hope had fled in the face of the Zid rock harvester. She drew her long-knife from its sheath, and struggled to her feet. Every movement brought physical pain as well as a deepening ache in her heart.

She knew what she had to do. The blade, as long as her arm from tip to haft, which she'd forged when her last molars came in, slid silently from its scabbard. The edge had been whetted, even to the point and the spine for the width of a hand, keen enough to split a tuber which was dropped on it. It was a blade meant for fighting, for killing. She gripped the haft with both hands and placed the gleaming point at the soft spot just below her ribs. For her betrayal, she would offer her own life as a penance to Veenah.

But the voices of her hearth mothers screamed in the back of her mind. *'Where there is breath, there is fight. Where there is fight, there is a chance for survival. Where a warrior survives, there is hope for the world. As long as you breathe, you must fight. To give up is to leave the entire world with no hope.'*

Her hands trembled and lost their grasp on the knife. It clattered to the rocky terrain. But, was there a world left to give hope to?

"Where can I possibly go?"

Her unsteady hand went to the necklace hidden under her tunic. A fresh stab of shame flooded her. A fem was not allowed to carry anything other than her knife and blanket. But she'd taken it in spite of the law. Her blood-mother, Lona, had crafted the multi-colored beads, adding five beautiful shells. Each bead had meaning in color or shape. Each shell represented her and her new sisters. It was a bonding gift that would forever remind her of her transgression.

A flood of tears spilled from her eyes. As Rok's fingers traced the intricate designs of the shells, an idea snuck into her mind.

Traders, wandering bands of homeless fems, often came to her village. As a young child, she was not allowed near these lawless Terians. But, she'd listened to their tales of surging, salt-filled waters which spanned the horizon to the edge of Terah, and trees so tall they reached into Veenah. Maybe she could join one of these traveling femtogs.

Lona had been a member of a roving band before coming to their village. Her fair skin and nearly white hair had earned her ridicule and torment, despite her enormous strength and cunning skill as a warrior and hunter. She'd snuck out of her village with the traders, but when they came into this valley, so long ago, the sister-wives of her syr, Cerian, were drawn to her. Lona had been accepted into the clan and into the femtog. It was natural that Rok do the same.

Maybe I'll find a femtog with a syr who will adopt me like my hearth mothers adopted Lona.

Rok considered the prophecy. She didn't really believe in it. But one verse stayed with her. Could she be the child who drew strength from the white breast? Could there be any truth to the old stories?

"I've been spared because Veenah has chosen me. I'll run until I find fems willing to follow me and learn what this prophecy means."

Her deadly weapon shimmered in Moonlight and she returned it to her sheath.

Speaking aloud into the darkness brought comfort and

encouragement. She could leave this place behind. But she'd never outdistance the pain in her heart. She'd given herself to the most loving fems anyone could hope for. She couldn't walk away. Instead, her feet turned back toward the place she'd once called home. The ground rolled under her feet as she ran.

A great sheet of rock appeared to stand on edge within the light cast by the rock harvester. The sight stunned her. Then she saw the reptilian beings riding their flying vessels within the light. And then two Zid slipped over the precipice, dropping down to walk on their hands and feet, with their scaly tails snaking behind them.

Zid never walked on all fours unless they were hunting Terians. Living Terians.

Rok drew her knife, jaw set, bitter rage boiling up in her throat. She took a step and another then ran toward the enemies who had destroyed her home.

Torn from your home
With never a breath
From deep you will soar
To life after death

3 Broken

Kia opened her eyes. She tried to move, but was glued in place by the fallout from the explosion. Her body laid twisted. She took a breath and choked as dust filled her lungs. Pain wracked her body.

"I have gone to Perg with all who have died." Tears washed the burning clay from her eyes. The ground rolled below her, grinding into her head and increasing her agony. "I never knew the pain followed someone into death. And why am I speaking if I'm dead?"

The ground quivered as if Terah were being shaken like a boar skin rug in the wind. Rocks and trees flew into the air. Kia remembered the blast of the Harvester. She'd never seen one so close, but she knew the damage they caused. And she knew the beings who controlled the giant machines. The Zid, rulers of Terah. The thought of them so close sent waves of terror through her.

"I'm not dead!" She struggled to free herself from the rubble. One arm finally loose, she scratched and dug the wet, rocky clay from around her and finally freed her other hand. She closed her eyes and held her breath as the air filled with flying dirt. Another layer of tephra settled over her and hardened like the adobe bricks which made up the village lodges and huts. Stones fell and she flinched as one struck her leg. She kicked her way to freedom, but her long, dark hair was trapped, permanently imbedded in the new rock.

"My knife!" Slashing her hair loose, she shrank back against the cliff.

Sheltered under the precipice from falling debris, she cleared mud from her eyes and realized Moonlight still ruled the dark sky. The gray haze of light covering the area came from the rock harvester.

"Stix! Rok! Where are you!" She screamed at the top of her voice then cringed, wondering if the Zid heard her. *No, they're inside that Harvester digging up the world.*

She screamed again and dashed for the tree line. Another explosion sent rubble into the sky and the stench of smelters filled the air. Poisonous gasses would quickly end all life.

"Stix! Rok! Vee! Song! Somebody answer me!" She untied her woolen cloak, the only other item besides a long-knife allowed a fem on her bonding quest, and shook it clean. Then she wrapped it around her head and face so she could breathe.

She had to find her sisters.

"Veenah, ruler of the day and night, help me!"

A gurgling croak sounded in the darkness. She shrank into the tangled remains of a tree. Zid rarely ventured out in the darkness. Their eyes didn't work in low light, but great birds of the night with yellow eyes the size of a fem's head did see well. Nightbird could appear on silent wings and pick up any creature, including Terians.

What made that noise?

"Rok? Are you there?"

"Quiet!" Rok growled, but reached through the darkness for Kia.

"You're alive!" Kia fell into Rok's arms, sobbing, and Rok's embrace lifted her off the ground.

"I'm here," Rok whispered, "but keep your voice low. I thought you'd been killed. Oh, your beautiful hair. Are you hurt?"

"I was nearly buried under the rocks and dirt. My hair was stuck and I cut it loose. Rok, you're covered in blood. What is that horrible smell?"

"I just killed one of those filthy Zid!"

"But they don't come out at night."

"I guess that story's a lie. It's over here. Hold its leg so I can skin it. The leather will give us strong shields."

"We don't have time. We have to find the others. The gas is coming."

"I'm nearly done."

Kia held her breath as Rok's knife did its work. "Ungh, that's nasty! Striped cat smells better than that! I might not eat for a moon phase."

"You'll thank me when we have new shields and boots. Watch your back. There might be more of these things running around."

Kia unsheathed her knife, studying the shadows for movement. Rok hefted the scaly hide of the Zid across her shoulder.

"Let's go," Rok whispered. "We need to get under cover."

Kia shook her head. "We need to find the others."

"They're all dead," Rok hissed, glancing around. "And we will be too if we don't get out of here."

"No! We have to find our sisters. We pledged."

Rok took a step backward. "You're right, we pledged, but I never followed you. You've been following me for the past season trying to convince me to pledge. Maybe that makes me the leader and I say we find shelter. Come on, Twisted Tree cave is not far from here."

"Fine. I'm going to look for our sisters alone then. I'm not leaving here without at least trying." The look on the warrior's face frightened and confused Kia.

"Wait." Rok shifted her load and took a step. "You can't go alone. You wouldn't have a chance."

"We were knocked off the trail halfway down. I lost them when the rocks fell. It's this way." Kia tried to hide the fear in her voice.

After a few steps, Rok stopped and glared. "I don't like it. We should both get away from this place."

Kia felt the sting of tears push at her eyes.

"But, I'll follow you. Don't worry, we'll find them." Rok pushed ahead.

"Ugh," Kia whispered. "You stink like dead Zid! Throw that hide over a tree branch. We'll get it later." Kia tightened the blanket around her face as another cloud of ash filled the air then led the way back toward the precipice where she last saw her bond sisters.

"Stix! Where are you? Vee! Song! Please answer me!"

The only response was the huffing and puffing of the harvester working just past the ridge – where her village used to be. She shoved the terrible thought from her mind and ducked as stones fell from another billowing cloud like an evil rain.

Rok held her close and they ran to the cliff for protection.

Rustling and a whimper from somewhere in the boulders turned her head. Rok stepped away, holding a finger to her lips and Kia held her breath.

The Zid were clever and knew how to mimic the voice of Terians, so Kia moved with caution. Her blade held ready, she peered around the brush and inched closer. A whistle, the sound of a night warbler tickled the night. Kia lay flat against the ground. It could be a warning call of a bird, or a Zid trap. Or it could be Stix, who could repeat the sound of every bird and animal known.

Another whistle, this time two day birds, the bleeding jay, and the spike headed water bird. Zid hunters would never use those two calls together because the birds lived in different places. Kia crept forward on her belly. Stix would have answered her by name if it had been safe. And why hadn't she come out of the shadows? She must be injured, or buried, but she was alive.

The sinister, rumbling voice of a Zid whispered through the night and Kia cast her blade to the rear just in time to see the forked tongue of a Zid flick over a boulder. She sprang to her feet, swinging her weapon, and split the thing's skull as it leaped into the air. In the blink of an eye, she could have been going down the throat of the long-nosed being. Instead it twitched silently as its musky purple blood spewed over the rocks. Kia stifled a scream when a giant nightbird swooped down and carried the carcass away.

"Kia! Over here!" A shining blade, the twin of her own knife, gleamed in the moonlight, signaling her bond-sister's location. Kia dove into the low cave.

"I thought I'd never see you again!" Kia cried, hugging Stix. "Are you hurt?"

Stix held her close and sobbed, "I'm sorry. I'm so sorry. I couldn't save her. And then those slimy lizards were looking for us and we couldn't breathe in the dust."

"Who, Stix, who couldn't you save?" Kia searched the dark cliff and finally saw Song huddled in the shadows, pointing.

Following Song's finger, Kia scrambled over the broken ground and found Vee, crushed and cold beneath a mound of dirt and rocks. Going limp, Kia screamed and writhed in new pain. Vee was so young.

She'd only had her second moon flow, but she'd passed all her tests and begged to be bonded with her hearth sister. Now she was gone.

Kia wrapped her arms around Song and wept with her.

Stix embraced both of them. "I tried to get her out. I saved Song. I dug her out of the dirt in time, but then I saw the Zid come over the ridge."

"I know." Kia wiped Stix's face with her blanket. "We must get away from here, fast."

"No," sobbed Song, "we can't leave her like this. We have to give her a death ceremony so she can go to Veenah."

"My little love," Kia said. "I know she's already there. But we're not safe here and I don't think our sister wants us to join her right now."

Stix pushed to the edge of the overhanging rock. "There's another Zid out there somewhere. You know they always hunt in pairs, and I saw them."

"Rok got it a while ago, but the poison gas is coming." Kia stood. "Let's go while the night bird is busy with that one I killed."

"Rok's alive? Where is she?" Song whimpered.

Kia glanced around. "I don't know. She was behind me when we heard something in the bushes."

Stix climbed to her feet, but sank back to the ground. Blood flowed from a gash in her leg.

Walk forward my beauty
Fear not for what's gone
New life is given
At breaking of dawn

4 Goodbye My Love

Stix fell back into the dark pool of blood. Kia thought the life would go out of her own body until she heard Song cry out. Kneeling, Kia pressed her fingers into Stix's neck searching for the pulse of life.

"Song! Help me stop the bleeding!"

"She needs something for a bandage, but we don't have anything," Song whimpered.

"Get the blanket from Vee. We can use that."

"No! I can't! I can't," Song sobbed.

Like a wild animal, Kia clawed the dirt from around Vee's body. "It's the only bandage we have and she doesn't need it anymore."

Cutting her hands on sharp rocks, she loosened the rope holding the blanket and knife to her hearth sister's body. The weapon felt heavy in her hand, as if it didn't want to leave its owner. Kia banished the thought and cut a strip from the blanket, wrapping it around Stix's blood-soaked leg. Quickly, she tied the grass rope tight.

"Is she going to die?" Song's voice quivered with fear.

"Not yet, but she needs water. And she needs medicine, but Vee knew more about that than I do. Her blood mother is a healer."

"I know some things. Vee taught me when we played." Song started crying again. "I wish Rok was here. Something must have happened to her."

Kia wiped the dust and sweat from her eyes and glanced into the moonlit night. "It's okay, don't cry. Rok's watching for other Zid

18

hunters. I'm sure of it. We have to be stronger than ever right now. Keep your eyes open. Help me lift Stix so I can carry her on my back." Kia staggered to her feet with her injured sister's arms hanging over her shoulders. Leaning on the dirt mound covering her hearth sister, she choked back a sob.

"Goodbye, my love. You'll never be forgotten."

Song handed Kia a broken branch to use as a walking stick. Kia balanced on it and, together, they stepped into the brilliant moonlight. Kia prayed that the illumination was the hand of Veenah promising to protect them.

"Where are we going?"

"First we find Rok. Watch those shadows!" Kia snapped. She stumbled and Stix cried out. Kia rested, leaning on the branch before struggling down the trail.

"I don't think Rok likes me very much."

"What? She loves you as much as she loves me – and as much as I love you."

"I'm scared of her."

"Yeah, so is everybody else in the village. She's a warrior like her hearth mothers." Kia stumbled again, nearly dropping Stix. "But didn't you hear her bonding promise? She pledged love and loyalty, and she's not the sort of fem who breaks a vow. I trust her with my life. And I love her."

Stix groaned. "But you love me more, don't you?"

"With my life and soul," Kia answered softly. "Can you walk?"

"I don't think so. Don't let go."

Branches crackled nearby, startling Kia, but then Rok appeared out of the darkness and lifted Stix by an arm. "This way. Wait! Where's Vee?"

Kia's eyes dropped. She could only shake her head. Song moaned, crying softly.

"She...she's..." Song choked.

"Veenah help us." Rok shifted under the weight of Stix and sighed. "She will be sorely missed, but we need to get to safety. And be quiet. The Zid can hear you all the way to the Forbidden Mountain."

"Let them come. We'll fight them all," Kia growled. "I got the other one just before it had me for dinner." She shuddered at the memory. "Where did you go?"

"Searching for whatever made that noise. Then I saw a giant mountain rat steal my Zid hide. I'm glad we left the thing in that tree or she would have been hunting us. I managed to get a blade into one of her cubs. Maybe I can follow the blood trail when Warmsun rises. We'll have fur as well as meat."

"I don't like mountain rat," Song whined.

"You would have liked her first kill even less." Kia laughed.

"Anything is better than rat."

"How about roasted Zid?" Rok said.

"Yuk! No way!" Song yelped.

Rok laughed deeply. "Oh, my beautiful bond sister," she told Song. "Since you were raised in a hearth of marvelous cooks, I trust you will be able to prepare anything I bring to the table and it will be a feast of Veenah. Besides, I'm not sure we're going to find much else to eat, after all this destruction."

Song began to cry again.

"Come walk by me." Rok held Song's hand and pulled her closer. "I think you've grown since last moon cycle. I know how you're feeling. I thought I was in Perg when my hearth sisters died last year. But you and I are bonded now, and we are going to survive this. We were five strong, but now we are four. We will make a powerful femtog."

Kia's heart swelled with pride. She'd courted Rok for many moon phases, even when Stix once flew into a jealous rage. She had visited the warrior's hearth for most of the turning of the seasons until Rok finally gave in during the last cold. Then Stix began to see the beauty in the blue eyed fem hunter. They'd all cried the night Rok had accepted her proposal to join her and Stix in a bonding. It was Rok who'd insisted they formally court Vee. She would have been a great healer. A tear escaped Kia's eye.

Rok turned them away from the dry river bed and into a forest where the trail narrowed to a path made by small animals.

"Hey," Kia said. "I thought we were finding shelter under Twisted Tree. There's a creek near it, and Stix needs water."

"That creek runs from our village. I doubt it's any good. Besides, I think the mountain rat went that way, and I don't want to risk a battle with her. We're going down by White River."

"I need to rest and I think Stix is sleeping again. She lost too much blood."

"Sit here by the calipsa tree," Rok said, lowering Stix to the ground. "I'll climb for some stink branches we can drag behind us and cover our trail."

Kia craned her neck to see the top of the tree. "You can't climb that. It's taller than a mountain."

"You have a lot to learn about me, sister. I climb calipsa trees much taller than this weed."

Song studied the brush, brilliant in Moonlight's full face. "I'll look for willa grass. If Stix can chew some, she'll feel better. And if I can get enough woody stem, I can make medicine for her leg."

"No." Rok's hard eyes softened when Song shrank back in fear. "Stay with the others until I climb back down. We can't get separated out here. You're safe by the calipsa. The only animal that will come close to this smelly thing is a tiny bear that eats the leaves. And he won't hurt you."

"But Stix needs medicine."

"I know. What does the plant look like? I'll try to find some when I climb."

"Almost like tall grass, only it has a trunk like a bush. The leaves shimmer in Moonlight if wind blows. But they're hard to see if they're growing near grass."

"Got it. Be right back down."

Kia thought Song looked suddenly taller when Rok asked her for knowledge. *Yes, my femtog is strong.* She held Stix's head in her lap and stroked her forehead. "You still with me?" Stix only groaned an answer.

Song propped up Stix's injured leg then sat cross legged on the ground facing her bond sisters. She broke off a handful of tough targus grass and started braiding it into rope. "What are we going to do now, Kia? What if we're the only Terians left alive?"

"I don't know. There must be other villages somewhere. Do you know Syr Brawn's femtog, the old ones on the other end of our village? My syr said his family adopted a young fem from a village far away when none of his fems were able to bear children."

Stix shifted and moved her leg. She groaned in pain and opened her eyes. "Syr Brawn traded his best hunter for two fems. They traveled

21

to the end of the river to find the village."

"How could he break up his femtog?" Song said. The sadness in her voice brought a lump into Kia's throat. Song kicked the ground with her heels and cried out. "They were bonded together! No wonder they live on the edge of the village. No one will have them near."

Stix tried to sit up, but slumped back into Kia's lap. "I don't think it was like that. My blood mother used to help the two young fems tan leather. Their femtog was strong. She told me that Jya chose to stay in that other village as a matron and help raise mems."

"Why would she do such a thing?"

"Because our village already has plenty of elders and matrons and most of theirs died from the fever. It was a good trade and Syr Brawn finally fathered some babes." She closed her eyes again, wincing from the pain in her leg.

"We'll talk to Rok about following the river and maybe we can join this other clan," Kia said. "I want us to be a strong femtog, but I also want to bear a child, or try to."

Song yanked another handful of grass to add to her rope as she sat listening. She sniffed and wiped her eye with the back of her hand. "I want to go back to our village and see if anyone else survived."

"There's probably not much left on that side of the ridge except a gigantic hole full of poison," Kia said. "If you could find a way to breathe, the Zid would kill you anyway. I don't know how we got out, except that we were blown over the cliff when the first blast hit. I didn't even hear the harvester coming. It was just there. I doubt if anyone else saw them either."

"I was just thinking of Kine." Song sniffled again. "He would have made such a good husband. He was the best singer and he believed so much in the prophecy. And he laughed all the time."

"How do you know that? We're forbidden to look at the mems after they go into training."

"Our hut was close enough to the mems' lodge so that we could hear most of what they were doing. I think I already loved him, and I never even knew him before he went into the lodge."

"I did love him. I knew him when we were little. He was born in the hut next to mine. The last thing I said to him was 'Please don't forget me' Now, I'll never forget him."

A tree branch crashed down behind the trunk of the calipsa. Another followed, then two more branches, thick with strong smelling leaves.

Song held her nose. "I hope she's not thinking of using those branches for firewood."

Rok called down from a high branch. "I heard that. You must think I got my head filled with dirt in that explosion. But it's an idea. If I could get some of this calipsa to burn under that Zid machine, maybe the stink would drive them back to the Forbidden Mountain."

"Good idea, I'll wait at the edge of Terah while you try to burn them out," Kia said laughing.

"Here, catch this. I found a good dinner this time. Two young tree-dogs, nearly the size of a toddling child. And I collected their entire cache of nuts and dry berries."

"Did you find their stash of water up there, too?" Kia grunted under the weight of the rodents. Their long thick tails covered her face."

"Try not to think about it. We're a half day's walk from fresh water. There's nothing much left of the river running through our valley." Rok climbed down the trunk, finding finger holds in the coarse bark.

Kia saw worry in the warrior's face, but when she started to speak, Rok shook her head *no*. Instead, Kia asked, "So what are you doing with so many branches?"

"I thought we could tie two of the branches together and make a carrier for Stix. Since calipsa is the strongest wood you can find, I figured this would bear her weight."

"That's a good idea. How did you think of it?

"I remember watching the little fems running and dragging sticks behind them. We need more rope to make it work."

"You're in luck. Song braided a length sitting here."

Song smiled, blushing. "I had to keep my fingers busy or I'd go crazy. Did you find the willa grass?"

Rok examined the length of rope which was nearly as long as she was tall. "You're really amazing. Yes, I think I found some. But I want you to stay and make more of this." She knelt and took Song in her arms, kissing her on the forehead. "Promise me you won't leave this tree, not even a pace. Stay with Stix. Kia and I will go after the plant."

23

Burying her face in Rok's neck, Song whispered, "I promise."

Kia leaped up, grabbing Rok by the hand and led her into the tall grass.

"Okay, Rok," Kia said when they were out of sight of the others. "I know when you are hiding something. What did you see?"

Hand of the innocent
Symbol of might
Defender of honor
Promise of life

5 Innocent

Moonlight shone bright enough to cast shadows from the retreating forms of Rok and Kia. Song stood trembling as her sisters faded from sight. Stix lay at her feet barely breathing. She knelt and touched Stix on the cheek then jerked away from the cold flesh.

She's dying, and I can do nothing. Song clutched her stomach, wanting to rid herself of the dull ache cutting through her. *Everyone is dying except me.* She rocked back and forth, crying silently through clenched teeth. The vision of stones pounding down upon Vee, crushing, killing, burned in her mind and sent waves of pain through her heart. She couldn't remember a day not spent with Vee. They'd played together as children and learned to hunt as they grew up. Vee had always been the strong one, now she was gone. She'd never be able to go on without her best friend.

Guilt and shame flooded into her and joined forces with her anguish. She had done nothing to help her beloved while Vee's screams echoed in the cavern. All she'd had to do was reach out and grab Vee by the arm. But she'd only sat there. Song cried out in her grief then covered her face with her hands, fear pushing away the guilt. What if she'd alerted the hunters of the night with her outburst?

Crouched at the base of the pungent calipsa tree, she peered into the night and tried to quiet her sobs. From far away the sounds of Terah being ripped apart drifted on the wind. Did anyone else survive? Her blood mother had been standing closest to the precipice. She could have escaped. And others could have fallen down the hillside when the blast came. The thought gave her a small bit of hope. The elderfems would have done anything to protect the mems they held. Someone else had to survive.

They can't all be gone. They just can't.

Song touched Stix again, feeling for warmth and breath. Stix groaned and opened her eyes.

"You're awake." Song moved closer and took her bond sister's hand.

"You're beautiful in the glow of Moonlight," Stix whispered. "But you've been crying. You know Vee wouldn't want you to grieve."

Another tear rolled from Song's eye. "I know. But I don't think this pain I feel inside will ever stop. Are you feeling okay?"

"A little cold. My leg hurts so bad I can hardly feel it anymore. Where's Kia?" She winced and groaned, breathing hard, then relaxed again.

"Kia and Rok went for medicine," Song said, glancing into the shadows. "They should be back by now. I hope nothing happened to them."

"Nothing can hurt Rok. And she'll protect Kia. They'll be back, don't worry."

"Do you think anyone else got out of there?" Song forced herself to breathe slowly, but a wave, almost like sickness, ran through her as she turned her face in the direction of the ruined village.

"I don't know. But if they didn't get far away, the Zid will get them, just like those two almost got us. We can only hope Veenah had mercy on them."

"I want to sneak back and search. If we cover ourselves with mud and only move in the shadows, the Zid won't see us. I know Rok can do it. I can go back with her."

"No good, my love. We got away. If anyone else survived the blast, they either got away, or they're dead by now. We will keep going. I'm just sorry I'm slowing us down. I probably won't heal from this. You and Kia and Rok should go on without me. Some of us have to live."

"No! Don't you ever say such a thing! We are bonded. That means we stay together for life, no matter what. I'm not leaving you."

"Good. That means you won't think about trying to go back to the village." Stix shifted a little and gasped in pain.

"Be still, sweet Stix. I know it hurts. Kia and Rok will be back soon with medicine. You'll be okay. I'll make sure of it." Song held her sister's head in her lap, but planned a way to search for others.

I'm strong even if I'm young. I can do this.

Another stab of guilt struck her. Yes, she was young, too young. The elders advised her to wait, but she convinced them. *I lied and told them I was old enough to join a femtog. I lied to all of them, even Vee. They trusted me and I brought this bad luck. I am nothing but an irresponsible child.*

The village had never been attacked before. However, the badlands had. The songs told of a once beautiful forest. Then, generations ago, Zid harvesters had turned Terah inside out, leaving nothing of the vast, life-filled land but death and waste. But the valley where her village lay had been spared. No one ever thought the Zid would come back. Why would they? Because of her deceit. The elders called such a thing speaking with a forked tongue; forked and evil–like the Zid. And it had brought down Veenah's wrath.

But, if she hadn't lied and joined with Kia, she would have been killed by that blast, instead of spared. She didn't even have a scratch. Maybe Veenah had other plans for her.

No! If I hadn't lied, none of this would have happened!

Song thought of the prophecy. An innocent hand would lead Terah. *I'm not innocent. I'm a liar.*

Tears filled her eyes again. She'd always believed that the chosen one would be some great warrior or hunter. The prophecy also said something about might and honor, but she was neither mighty nor honorable. Could a warrior be innocent?

Her head spun with confusion and a new sadness filled her. She didn't understand the prophecy any better than other fems. She hardly ever thought of it, except when Loresinger chanted it at ceremonies. She took a deep breath and wiped her face with the back of her hand.

"Are you still awake, dear Stix?"

"Barely. Your hand on my head feels good."

"Do you ever think of the prophecy?"

"Not really. I don't think it's real. It's only a song they sing. No one even knows what it means. I think it's just a reason to make us go away for a moonphase, so we learn to work together."

"That's crazy," Song said, sitting a little straighter. "We already know we work well together."

"My blood mother said it's a time for us to enjoy each other before we take our place in the village. It takes more than just love to build a hut, grow our gardens, and one day take a husband to our hearth and have babies."

Song felt her face grow hot. She wasn't even sure how a fem got the babe inside her. Even though she had looked forward to having Kine as a husband, she shuddered, wondering what it would be like.

A rustling sound came from the direction Kia and Rok had gone. "Hey, love," Song whispered. "I think our sisters are returning. You will soon have medicine." She prayed silently that the noise wasn't a predator, or the Zid.

Heart of a child
Look to the sky
Courage to answer
A new battle cry

6 From The Killer Comes Shelter

Rok glanced behind her, making sure they were beyond sight of Song. The twisting in her gut reached up into her head and down into her legs, making her weak and wobbly.

Kia reached for her. "What is it?" Her grip spun the warrior around.

Rok flinched and shouldered away from Kia. "Don't…I can't…I don't want to talk about it right now. Let's just go get the medicine plant for Song."

"Stop and talk to me. I have to know what you saw."

Surrendering to Kia's embrace, Rok tried to hold back a sob.

"Go ahead, love," Kia whispered. "Cleanse yourself. I'm here."

"I don't know if we can do this," Rok cried out with jerky breaths. "It's all gone. Those filthy creatures… If I could I, would kill every one of them. At least when we hunt, we leave the strongest of the herds so they can rebuild their numbers. My hearth mothers all pleaded for sentries to be set, but the Zid haven't been back to this land since they created the badlands two or three lifetimes ago. The elders wouldn't even talk about it."

"My love, they came so fast not even a sentry could have saved our village. We can't give up as long as we have breath. We can't let the memory of our people disappear. Veenah saved us for a reason."

"I don't think I believe in Veenah right now."

Spent of her tears, Rok lowered her arms, wiping her face with the back of her hand. "I don't believe in something invisible, but I do believe in us. Thank you for holding me. Now, we just have to find a place to live, or maybe we'll become a lost, traveling band of traders. Let's go, the medicine plant is just up the trail. And please, don't tell them, um, that I…"

"That you have feelings?"

"I was taught to be strong, not to cry like a babe. It means I am weak."

"Sister, you are far from weak. We are fems. That means we are not just strong, but passionate and filled with love. We must shed tears or they build up in us and can burst our hearts."

*****

Kia assembled the poles and began tying a carrier together with the grass rope Song had braided. Strong, flexible branches tied between the two long calipsa poles kept the creation stable, while a net of ropes, covered with their blankets, made a comfortable sling for Stix. Kia hadn't said a word since she and Rok had returned, and Rok stayed busy directing the building project as well as keeping the fire as low as possible while she worked on the luxurious thick fur of the animals. The tree dogs roasted over the fire.

Song tended Stix as best she could. "You have to chew these leaves. You can spit out the pulp, but you have to swallow the juice. It will help with the pain."

"It's bitter. I'm so thirsty," Stix groaned, but complied.

When Song untied the bindings from Stix's leg, she gasped. "I didn't know it was so bad," she whispered. "We need more willa. And many other medicines, but I'm not sure what they are." She peeled the bark from the thicker branches and crushed it into a slimy poultice with a smooth stone. As carefully as possible, she laid the dressing along the cut. Blood still oozed from the deepest part of the wound, but at the ends, near Stix's right hip and back of her knee, heavy, dark clots were forming.

"I can use a claw from one of those tree dogs to try and close that cut, but I need sinew," Song said. "And we need water. This can turn bad and she will die."

Kia finally spoke. "We'll stay here long enough to get that meat cooked and dried so it won't rot. It's enough to feed us for two days, if we're careful. The nuts will keep us strong even longer. "We have to walk all night to get to White River, but we can't stay here."

Song's jaw dropped. "We aren't going back to find survivors?"

Rok stopped working the furs long enough to answer. "There's nothing left. No one got out of there."

"But we got out so others must have gotten away! We can't just leave without trying! I'll go back by myself if I have to!" Tears flowed down her fair cheeks, cutting mud trails all the way to her chin.

Kia dropped the last of the rope and embraced her. "I'm sorry. We can't go back. Rok saw the poison gas already filling the plains. Terah is dug up for a day's run in both directions. And more Zid are arriving in their flyers, even in the dark. If even one Terian living or dead was anywhere to be found, they've been taken for food. The attack was just too fast. If we go back, we'll just be some lizard's lunch. We can't do that." Kia held her bond sister until Song began to relax.

Rok finally spoke. "Hey, you two, we've got work to do."

Song wiped her face. "Okay, I'm done. I guess I had to get that out of my system."

"I know," Rok said. "Come over here. I need help stretching these skins. I want to get at least a little smoke on them before we go. Kia, can you cut that meat so it will dry faster? We need trail food. I wish it would cook faster. I'm about to starve."

"I wonder what a normal bonding quest is like," Song said, almost smiling. "Find food, water, shelter, laugh and have a good time? Pretend we're searching for some magical jewel? Then build a home and marry the best mem with the most beautiful voice?"

Stix interrupted, "And the biggest seeder. And we'll all bear a child every year."

Song gasped, plumes of red flowing up her neck to her cheeks.

"We'll need to adopt another hunter," Kia said, grinning.

Roc chuckled. "If we all have children we will make a whole village by ourselves."

"I just hope at least one of us is fertile." Kia glanced around her little band.

Rok nodded. "We also need to survive long enough to at least find a village with a mem so we'll have a husband."

"Well," Song said. "I'll just pretend this is a real bonding quest. I don't deserve you three. You're so strong." She unsheathed her knife and carved strips of meat from a sizzling roast. "I thought we'd save the good plates and eat with our fingers."

Kia accepted the first slice. "Song, our femtog will be stronger than most. We have a healer, who also makes us smile. I love you."

"I love her more," Stix said, struggling to sit up. "My leg doesn't hurt so much anymore."

"Mmmm, I love her most, she cooks," Rok said stuffing her mouth full, not caring about the juices dribbling down her chin. "I guess I'm glad you finally convinced me to join you, Kia. I never really thought of myself as femtog material. You know I have a bad temper, so if I yell, don't think too much of it. Okay?"

"I never do," Kia said.

"I'll yell back." Stix slumped into Kia's lap and chewed weakly on a piece of meat.

"I'll hide until you get over it," Song said quietly. She cut another slice of roast for Rok.

The ground rumbled around them and they all crouched closer to the Calipsa trunk.

"I think it's time to go," Kia announced. "Zid might not hunt at night, but who knows what they'll do when the light comes."

They eased Stix onto the carrier, wrapped their meat and the cache of nuts in blankets to carry. Rok covered the little fire while Song and Kia lifted the front of the carrier.

"I'll bring up the rear and cover the trail," Rok said. "Let's go."

Moving downhill was easy, unless the carrier bounced over a rock. Stix cried out more than once.

"Do you need us to stop?" Kia said. Sweat covered her body. Song staggered under the load.

"No, keep going. But I'd like another one of those leaves."

Song panted and nearly stumbled. "We should all chew some. We won't feel so thirsty and the willa may give us more strength. The branch is tied to the pack just above your head."

A shadow flashed through Moonlight. "Get under cover!" Rok screamed a war cry and swung the Calipsa branch into the air, fouling the talons of a nightbird. "Trees! Get under the trees!"

Song fell and cried out. Stix screamed in pain and fear as

Nightbird turned to attack again. She rolled out of the carrier and yanked it to cover her. Nightbird hooked the carrier and lifted it into the air, then dropped it a few paces away. Its beak snapped together in a fearful warning then it circled on eerily silent wings for one more attack.

Kia grabbed Song and dove for the thick grass and brush. Song whimpered and Kia covered her mouth. Moving slower than a slug, Kia pulled the branches of a thorn bush across them. "Don't move," she breathed. "I'll try to get to Stix when that thing circles again."

Stix screamed again and hurled herself to the spot where Nightbird had dropped the carrier. As she rolled over, she spun the lower ends of the poles toward the oncoming creature and waved her arms, screeching at the top of her lungs. Giant yellow eyes flashed in Moonlight and Nightbird folded its wings to dive for the sure meal. Stix raised the poles just before the talons struck and the sharp wood pierced the beast. It fell straight down, flopping only once as its life drained away.

Kia gasped, frozen in place, fearing that Stix had just given her life to save her sisters. She couldn't even cry. Song's entire body shook from the terror of the attack. Rok took a step toward the hulk, raising her knife, ready in case the beast came back to life. Its wing, twice as long as a fem's height, moved slightly and Rok crouched to pounce on top of the thing's head and kill it. Kia scrambled to her side. Song picked up the Calipsa branch and leaped for the other side of the beast.

A massive feather moved to the side and Stix pushed her head through the wing. "Don't hit me!" she said, ducking back down. "Get this heavy thing off me!"

"By the fires of Perg," shouted Kia. "You scared the life out of me! What were you thinking, jumping in front of that thing?"

"I'm sorry, but I think I broke the carrier," Stix said.

"Who cares about the carrier! Are you okay?" Kia dragged the wing to the side and Song examined Stix's injured leg.

"She's bleeding again." Song glanced at the sky. "Warmsun is coming and we need to find shelter. And water. How much farther to White River?" The three of them looked at Rok, waiting for the answer. Their bond sister was hacking furiously at the huge bird's head.

"Water is a short run from here," Rok said. She tugged and twisted the hooked beak and finally hacked it loose with her knife.

"We'll make a shelter under that wing. I can carry a day's ration of water in this. Kia, will you stay with Stix? I want Song to run with me and look for more medicine, and more enemies."

Song shrugged out of the ropes holding her blanket and the cache of nuts and dropped the pack beside the dead bird. Then she hacked the leafy twigs from the Calipsa branch. Both Rok and Kia lifted the first joint in the wing high enough for Song to prop it up with the branch, creating a tent-like half-shelter.

"This will protect us even from the Zid." Song shook the wing a little to test its stability. "It's already going stiff, but it will cover us well." She hugged Kia and took Stix's hand. "We'll be back soon."

Kia watched them zip into the darkness. Song may be smaller than Rok, but she certainly could run as fast. "Be safe, my sisters," she whispered then turned back to Stix. "Let's get you inside our first home."

"I've already been in there. I don't want to move. I'll never be afraid of anything again. Not after that."

"How'd you figure it out, I mean using the carrier like that?" Kia sat down and held Stix's head in her lap.

"I didn't really have time to think about it, just react. I wished I had a spear, you know, long and pointed. I remembered how sharp the poles of the carrier got dragging over the hard ground. I knew I couldn't throw it, but I thought if I got the nightbird to dive at me, it would spear itself."

"I'm glad it worked. This is something to remember. A weapon the enemy can kill itself with."

Stix moaned, "I'm cold."

"No!" Kia felt her bond sister's head then pulled back her eyelid. "You've lost too much blood and you have a fever. Stix, stay awake and talk to me!" She tied the rope tighter around the wound hoping it would slow the bleeding again. "I'm going to make you a sleeping place where you'll be warmer. Keep talking to me!" Kia leaped up and cut handfuls of grass with her knife.

"What do you want me to say?"

"Anything. Tell me about your hearth mothers." Kia piled the grass under the bird-wing shelter. When she stood to gather more grass, she discovered the soft feathers on the bottom of the wing and pulled a few out. "Stix! What are your hearth mothers' names?"

"Rem... Flower... Zina ... Cali..."

Kia yanked a few more feathers and covered the sleeping place with their softness. "Stix! Talk! Who else in their femtog?"

"My blood mother is Dox. She's our hunter.... I guess that's why I'm good at hunting."

Kia knelt beside her. "I've made you the best sleeping place. You'll be warm inside." She lifted her weak sister and half dragged her under the wing-turned-shelter.

"You're right, this is soft. Now that we know how to kill Nightbird, everyone can have a soft sleeping place. I'm still cold."

"Well, keep talking to me. I'll get some bigger feathers to cover you."

"We can't stay in here for very long. It will stink in a day and the carrion eaters will find us." Stix shifted and settled lower into the soft bed.

"How about we let Rok solve that problem later. Stay awake and tell me about your first hunt."

"Why? You were there. You can tell me about it."

"Talk to me."

"When is Rok coming back with the water?" She shivered so hard that Kia could see it.

"Soon, I hope. And maybe Song will find more medicine."

"Under the other wing ... the Willa branch ... blanket...." Stix gasped for air. "I'm so thirsty."

"Hang on sister, don't you dare close your eyes! I'll be right back." Kia crawled from under the wing shelter and dashed around the bird's mangled head. Its other wing lay twisted in a grotesque angle, as if the dying plea of Nightbird was to rejoin Veenah. She parted the feathers and pushed her way under the stiffened wing, searching for any sign of the carrier which had taken the beast's life.

The blunt end of a Calipsa pole protruded from the thing's breast and Kia clawed away blood-soaked feathers, hoping to find the willa somewhere in the mess. The darkness nearly suffocated her and fine feathers entwined her head and face while she probed for the second pole. The medicine had to be here somewhere. But, both poles had impaled the bird to their fullest and Kia only found broken grass ropes.

Her foot hit the soft mass of a blanket roll. She crouched to gather it and found the Willa branch still tied firmly. The impact had thrown it clear of the blood flow and Kia knew it was safe to use. She squeezed free from the wing, her bruised and scraped body screaming in protest.

"I've got it!" She yelled. "Stix! Talk to me! I found the medicine!" She scooped up Song's pack with the nuts and berries and scrambled back to the shelter.

"I'm still here," came the weak reply.

"Here, chew." Kia stuffed a leaf into Stix's mouth.

"Ugh, it stinks."

"Yeah, so do you. Chew."

"Our first bonding sleep should not be under a dead bird. It's bad luck."

"Like our luck has been wonderful so far." Kia stripped a couple more leaves from the willa branch. The long, low howl of a wolf made them both tremble.

Turn not from the struggle
Rise out of the mist
As one you will rally
And heal the rift

7 Healing Stix

Moonlight moved toward the Forbidden Mountains and Kia struggled to see. As much as she feared Zid hunters, she feared darkness more. And, Stix was still cold.

Kia ventured from the shelter to find stones for a fire ring. With luck she may locate a flat rock to use as a cooking plate. With more luck she could find flintrock which would break apart in a fire, and she could make spear points.

Near the base of a giant cone tree she found all the rocks she needed and several cones which would burn hot and bright. She gave thanks for the find, then instant bitterness rose in her belly. Why was Veenah punishing her? What had she done that had been so wrong to deserve such punishment? Why had Veenah taken her blood sister and tried to destroy her femtog? Why had Veenah allowed the destruction of her entire village?

Prayers and worries had to wait. Kia had one goal at the moment – save Stix. She stumbled across the uneven ground, back to the shelter and prepared her fire ring just beyond the edge of the wing. Nuts fell easily from the cones and she wondered why tree dogs hadn't found the treasure. She popped some into her mouth. "Probably this Nightbird ate all the tree dogs in the area." She clumped up a wad of dry grass and stripped a bit of soft feather from the wing, then struck her fire rocks. The spark hit the feather-fluff and burst into an instant flame which took up residence in the grass. She gently blew into the tiny flame and added

37

cone chips one at a time. Quickly, a warm, flickering light filled the shelter.

Rok and Song had not yet returned.

Kia stayed busy finding firewood and feeding Stix cone nuts and willa leaves.

"Here, eat a piece of tree dog meat. You must keep up your strength."

Stix coughed. "You eat it. I can't chew anymore," she croaked. "Thirsty."

"Try to stay awake. Rok and Song will be back soon. They have to walk slow so they won't spill the water they're bringing. Morning fog will also come, and water will gather on the grass. Maybe I can find a cape plant and make a water basket out of one of the wide leaves."

"Look for a spine plant. They always have water in their meat." Stix coughed then cried out in pain. "I'm so cold."

"I don't know why I didn't think of that before. Let me bring you more warm stones then I'll look for it."

In the glow of Moonlight, Kia stumbled along a narrow game trail. Fearing she would travel too far from her ailing sister, she finally found what she searched for. Broad green segments were still engorged with water from the recent rains. But they were also covered with sharp spines which were painful and difficult to remove if they punctured the skin. She knocked two fat pads loose and held them with a stick while she shaved the spines from the thick skin. Then she skewered the prize with her knife and raced back to the shelter.

Stix was asleep. At least Kia hoped so. She fell to her knees and pressed her ear to her sister's chest. Her heart still beat, barely. But her mouth was turning blue. Kia cut a wedge from the spine plant and squeezed the juice on to Stix's lips.

"Wake up," Kia pleaded. "Please wake up. You cannot leave me. Without you we cannot survive."

Stix licked the syrupy juice and Kia pressed more into her mouth. She peeled back the leathery skin from the juice filled meat.

"Chew this and I'll get you some more."

Kia's own mouth begged for water, but she tended her sister until finally Stix's eyes fluttered open.

"Now you're trying to drown me?" Stix chewed the stringy

tissue and swallowed the life-giving fluid. "Did you find enough for yourself, too?"

"I'll get more when you're better. Eat." She peeled another wedge.

A racket outside the shelter made them both tremble, then Song's bright face, haloed by her gold colored hair, appeared in the firelight.

"You know, the thin pieces are tender and taste better," Song said.

Kia leapt to hug Song. "Yes, my love, I know, but the big ones hold more water. Where's Rok? Did you two have any trouble? I was so worried."

"Rok is right behind me, she has to walk carefully. How is Stix?"

"I'm hurt, sick, tired, cold, and thirsty, but I'm the happiest fem alive to see you!"

"At least you're still alive. I have more medicine, and I know where we can get sinew to close your wound."

Kia dashed out the door to meet Rok.

In the chill of the predawn fog, sweat rolled down Rok's face. She cradled the huge beak like an infant. It was full, nearly to the top, with fresh water.

"This is enough water to last for a changing of the moon! Let me carry it the rest of the way," Kia said.

"It won't last that long, I'm afraid. I can't let go. More will spill. We lost so much when Song helped me carry it. She spilled less than I did, but when we trade, water runs out. Just hold my arm so I don't stumble on the trail."

"Well, stop so I can take a drink. I'm about to die of thirst." She held her lips to the edge of the vessel and gulped while Rok tilted it. Satisfied at last, she looked into her bond-sister's face. "You're tired. You should have taken some of the meat or nuts to eat on the way."

"We found berries and cone nuts. I even caught a small fish and ate it raw. Song didn't like it." Rok chuckled. "I guess I did look like a bear ripping the flesh from a live fish, but I was hungry." She saw the small fire. "I think I love you more than ever. Your fire makes me almost as happy as finding the water did."

"I'm glad you approve, but you build fires so much better. I guess we all have our talents."

"She's precious, you know," Rok said quietly, kneeling to set the water vessel near the fire where it could heat.

"You mean Song?"

"I had already lost my milk teeth when she was born, and I liked her right away. Her hearth mothers didn't really get along with my hearth mothers, so I never got to know her. When we moved to the edge of the village I hardly got to see anyone, especially Song. My blood mother is a warrior and wanted all of my hearth sisters to be the same. My syr teaches us this way, he believes in the prophesy and wants us all ready. We are a rough hearth."

"I know. I was always a little afraid of your mothers." Together they gathered stones and a few sticks to balance the valuable water.

"But you came to visit me anyway. Other fems have courted me, but they quit. I guess my mothers frighten them. You gave me the chance to get to know Song and for that, I love you."

"Stix and I both wanted you, and that gave us courage. If I'd known you loved Song, I may have courted her first, but she and Vee were really scared of your hearth. All of your mothers are warriors aren't they?"

"Yes, but they have many skills."

"Your hearth mother, Lona, makes beads that my blood mother trades for. I have…had… a headpiece made from her beads." Kia covered her face with her hands to hide the sudden grief. "What are we going to do without them?" she sobbed.

Rok embraced Kia. "We will do what we were born to do – survive and rebuild. That's what our mothers and our syrs would hope for us." Rok pushed herself to her feet and pulled Kia after her. "Right now, we have two sisters who need us. While this water heats, we need to cut some sinew off this bird. I think we'll find some under that other wing."

"Don't you want to see Stix before we get to work?"

"I'm thinking she would rather be healed than have a long chat over nuts and tea. You'll need that." She nodded and Kia grabbed her knife from what was left of the spine plant.

"We'll be right back, love. Take care of her." Kia touched Song on the cheek and ducked out of the shelter.

Rok was already pushing her way under the wing when Kia joined her.

"What do you expect to find in the dark, Rok?"

"Put your hand on this joint." Rok held Kia's hand to a knuckle in the giant bird's wing. "Do you feel the cord running from the bone to the muscle?"

"Yeah. That's the sinew?"

"Right. We don't need light to find what we know is there, just trust your skill and knowledge." She slid her sharp blade under the skin and exposed the tough tendon and Kia helped pull the skin away from the muscle. "We also need a roast. Get ready to grab this when I cut it loose. It might be heavy." Rok cut the meat from the bone and it swung down, knocking the breath out of Kia. "I told you it was heavy. Now pull on it while I cut the tendon."

In moments the roast was cooking over the fire and Song was splitting the tendon into sinew. "Is the water hot yet?" she called. "We're going to have plenty sinew to heal Stix and have some left over for the next time."

"I pray to Veenah we never need it," Kia whispered.

Song smiled grimly. "Will one of you please heat a tree dog claw in the fire? And I need the bloody parts to be cut from this blanket."

Rok had just sat down and was massaging the back of her neck. "Song, I don't know how you can keep going." She fished a claw from one of the packs and had it on the fire in moments.

Kia dropped an armload of soft feathers in the shelter and held up the blanket which had been wrapped around Stix's leg. "There's not much on here that's not bloody. Do you need a piece for a bandage?"

"Yes, but I also need a piece to wash the cut."

"Hey, what's wrong with Stix? She's not moving!" Kia dropped the blanket and rushed to Stix.

"Relax, I gave her some medicine to make her sleep. When I close the cut it will hurt too much if she's awake. You did the most good by feeding her the juice of the spine plant. It saved her life. I'll need more of it to make a poultice for the wound."

"I thought you didn't know much about healing."

"I don't, not like Vee." Song sat back from her work cleaning stones, leaves, and shreds of the woolen blanket from the sticky wound.

41

"I miss her so much." She brushed the hair from her face. Kia thought she looked more tired than Rok. "I made a cup from the spine plant skin, bring me some hot water."

Kia dribbled water into the gash and ran back for more. When it was clean enough to suit Song, she sat by Stix's head while Rok held her leg. By the light of the small fire, Song punctured the skin at the edge of the wound with the sharp tree dog claw and pressed the end of the sinew through the hole. Slowly she progressed, closing jagged edges, while Kia and Rok both watched in awe and horror.

Stix began to breathe harder and she threw her head to the side crying out. Kia held her tight. "It's okay, love, we're all here. I'm sorry, but we have to do this to save you. I know it hurts."

Stix shrieked and threw her head to the side.

"Song, where is the medicine to make her sleep? She's in pain. We've got to help her," Kia pleaded.

"I can't. She'll see strange things when she wakes up. Just hold her. I'm almost finished."

Stix screamed again.

Kia held Stix's head and shoulders on her lap and gripped her hands. "Shhh, my love, I know it hurts."

"I need more water to wash this blood away!" Song cried out. Rok jumped to get it, but Song stopped her. "No, you have to hold her down or she'll tear out the sinew. Oh, I know why we have to be five! Veenah, why did you have to take my beautiful Vee! I need her so much!"

Kia sobbed silently while Stix thrashed in pain. "Be still. Please be still, dear Stix, we're trying to help you." Kia thought of a time long ago when she and Stix watched a pair of bleeding jays feeding their chicks. In a low voice she recounted the story for Stix. Slowly she relaxed.

Song washed the wound clean with several cups of water. At last, she sat back. "Finished." She covered the stitches with a poultice of willa bark and spine plant. Rok helped her wrap a fresh piece of woolen blanket tight around the leg and she tied it.

Warmsun shed light into the shelter and Stix slept.

Rok staggered out to the smoldering fire and drank her fill of the warm water. She dipped a cupful for Song, hoisted the browned roast and returned to the shelter. With the last of her strength, she tied the meat to a massive feather and cut slices for each of them. Still chewing, she slumped to the sleeping mat with Song in her arms. Kia settled into the soft feathers beside Stix after she knew her sisters were comfortable. She fell asleep asking Veenah to give strength to her fems. But she feared the strength would never come.

The leader will follow
The warrior will plea
The healer is coming
To set Terah free

8 Refugees

Kia opened her eyes to the blinding light of Warmsun wondering what had startled her. Rok slept soundly a few inches away, nestled down in the mound of feathers. Song was between them, her head resting on Rok's arm. Stix thrashed her head side to side and moaned, her hands worked – stretching out and balling up in tight fists and her healthy leg twitched. Again she moaned. Kia managed to capture a few words between the groans.

Run. Fire. Kill. Her breath came faster and beads of sweat popped out on her forehead. Suddenly she opened her eyes and screamed, "No! Kia!"

Kia sat straight up.

Song screamed.

Rok leaped to a crouch, clutching her knife.

"It's okay. Stix has sleep terrors." Kia cradled Stix, rocking and holding her tight. "We're here, sweet Stix, you're safe." Kia stroked her forehead, but jerked back from the burning hot skin.

Stix groaned, but lay limp in Kia's arms.

"Song..." Kia glanced around but Song only huddled in the far corner of the shelter, sobbing. Kia's eyes met Rok's. "Help me."

Rok, moved to the sleeping place beside Stix. "What's wrong?" With a gasp, she yanked the soft tunic off over Stix's head. "She's on fire! Song! Get water!"

Song cried harder, but grabbed the spine plant cup and dove out of the shelter. She spilled much of the precious liquid stumbling back with it. Before either of the fems staring at her could say anything, she ran for more water. This time she also brought a blanket with the corner dripping wet. She wiped it over Stix's arms and body while Kia dribbled water into her mouth. Rok stared at Song, but didn't speak.

"We need more of the spine plant," Song whispered. "Kia, do you think you could find it again?"

"Of course, but what's wrong with you? Why are you still crying?"

"This happened because of me," Song sobbed and turned away. "I brought the bad luck. I...I..."

Kia almost laughed. "If you're thinking about you and Vee whispering to each other in the middle of the ceremony, I highly doubt it. I don't think you have the power to call a Zid harvester."

Rok, still crouched, sitting on her heels, growled through clenched teeth. "I think you've all forgotten that I'm a trained warrior, and I can tell when someone hides the truth."

Kia's heart turned cold with fear. She'd seen Rok's temper and knew the horrible consequences of crossing the warrior. Once, Rok had snapped the neck of a swamp wolf when it attacked. Another time, she caught an elderfem stealing food and beat her nearly senseless, breaking the elder's arm in the process. The Eldermems and council had declared Rok justified and punished the offending fem. After that the whole village feared Rok. Now Kia feared for Song.

Rok roared, fists clenched in fury. "What are you hiding from us? Are you such an infant you can't speak?"

"Stop it," Kia screamed. "Stop now, Rok. This is not the time! No matter what, we have to work together, twice as hard because we are only half of a femtog. And that's no one's fault! You're scaring me and Song, and you're upsetting Stix!"

"Stix is out of it. She can't hear a thing. Come with me. We'll get the spine plant." She glared at Song. "Get over here and take care of *our* sister. If you think all this is your fault, then *do* something about it instead of bawling like a child!" Rok stomped out of the shelter and Song scrambled on hands and knees to Stix's side.

Trembling, Kia touched Song on the cheek, but had no words. She hurried after Rok.

"Don't say a word!" Rok growled. "Just lead."

After a few steps down the trail Kia spoke anyway. "Sounds to me like you'd like to lead us."

"I told you in the beginning I wasn't femtog material."

"You wish you hadn't pledged?"

"If I hadn't pledged my love and loyalty I'd be ash under that Zid Perg-hole, or worse, I'd be a slave."

"That's not an answer. If the Zid hadn't attacked, would you leave us and go back?"

"No, and don't ever ask me that again. I don't break a promise. And I don't hide the truth."

"And just what truth do you think little Song is hiding?"

"If I knew, it wouldn't be hidden." Rok swiped her hands over her face and lowered her voice. "I just don't know, and that bothers me. She should trust us more."

"The way you trust us?"

Rok shot a hard stare at Kia and walked on without speaking.

"You didn't answer the other question," Kia said.

"You didn't ask another question, you made a statement."

"Well?"

"No, I don't want to lead. It's enough responsibility to protect your hides. I can't be anchored down with decisions as well."

Kia thought Rok might be calming down a bit, but she was still wary. She took a deep breath and chose her next words carefully, trying to push the image of Rok beating the elderfem from her mind. "Do the rest of us need to fear you?"

Rok stopped in the trail. "No. I pledged to protect you with my love, my loyalty, and my life. I would take my own arm off before I laid a hand on any of you. I wouldn't be protecting if I harmed you, would I? In fact, I'd like to take my tongue out for yelling." Rok embraced Kia tightly. "That's all I have to say and I don't want to say it over and over. I can't change who I am."

"You'd better make sure Song knows what you just told me. You scared her."

"She's the last person in Terah who needs to fear me. And I've told her that already."

"Good. The spine plant is over here." Kia turned off the narrow trail and pointed to a jumble of boulders. "Behind those. But watch for slitherbeasts."

"And wolves. How did you ever find this in Moonlight?"

"The hand of Veenah."

"Humph." Rok took the lead with her knife bared, peering under brush and behind stones possibly hiding a serpent big enough to swallow a fem whole. Suddenly she yanked Kia protectively behind her and drew her hand back, prepared to throw the knife.

A coppery-haired fem stood up from behind a boulder with her hands held over her head. She gripped a bow and arrow in one hand. "Don't kill me!" she yelped. "I thought you were a swamp wolf or a Zid!"

"Put that weapon down, fem. Where did you come from?" Rok said, still poised to throw her knife.

"We've been walking for three days," the fem said as she eased around the boulder to drop the bow and arrows. "We came from a mountain village on the other side of the valley. The Zid attacked before the rock diggers came." She ducked back behind the boulder.

"Who is with you?" Kia struggled out of Rok's grip and stood beside her.

"Only Fem'ma and a mem."

"How did you escape and get so far from the mountain?" Kia was still suspicious.

"I was away from the village trying to hunt."

"Trying?"

"I'm useless with that thing, but I had to gain skill if I ever wanted to be part of a femtog."

"Where are the others? I think you are a raider, or spy for the Zid." Rok stepped away glancing in all directions.

A jolt of panic swept Kia's body when she realized the rocky area was a perfect ambush site. She unsheathed her knife and backed down the trail, holding Rok's tunic tight in her left hand.

The strange fem climbed up on the boulder. "That's the stupidest thing I've ever heard in my life. If those wretched spawns of Perg had taken me – and I was still alive – do you think there is any way I would still look like this?"

She wore a necklace of bear's claws and a long, white tunic

made of mountain ram's skin, adorned with beads and the velvety white tails of rock mink. Seamless slitherbeast skins covered her legs, down to thick, bear-hide foot coverings.

"I had no idea the mountain village was so wealthy," Rok said. "Still, I don't see the rest of your troupe." She and Kia backed down the trail until they were clear of the boulders.

"Don't worry, young warrior." The rich, tenor voice of a mem came from the high bushes. He emerged, perched on the shoulder of a tall elderfem who wore a long buckskin dress. He wore a white cloak adorned with river clam shells and closed with buttons made from small animal leg bones.

Kia's heart flopped and she was positive her eyes left their sockets. The elderfem wasn't holding the helpless mem. He was barely balanced on her shoulder!

Kia turned her head away, ashamed that she'd stared at the mem.

He spoke again. "Fems, stand down, all of you. Not enough of us remain in this part of Terah to risk a battle. I assure you, we are harmless. In fact, we are so harmless we cannot even get meat. Let me introduce my little clan. I am called Moon. I am carried by Fem'ma. I don't know her birth name. Ch`e is the one who cannot scare the side of a hut with her bow."

"Shut up, Moon. That was mean," Ch`e huffed.

Kia cringed to hear such disrespect. Even if he was young, all mems deserved to be honored.

"Forgive me dear Ch`e. Fem'ma, lower me to the ground so I may present our weapon to the warrior.

The matron's face seemed to drain of its color. "No!" she whispered. "Not here!"

"You must!" Moon's voice kicked up a notch.

"It's the law."

"Ma, Please! I'm sure she can make better use of it than we can and possibly she will be willing to hunt for us."

With visibly shaking hands, Fem'ma unfurled a small blanket and spread it on the ground beside the bow.

Rok gasped and took a step forward. Kia covered her mouth to keep from crying out. The matron placed Moon on the ground. It was unheard of. What if he toppled and injured his head? Worse, what if he

48

injured his seeder? She ran forward, instinctively, to lift him out of danger. The matron grabbed her arm.

"It's okay. He's protected. I keep him wrapped so he won't injure himself. He likes to stand on the ground, and he hasn't toppled in years."

"What? How?" Rok and Kia spoke as one.

Moon tipped his head back and laughed hard. "You've never seen one like me! Watch!" He wobbled a bit and leaned forward, twisting his thick torso, and took a step, then another. He shuffled forward until he was clear of the hem of his cloak then twisted again. Protruding from his tightly swaddled wrap was a foot.

"See? I have two of them! And," he shrugged the cloak to the side to expose his shoulder, "I have hands! Well, tiny hands, but my fingers bend and I can hold onto Fem'ma when we travel." He hobbled to the bow and. "Let's see if I can do this." He curled his torso and twisted, reaching his exposed hand toward the weapon.

Rok stepped toward him, watching Ch'e and Fem'ma with caution.

Moon hooked a finger around the bow, but dropped it. "Wait," he said. "I got this." He bent again and this time secured the bow. Lifting the end from the ground, he hobbled a circle to face Rok. "May I present our weapon? We would like meat. What do you say, warrior, is it a trade?"

Rok averted her eyes and bowed her head as she reached for the bow. "I accept your trade, Syr Moon. With my leader's permission, we have meat at our shelter. However, we came this way to collect spine plants for medicine."

"Warrior, let's get something straight right away. I'm not a father, nor even out of training yet, so you should not call me syr. And please look at me. You make me feel like a freak when you turn away. What are your names? I don't want to call you Warrior and Hey You forever."

"I am Rok of Cerian hearth. My bond sister and leader is Kia of-"

"Greetings, Rok and Kia of your own hearth," Moon cut in. "I would venture to guess your village, along with your fathers' hearths, is gone. And we should drop the formalities, at least while we are refugees."

Kia whispered to Rok, "What's refugees?"

"I heard that," Moon said. "A refugee is what we are. Wandering, homeless, because the enemy has destroyed our homes. You were here looking for medicine? Which of you is sick, or are there more of you?"

Kia answered. "We were five starting our bonding quest. One sister was killed in the first blast and another is badly hurt."

Ch`e hopped down from the boulder. "Why didn't you say so before? We're wasting time!"

"Are you a healer?" Kia asked.

"The best. I'll help you." Ch`e dove for the spine plant and knocked loose several pads along with some of the purple fruits. "Can one of you scrape those? Fem'ma, will you weave a basket?"

Everyone burst into action. Moon wobbled dangerously close to the spine plant. "What can I do to help you?"

"Don't get hurt," Kia said, feeling heat rise in her cheeks.

"He's a mem, not an infant!" Ch`e grumped. "Here, Moon, use this stick and hold the pads down so they can clean them faster."

Again Kia's jaw dropped.

Moon deftly flipped the stick to his shoulder and braced it with his jaw while he held it down with his fingers. Chuckling at Kia's surprise, he said, "We are a progressive clan. Mems are expected to participate. Get busy, our medicine woman has a temper."

"Great," Kia mumbled. "Just what I need, a hearth full of angry fems."

"What kind of injury does your sister have?" Ch`e hollered from across the field.

"Hey!" Rok yelled. "Don't wander off alone!" She glanced at Kia then Fem'ma, who was half finished with the basket.

"I'll stand watch. You go with her," Kia said.

Rok took off like an arrow to catch up with Ch`e. They stopped at a thick tree several paces away.

Rok eyed the fem while glancing around the clearing. "Stix has a bad cut on her leg. Our sister, Song, used sinew and a tree dog claw to close the wound. She gave Stix something to help her sleep while she sewed."

"Good, I know what to get. Lift me up on your shoulder so I can reach that tree moss." Ch`e pulled several wads of silvery moss from the tree. "Now, see that fallen log? Let's see if it has some lichen. And I need a couple of small green plants that should be growing somewhere in this damp soil. Ha! Got it. Hey, I can get used to hunting medicine with my own guard."

Rok grunted and led the way back to Kia.

Fem'ma lifted Moon to her shoulder and carried her basket loaded with much needed medicines. The troupe followed the trail back to the shelter at a fast jog. Kia glanced over her shoulder to see Moon grinning, sitting sideways so he could hold Fem'ma's hair with both hands.

They slowed before emerging from the tall grasses when they approached the dead nightbird, and the shelter under its wing. A shriek from a carrion bird split the air, followed immediately by the snarl of a short-tailed lion. Kia peered through the reeds in horror. The nightbird had been ripped to shreds and was completely turned on its back.

Song and Stix were nowhere to be seen.

Death rains upon us
From out of the sky
Evil pours forth
To silence our cry

9 Death Birds

Kia screamed and hurled herself at the carrion eaters, lean, dirty brown birds with thick red skin hanging in folds from their heads all the way down their necks. Defending their meal, the two nearest birds screeched and swatted at her with their wings which were as long as the tallest fem. She slung rocks and broken pieces of firewood, irritating them to a frenzy. A large stone from the remnants of the fire ring met its mark, hitting a giant bird just under its eye. It took flight and one by one the rest followed, taking to the air and escaping the maddened fem.

All that remained of a once comfortable sleeping place was a bit of scattered grass and feathers. Kia fell to her knees panting for breath.

One bird hobbled into the brush, its wing broken and pinned to its side by an arrow. Rok retrieved her arrow from a dead shorttail lion and followed a blood trail to where the second lion had fallen and pulled the arrow from its tawny hide. She lay her hand on the beast's head.

"I'm sorry I had to take your life to save my own. We need your fur, but there's no time. We have to find Song and Stix." She stood and searched for foot tracks. "I should have known the death eaters would come. We should have never left them alone!" She leaped to the branch of a nut tree and climbed to get a better view.

Kia yanked at the mutilated wing of Nightbird, searching for any sign of their missing sisters. She found the bag holding the nuts and the tree dog pelts and rolled the three remaining blankets.

"There's no fresh blood here. They must have escaped. But they

52

can't go far with Stix's injury."

Ch`e emerged from hiding, "Why are you looking under a dead nightbird? You're all cracked!"

"Stix was injured bad and couldn't walk, the nightbird attacked and we killed it. Well, Stix killed it. We sheltered under its wing. Cast around for tracks."

"I would have never thought of that. I don't see tracks, but here is a piece of rope." She walked a few paces away from the carcass, pointing to a thorn bush.

"That would be Song's marker. Hey, where's Fem'ma and Moon?"

"Duh, under cover. Fem'ma was a hunter before she was a matron. And she's protecting Moon." Ch`e cupped her hands around her mouth. "Come on out, it's safe."

Not far from the trail, in the deep reeds, Fem'ma stood holding two poles cut from young trees. "The death eaters aren't gone," she said, hacking the end of one pole into a point. "They're planning a way to make us their dinner along with the nightbird. I saw a movement three hand's paces behind you. That is either the mate of your dead lions, or your sister's next marker. Take this, just in case." She tossed one of her crude spears to Kia and ducked back into the grass.

Along a narrow trail, well past the ravaged camp, Kia found a third hastily woven length of grass rope. "Song! Stix! Where are you?"

Rok pushed ahead pointing toward a low mound in the grass ahead. Ch`e took position a few paces to the side and the three fems approached the structure. Wide blades of targus grass had been bent and woven together. Kia had never seen such a thing. She circled closer and prodded the mat with the spear. "Song? Please tell me you made a grass hut. Are you in there?"

A whimper was all the reply she needed. Kia and Rok tore the grass away. Song lay huddled in a small depression with Stix.

Falling into the nest, almost with a sob, Rok wrapped her arms around Song. "I was so afraid I'd lost you forever."

"They came so fast...and...I was sleeping. I'm sorry, I should have been standing watch, but I was so tired. Memlore was right. I'm too young to have a femtog of my own."

"It's over," Kia said. "You're alive, and you were clever enough to leave us a trail. We should have been back sooner. How's Stix?"

Rok knelt beside Stix, one arm still around Song.

"She's sleeping," Song said. "She ran with me when the carrion birds came, but her pain was so bad she was screaming. I gave her more of the sleeping medicine." Almost in a whisper, she added, "I made her chew it. I hope it's not too strong."

"She's not burning so much now. You're a good healer."

"This is your injured sister?" Ch`e asked, approaching from behind.

Song leaped to her feet. "Who are you?"

"I am called Ch`e."

"I am Song. Are there more survivors?"

"Not many came through the first attack, certainly few from the plains. I come from the mountain, but the rumbling terah caused rocks to fall on my village. I was gathering herbs when it happened. Your patient, how bad is she?"

Kia looked up from where she knelt beside Stix. "You can see the blood from her cut. She burned from fever when we left to find medicine."

"I'll look at her. My hearth mothers were all healers. I'm a great healer."

"You are?" Song said. "I know little, but I sewed the wound with sinew."

"You said you gave her something to make her sleep?"

"I gave her Mountain Doc. Also when we closed the cut."

"No! How much did you give her? If she sleeps this hard, you gave her too much!" Ch`e threw down her pack and immediately examined Stix, opening her eyelids, looking into her mouth, and testing her fever with lips to the forehead. "I must look at the injury." She used her knife to cut the bindings and expose Stix's leg. "This is hot, too hot. However, you did well closing the cut. If she lives she will have a grand story to tell the children of her hearth."

"What do you mean, *if she lives*?" Kia nearly choked on the words.

"Poison can grow in a tiny wound or a large one. We need to prevent the poison from spreading." Ch`e opened her pack then stopped and stood, looking toward the sky. Carrion birds still circled and dipped, feasting on the giant night bird and no doubt on the dead shorttail lions. Warmsun had passed his high point and was traveling back toward Terah, but thick, black clouds loomed on the horizon. "We have to find good shelter, and more water." She whistled, shrill and long.

Fem'ma raised herself from the targus grass, twenty paces away, with her weapons ready. "Who are these fems?" the elder called.

Rok moved between the elderfem and her sisters, her own knife in hand. "These are the rest of my sisters. Lower your spear, Elder. They welcome you."

Ch`e waved Fem'ma closer. "It's all right. Bring Moon. We may as well get acquainted. We need to find shelter, and I may need some different medicines for this one."

Fem'ma ducked into the grass and reemerged with two heavy packs and Moon on her shoulder.

Song turned her head, cheeks flushing. "Kia! She carries a mem! What are we going to do?"

"Shhh, sister. Right now we must pull together."

"But it's forbidden!"

"And just who is going to say anything to us about laying eyes on a mem?" Rok raised her voice then grabbed Song's hand. "I'm sorry, I didn't mean to yell. We are a small band, alone in Terah. Now we have one more fem to help us. And if there are no more villages left, at least we have a mem."

Ch`e ignored their outburst. "Fem'ma, you know the land better than most fems, guide us. Moon, you watch behind us. Danger can come from anywhere." Ch`e studied the still, sleeping form on the ground. She raked the soiled dressing away and spread a bit of tree moss on the wound then retied the bandages. "Kia, Rok I don't know if this will work, but instead of one of you carrying her on your back, we will try to carry her between you. Hold her arms over your shoulders then lift her and hold her legs up, as if she was sitting on your arms. Grip your hands under her legs so you won't drop her."

"Won't that give her more pain?" Song asked.

"Hopefully it will give her enough pain to wake up. And when she wakes, she will need water. We carry only a small amount and it is for Moon."

Song pointed to a fat, round spine plant as tall as her knee. "We can find water from those, and the river isn't far from here."

"You have a sharp eye, healer," Ch`e said smiling. "I'll need you on the trail with me looking for herbs and berries. Okay, fems, let's get going."

Rok put her hands on her hips. "Just because you bring an elderfem and a mem with you doesn't put you in charge."

Kia huffed. "C'mon, help me get Stix up. We'll work this out later."

"But you are leader of this femtog," Rok said between her teeth.

"And I say we take her advice and carry our sister to safety. I'm too tired to even think straight right now."

Kia gazed into the faraway mountains, the forbidden place. Her world, once so big, so lovely and giving, had become small and cruel. She wondered why Terians weren't allowed to travel there. It looked like more than a few days run. But then, they had more than a few days to spare. She wondered why those mountains now called out to her. She also wondered why making a decision suddenly was so very difficult.

"Which way to the river?" Kia said with a sigh.

Fem'ma glanced around. "I've never traveled this far when I was a hunter, but I'd say downhill."

Rok grunted. "You are wise, Elder, that is the direction of the White River."

Kia helped Rok hoist Stix and they trudged along the ragged trail. In the distance, a rumble rolled across the sky.

"If you still think Veenah is listening to you, Kia," Rok panted, "you could ask her to turn that storm aside. We don't need to fight that as well."

Kia couldn't answer. *Are you still with us, Blessed Veenah?* In her heart, she had doubt, and it left bitterness oozing into what once held love and faith.

Ch`e and Song walked together farther ahead of the group, both using crude spears to part targus grass and thorn bushes looking for medicines and food. Once Song thrust her spear into the base of a tree and retrieved a long-ear nearly as big as a child when her first tooth falls.

Kia's stomach rumbled at the thought of how many ways the tenderest of meats could be prepared. Ch`e held the animal while Song made fast work of cleaning it. They buried the entrails so the death birds

56

couldn't follow them.

Ch'e dropped the meat into her bag, slinging it over her shoulder, and called out to Fem'ma. "See, I told you I'd find us help. We will have full bellies tonight. Let's hurry to this river of yours, fems."

Kia ground her teeth together as the stranger claimed meat which her sister had taken. Leadership might be difficult, but giving in to this loud-mouthed Terian would be much worse.

A cold wind announced the first heavy drops of rain.

Cover me in dearth and rot
Where enemies dare not follow
Feed me, heal me, teach and guide me
Give me strength to face tomorrow

10 The Den

The small stand of trees did little to deflect the pounding rain. Rok did her best to cover Kia and Stix with her small blanket tented over their heads, but the wind buffeted them and nearly ripped the blanket from her hands.

Song crouched, alone, under a tree branch, holding her hands over her ears. Lightning tore through the sky, followed by a clap of thunder, and Song screamed.

Ch`e huddled closer to the hunched form of Fem'ma. Rok watched her closely and wondered why the healer wasn't trying to help protect her elder.

"There's still something about that one I don't trust," Rok whispered, nodding her head toward Ch`e. "But I trust you, and I trust my own knife. You and I will have to take turns keeping watch no matter what these other fems say. I don't want them standing watch without one of us." She waited until Kia agreed. They both looked toward their youngest sister. "I love Song, but she may not be able to stay awake to help. She's different, maybe injured in a hidden way."

"All of us are changed. We're not supposed to be the same." Kia said.

Rok studied the slight form of the young fem she loved. Her heart hurt with every beat. Only a few days ago, Song had been laughing, running, and jumping out of sheer happiness. Now she sat, stoop shouldered, like an aged elder. And the hollow look in her eyes almost

58

made Rok's blood run cold. She knew Song was still grieving for the loss of Vee. But what could be haunting her?

Water fell in sheets as the tempest strengthened and Rok felt herself growing weaker. She turned her head to allow some of the rain to flow into her mouth, but the huge, cold drops stung her face and she hunched lower. The air erupted with light and the crackle of the thunderclap and even Rok jumped in fear when the bolt of lightning struck a nearby tree.

Images of the blast, the destruction of their home, intruded into her mind. The memory of her selfish escape would haunt her dreams forever. Did that sin, that betrayal of trust when she'd run from the blast in fear, stand out in her face the way Song's pain glared out through the child's eyes? No one could ever know what a coward she had been. A growl grew deep in her chest as Rok struggled to drive out her guilt.

The wind eased and the rain no longer fell like a waterfall over a cliff. Stix's cheeks glowed red. Rok stiffened her back against the storm and shouted, "We've got to get out of here and find better shelter. Stay close together!" The force of her words caused her to cough.

Lifting Stix took all her strength. Again, she locked arms with Kia and together they gained their balanced and supported their sister. The wind drove into her, as if it still wanted to punish her. She leaned into her steps to outdistance her past and slowly re-focused on the present.

As a warrior and protector, Rok steadily scanned the brush and tree line for dangers. The storm broke up as fast as it had started and Warmsun cast her mottled light between the spent and shredded clouds. As her tunic slowly dried, the stiff leather began to chafe and her skin itched.

Rok glanced behind her. Fem'ma followed a short distance, using her spear as a walking stick. She didn't hold Moon in her arms or carry him in a sling, which was the respectful way. Nor did she bother to help him balance on her shoulder. Instead, the mem clutched her dripping wet hair with his pudgy fingers and kept his seat by gripping with his feet.

Moon's head swiveled in all directions. Rok knew he could see farther than the rest of them, but that fact angered her as well as alarmed her. Someone untrained could panic in the face of danger. Worse, in her heart she knew it was wrong to put that much pressure on any mem. Protection was the responsibility of the hunters and warriors, not a helpless mem.

Song trudged along a few paces ahead. In spite of the sweet smell of a freshly washed world, and the raucous noise of birds playing in the aftermath of the storm, she still looked downcast. The sight brought even more pain to the warrior's heart. She swallowed hard, and then hoped the pain in her throat was only her grief, and not a curse of illness sent by the storm. She tried to stifle another cough.

Kia had been silent since they'd spoken about Song in the middle of the raging storm. At length, she spoke again, startling Rok out of her thoughts. "Yes, Song has changed. We all have. We are on our bonding quest, which itself, should change us. We will be changed more than usual because our bonding has been anything but normal."

"That's not what I mean and you know it," Rok growled. She shifted her grip to relieve her arm a bit and cradle Stix a little better. Stix groaned, but slept on. "Song was happy and smiling. She was radiant like sky in summer. Now she's dark, as if life has faded. I'm so afraid we lost two sisters instead of only one. Something is just not right."

"It's all the danger and fear we have faced. She grew up with strong values and faith, and then we meet these strange Terians who don't have any respect for a mem," Kia whispered lower. "Why does he take the name of the ruler of the night sky? Does he count himself as a deity?"

Rok considered her leader's words. Her beloved Song had indeed grown quieter since the arrival of the strangers, and the presence of a nearly grown mem upset all of them. "I don't know, maybe he believes it because he has what no other mem has ever had before. But how did he escape? Ch'e told us she was practicing with her bow in a ravine away from the village when the attack came, but what about Fem'ma and… him? Where were they?"

Kia stumbled and nearly fell, jarring Stix and knocking Rok off balance. Stix cried out, but didn't awaken.

Rok continued. "I wonder why we've never heard of the mountain village. Our warriors travel far. And another thing; that young fem hides the truth. She may have told us she was practicing, but she told Song she was gathering medicines."

Warmsun was close to her resting place when Kia finally heard the roaring of White River. Boulders, fallen trees, and thick tangles of vines and thorn bushes created an almost impenetrable wall before them. Song pointed to a narrow trail winding down to the river, and the troupe inched their way closer to the life giving water. Sweat rolled down Rok's body, and she could feel Kia shaking with exhaustion.

Stix groaned again. Her clutch on Rok's neck tightened as she roused herself. "Thirsty," she croaked. "Water! Hurt! Put me down!"

Rok struggled to maintain her hold on Kia's arms and not drop their sister.

"Calm yourself, love," Kia said. "We're almost there."

"I had such a strange dream," Stix said, coughing to clear her throat. Her words slurred and ran together. "I saw two of you. Two Kias and two Roks. And two Songs between you."

"And where were you?" Rok asked. A chill ran through her. Ch`e had warned them about this. Rok had seen the effects of an overdose before. The fem who had been injured on a hunt, took too much of the pain-relieving Mountain Doc tea. She recovered in due time, but saw strange and terrifying things for the rest of her life.

"I don't know. I only saw it. You were in a circle, but it was bigger than only us and I couldn't see the rest. It was a strange dream. And black fliers were all around and the whole world was green. Then I was riding a flier. I wonder if a fem could really ride a flier. I could ride a nightbird all the way to the Forbidden Mountain. Isn't that funny?" She coughed again. "Please loosen my leg, Kia, it hurts."

Stix chattered senselessly for a while then just sat with her head drooping lower and lower. Rok trembled with exhaustion and no longer tried to contain her coughing.

Kia called down the trail to Ch`e and Song. "We need to find a good cave. Stix is awake and needs to rest."

Ch`e chopped at thick vines to open the trail. "I think you're just tired of carrying her. Better shelter will be close to the river in the rocks."

Stix jerked in surprise, pulling Rok off balance. "Who is that?"

Rok answered, "That is part of what's back there."

Kia stumbled, nearly throwing them all off the trail, when Stix twisted to look backward.

Stix squeaked in surprise. "Did you know there's a mem

61

following us?"

"Yeah, first we were five, then four and almost three. Now we are a full hand complete with an elder." Rok grumbled.

"But we have not bonded! The mem can't be here! It's bad luck," Stix again struggled to free herself, then slumped, groaning in pain. "Where did they come from? Who are they?"

Kia puffed, "We pray to Veenah they are friends."

Rok ground her teeth together. "But we trust our weapons in case they are not." She stopped at a huge fallen tree. "Kia, this is the place I think we need to stay. Song and I found it when we went for water. We planned to bring you here. I think the brown bear sleeps in this den when the cold comes. It's dry and safe. You must tell the others we stop here."

They lowered Stix to rest on an exposed root that was high enough to support her comfortably. The ground called to Rok and promised soothing rest, but she pushed the temptation away and surveyed the camp. A den large enough for many brown bears lay beneath the tree trunk. Warmsun shone through the opening, assuring light and heat for much of the day and boulders, wedged under the wood, collected the heat to deliver it throughout the cold night. The shelter would be safe; not only from storms, but from predators who would dare not approach a fire. *And I can even defend us from a Zid attack in this shelter.*

"It is a good place for us to rest." Satisfied, Rok shrugged the bow from her shoulder and inspected it for damage. The few arrows wrapped in the sheath needed sharp points to be useful, but they were straight and sturdy and even well fletched with the feathers of a waterbird. She waited while Kia made the decision.

Song and Ch`e had disappeared through the brush. Glancing after her beloved, small sister, Rok felt the flame of anger and jealousy toward the newcomer rise in her chest. *That one will try to be leader, but I will never betray my Kia.* She scanned the area again. Fem'ma stood a few paces away. Rok knew the matron would be ready to carry her charge to safety if needed. Moon perched tall on her shoulder and simply grinned.

"We stay here." Kia trembled. "We have to watch for the brown bear, but the cold is still far away, and he's likely out filling his belly. And we need to post a watch in the darkness because a slitherbeast or even a short-tailed lion can slink into the den in the night and make a meal of us."

"A den close to the roaring water would be safer from bear, wolf, and serpent, but it would not be safe from a rising flood," Rok said quietly.

Kia swayed and Rok leaped to support her. But, Fem'ma was beside her sister instantly.

Fem'ma said gently, "Rest, child. If you will allow, I will inspect the shelter and assist you in preparing it. Give me direction."

"You mean you will follow me rather than your own clan?" Kia said.

Rok's cold and untrusting heart stilled, waiting for the elder's response.

"Ch`e is young and strong. She may be a healer, but she has much to learn, as do you. However, she is headstrong. She does not have the wisdom to put her clan's safety above her pride."

The weight of responsibility softened with a warming deep inside Rok at the thought of these strangers entrusting their lives with her small family so easily.

And now I have more to protect, but if we were a family in a village I would protect this many and more.

Leaves rustled and branches cracked under Ch`e's knife, and she pushed her way back to the small clearing of the bear's den. "Why aren't you following? Song is preparing a fire ring in a good shelter near the water. There are no trees to hide our enemies' approach and a calm pool of water is only a few paces away. I have found grapes and figs and a giant shell of a land slug that will make a perfect stew pot for our longear."

Kia stepped away from Rok and Fem'ma, hands on her hips. "There is a reason no trees grow in that place, Healer. Water will come up and sweep everything away. We stay here. Veenah will provide and protect us."

"Oh really!" Ch`e snapped. "So you are one of those fools who believe in something unseen? I suppose you believe in that stupid prophecy as well. Today's little bit of rain can't turn this wide river into a flood, and I doubt that it ever will. Fem'ma, Moon, I have not been wrong yet and I've kept you safe. Follow me. A separate shelter is down there for you. In every way my shelter is superior to this hole in the ground!"

Fem'ma remained silent and Rok thought she detected Moon chuckling. Everyone looked at Kia.

Finally, her leader spoke. "When the rain falls here, it also falls in the hills and mountains. It takes a day or two before it flows down this far. And Warmsun melts the snows in the mountains which will make the river run wild. We stay here." Kia slumped onto the branch beside Stix.

"Ha. Stay if you wish, I have the food!" Ch`e whirled, throwing her long hair in an arc.

Song climbed through the tangle of branches and sidestepped the angry fem. "No, Ch`e. I have the food."

Cold, alone, the hunter stands
And waits without a sound.
Now, belly full and heart content,
A village saved, a hero crowned.

11 Never A Silent Watch

Ch`e glowered in the flickering firelight. She sat outside the bear den chewing the last shreds of meat from a juicy leg bone. Kia watched her, not sure if this fem would become a friend, or a sister, or possibly an enemy. But she needed Ch`e, not only for her skill as healer, and not because she brought with her a mem, which would ensure their life would continue. She needed this angry fem to love her and her sisters.

A pang of loss seared through Kia, but she buried it deeper in her heart as her gaze wandered over Ch`e's slender form. The fire in her eyes, and the swift, sure way she moved meant this fem would be strong and loyal. If she looked past the anger, Kia easily saw the passion and beauty which would be passed to her children – if she could bear them. This fem would be a fierce part of any femtog. She had to win Ch`e's trust.

Not tonight.

Stix sat upright, sipping meat broth from a spine plant cup. The tea that Ch`e had prepared for her seemed to have cured the fever–at least for now. Stix dipped a tuber from her broth and dropped the whole thing into her mouth, chewing until the juices ran down her chin.

"Are you feeling better?" Kia asked her.

"Hmm," Stix mumbled through her food. "It doesn't hurt so much, but I don't think I'll ever get the horrible taste of Ch`e's medicine out of my mouth."

Ch`e huffed. "It has to be strong enough to kill the poison.

Would you rather suffer and die? Humph, none of you appreciate me." She turned her back to them without waiting for any answer.

Rok sat with her back against the front of the den, chewing on a slender willa branch. She'd hardly eaten that night. Kia guessed that the strong warrior might be suffering from the pain of her many bruises – or possibly a sore throat from the rain. One eye was nearly swollen shut and a great, purple bruise covered half of her face, and blood oozed from a dozen small cuts. She's sipped only a bit of Ch'e's medicine, but had refused any other medical treatment. At least she didn't cough as bad.

Song had fallen asleep with her head in Rok's lap. Dark circles around her eyes betrayed the young fem. She was not well, but it was in spirit, not in body. Kia knew that medicine couldn't cure that. She didn't know if anything could. The thing which had taken Song's joy could never be healed.

Rok's head drooped, her eyes closed. Kia's heart squeezed shut, its pressure tingling in her eyes, forcing tears to cloud her vision. *How can I lead such a strong warrior?*

Despite her strict upbringing, she stole a glance at Moon. He was happily feasting on chunks of meat and the brilliant orange roots Song had located. Other than her father, Trog, Kia had never seen a mem take food, except an infant on his mother's milk. Trog rarely asked for more food or different food. He only accepted what his wives offered him. This mem was so different.

Moon sat on his feet and motioned to Fem'ma that he wanted more. Of course his mouth was so full his cheeks bulged. Fem'ma placed several different pieces of food on her hand and held them where he could reach. He caught a chunk of meat with his longest finger and rolled it to the edge of her hand and into his mouth. He smacked and licked his lips.

Kia wondered how much he could eat as he grunted and filled his mouth again. She decided to plan a hunt for a targus beast. A shoulder bone from the huge grass eater would make a more dignified food tray for both the mem and his matron.

Rok nodded awake and rose to her feet, then gently lifted Song and carried her to the sleeping place in the larger nest of the den. A moment later she re-emerged to help Stix lie down. Before Rok ducked back into the den, she looked back at Kia. Almost drowning in the sky-blue eyes, Kia raised a finger to her lips, then held her fist over her heart; a silent affirmation of love which Rok returned.

In the dimming light, Kia watched the powerful fem settle into the fresh pile of grasses with Song in her arms. Stix quickly fell asleep in the thick mat near the back wall. Kia could just see her in the soft glow of evening. Fem'ma and Moon disappeared into a private corner of the den which she'd prepared earlier. Inside the den, all was safe.

None of them had spoken about standing watch. They'd hardly spoken at all that evening. Later, she would awaken Rok to take over guard duty as they'd agreed on the trail that day. Kia forced out any thought of her own pain and listened to the bubbling and rushing of water. She could almost see the riverbank through the wide pathway Rok had chopped out. The afterglow of Warmsun's setting illuminated the forbidden mountain in a red glow then faded into night. A peaceful darkness settled over the camp.

Firelight dimmed and Kia rose from her seat to add wood. Since Ch`e had stayed at the far side of the camp, pouting, she was likely planning to sleep outside. A dangerous choice, but not as uncomfortable as sharing the space with an angry fem. And with someone on lookout, Ch`e would be safer. But Ch`e wasn't by the fire, or sitting on top of the fallen tree. Kia laid a few branches and chunks of dry drift wood on the fire and flames danced higher, casting eerie shadows. Ch`e was nowhere to be seen. Kia cut a sapling cone tree and trimmed it into a long spear, hardening and sharpening the point in the fire. Soon she would have to find a supply of grinding stones to hone her blade.

Moonlight shone through the trees and bushes. The sounds of night, insects, birds, and frogs, told her that all was well. She wasn't so sure. Nightbirds flew silently. Mountain lions and wolves prowled or waited in ambush for prey. Slitherbeasts lay invisible in the shadows next to game-trails waiting for their next meal to walk into their grips. And the Zid had ways of seeing through the darkness when flying in their skimmers; and Zid were in the territory.

Where was Ch`e? A fem would never wander alone in the night, even with Moonlight to guide the way. But Ch`e seemed oblivious to those dangers. The thought sent chills of fear through Kia. Did the healer just not care? Or had Ch`e never been trained and taught about such things?

Kia pondered the issue while she scraped the charred point of her spear which was now sharp enough to pierce even the tough hide of a targus beast. Moonlight climbed higher in the sky, smiling down on Terah as if no pain or terror existed, but Kia still felt the terror of the Zid's sudden attack. Her head pounded in time with the beating of her heart.

Trees and brush provided a protective screen which camouflaged the den. A small clearing ensured that enemies approaching from the front or sides would be seen long before they arrived, but Kia would speak with Rok and Fem'ma about setting traps and alarms for even more protection. She climbed to the top of the fallen tree to study the ascent to the top of the valley on the far side of the river.

Is that the direction of the Jewel of the Prophecy?

The thought quickened her pulse. No fems she knew of had ever crossed the river. She didn't know if a crossing was possible in the wide, sparkling torrent.

In spite of the occasional rumble pulsing through the rocks as Terah groaned in pain, nothing could be seen of the devastation occurring in her previous territory. Even the false suns casting light in the Zid mining zone were hidden by the ridge and forests. Wind traveling through the valley would carry smoke from the hearth-fire away from their enemy but Kia understood too well she had to keep her tiny clan alert.

But how to keep control of my clan when the angry one tries so hard to disrupt us?

Twisted roots from the old tree pointed jagged fingers in every direction. A few vines had taken possession of the tallest spires and Kia pushed them away to take a seat. A more perfect lookout could never be found. Still, she saw no sign of Ch`e. The song of a wolf somewhere in the badlands was joined by another until the night air chorused with their mournful howls.

They could slip in here and attack without anyone even knowing. Wolves as well as...

Fear jolted her at the thought of a slitherbeast, which may have crept into camp and taken her. But there would be sign; tracks and broken grass or brush where such a serpent would travel, and Ch`e's pack and weapons would still be on the ground. No, Ch`e had gone off somewhere. Kia scowled.

Exhaustion overtook her as she sat in the lookout and her head drooped. Startling herself awake, she stood and cast one last glance around the den. It was too quiet, and she was no longer alert. It was time for her to take her rest and awaken Rok. Without a sound, she slipped from her perch and walked the length of the dead tree to flatter ground. She poked at the fire and added more wood, then stretched and yawned, and turned for the entrance of the den.

A shriek and splashing of water at the river awakened everyone instantly. Rok was beside her, bow in hand. Song crouched in the doorway with two spears.

"Stay with Stix," Kia told Song.

"Where did it come from?" Rok whispered.

Kia pointed toward the river and the two of them crept toward the path, but crawled through the brush at the side, rather than expose themselves to danger. Rok took the lead moving more silent than air, but Kia stepped on a dry twig, sending the 'snap' echoing through the night. They crouched lower, listening. Something splashed in the river, and then a muffled growl, not from animal or bird, met them.

Kia whispered into Rok's ear, "Ch`e is missing." The strange sound must have come from a Terian, but it still could be a trap. They eased to the edge of the bushes.

Moonlight shined on the rocky riverbank revealing two thrashing forms at the water's edge. A creature as long as three fems end to end had Ch`e pinned to the ground. Separating to flank the beast, Kia and Rok rushed in.

"What in Perg is *that*?" Kia breathed. The creature obviously came from the water. Its tail beat the water to a froth. Eyes too small for such a beast sat on the sides of its head, just behind a gaping mouth which emitted frightful croaks and grunts. Its arms, pointed and without hands, lifted the giant body enough to once again flop on Ch`e, crushing her body. A third arm rose up from the thing's back. Its tail thrashed again and this time Ch`e growled a garbled threat. Kia raised her sharpened spear, unsure of where to strike and hit the beast's heart.

Rok stepped to the opposite side of it. "All I want to know is how to kill it."

Another voice almost caused Rok to sling her knife – straight into Fem'ma.

"Don't kill me! And for sure don't send your spear into that thing's side. We call it a water cat because it is the only fish that roars like a lion. Kia, your spear is longest, put the point into the opening behind its eye and shove it out the slit in the other side. Then we can lift it from Ch`e. Rok, you hold its spear arm to the ground, I'll hold this side."

Kia shoved the spear through the fish's gills and blood began to flow. Its tail thrashed wildly and again it tried to lift itself. Kia was thrown to the side and tripped over a thick targus grass rope tied to a boulder and running all the way into the creature's mouth. She leaped to her feet, gripping the spear, and braced herself for the fight. She finally understood the thing wasn't trying to crush Ch`e as much as it was trying to get back to the river.

Ch`e removed her blood-soaked arms from the bottom of the gill slits and scrambled to safety. She grabbed a heavy stone and brought it down on the monster's head again and again until it quivered in death. She sat, shaking almost as much as the monster, and glared at Kia. "It took you long enough! Didn't you hear my call?"

Anger rose up from the pit of Kia's stomach like the hot water that shoots from the ground. "The whole of Terah heard you! Probably those Zid back there as well! And if I had known where you were and what you were doing I would have been closer! What were you thinking wandering off by yourself? Even an infant knows better!" She gasped for breath as even more rage boiled inside her. The fem had changed her beautiful white dress for a plain, leather tunic. She had packed supplies before venturing from her village at the time of the attack!

Rok restrained Kia, holding her by the shoulders. "Sister, quiet! I think I understand why she came out here. But I agree, she – none of us – should ever again go to the hunt or even search the brush for berries alone." Kia relaxed her attack pose, but couldn't un-ball her fists. Rok released her to examine the massive fish. "I've never seen something this big, and never one with spears for fins. Our clan sets trap in the river to catch the red meated fish that come after the cold has left." She faced Ch`e directly. "I honor you, Hunter, and would learn to hunt this creature, if it pleases you."

Kia ground her teeth, still angry, now even more that Rok would try to flatter this rogue fem. Her thoughts whirled in mind boggling confusion as she suddenly realized Fem'ma had come alone. "Where's the mem?" she shouted. "Did you leave him?"

"Of course not, Song and Stix will provide protection. I assure you, he is safe."

"But are they safe from him? It's so wrong to leave them together without an elder." With a glance toward Rok, she dashed back to the den with Fem'ma behind her.

Song ran to meet her. "I didn't lay eyes on him. I didn't break the taboo. But he spoke to me and tried to make me laugh. Stix kept her eyes averted, too, but she spoke to him. She's so worried about you. What happened?"

"Slow down, love, breathe." Kia embraced her bond sister until they both stopped shaking. "I guess we're going to have to learn a new set of laws while we're forced to live this way. You can't be so afraid. I don't think Veenah will send a bolt to strike you down because of something you cannot help."

Song burst into tears. "You don't understand. I have broken more taboos than speaking to a mem." Her knees gave way and she collapsed to the ground in a sobbing heap.

With gratitude I accept your gifts
And take comfort in your care
Abundant wealth, I rejoice in bounty
But only if I share

12 The Breaking Of Meat

Fem'ma walked up to Kia carrying Moon in a more dignified sling. Song scrambled to her feet and wiped her face with the back of her hand. She looked down and drew designs in the dirt with her toe.

Moon cleared his throat. "I was afraid we were under attack, but now I'm guessing something less horrible has happened."

"Ch`e has captured a giant fish." Kia spoke, but kept her head bowed in respect.

"That is like Ch`e." Moon chuckled. "If there is water, she will be hunting. The eldermems have spoken of her skill often. I don't know why she ever wanted to learn the bow or throwing stick. What type did she kill?"

Kia looked at Fem'ma for the answer.

"It was the biggest water cat I've ever seen," the elder said.

"A great gift from Veenah. Not my favorite, but tasty, and the skin makes valuable leather. Fems, I suggest you go back to sleep. The warrior and the hunter will return when their work is finished. When Warmsun is once again in the sky, I wish to speak to all of you."

Song trembled at the mem's words and Kia held her close.

Moon continued, "I advised Stix to remain seated. I'm not sure she can move, though, but I know she needs you two more than anything, so go to her. Fem'ma will take care of me. I want to see this giant water cat with my own eyes."

Still clinging to Song's hand, Kia bolted for the den. She sunk

72

into the sleeping mat beside Stix and pulled Song down between them. "Moon is going to teach us something tomorrow," Kia told Stix. "I don't know how I feel about that."

"He acts as if he's already an elder or a Lore," Song whispered.

Kia nodded in agreement. "I wonder if he has been united with Ch`e and the rest of their femtog was killed. If that's true, then all of them are guilty of deceit."

Stix raised her head in shock. "If they are already united, we can never really adopt her as a bond sister, we would never be equal. But if he is not a syr, then he has no right to teach us."

"Shhh. I hear Fem'ma coming. Close your eyes."

Kia's exhaustion claimed her before Fem'ma and Moon returned to the den. She didn't even move until Warmsun seared her eyes beneath their lids. Her arm had gone numb under Song's head. Stretching the stiffness from her muscles, she freed herself and sat up. Stix leaned on her elbow watching Song sleep. Kia thought by her wrinkled brow and dark circles under her eyes that Stix's pain had returned.

"I'm okay," Stix whispered. "Sore, but Ch`e will take care of that soon, I hope."

"I smell a cooking fire. They might be back now." Kia cast a quick glance toward Moon's sleeping place. Her face flushed at the boldness, but he and Fem'ma were already outside. Then the same heat covered her body, thinking of the lecture Moon planned to give them.

As if he has the right.

"I'll bring you water. Hold her and let her sleep." Kia indicated the peaceful, sleeping Song.

"I wish we could all just lie together and sleep late. Why did all this happen to us, Kia?"

"I don't know," Kia whispered, then ducked out of the cave.

The clearing bustled with activity almost like a village. A drying rack had been erected over a smoky fire, and fragrant branches now smoldered under slabs of white meat. Kia's stomach twisted, telling her she hadn't filled it for far too long. She crouched behind a bush to relieve herself, and study the goings-on.

Ch`e and Rok hung meat on poles and Fem'ma braided grass into rope as fast as she could. Moon wobbled along the edge of the clearing looking into the forest. Kia didn't think she would ever get used to seeing such a thing. She'd never seen a mem, either infant, or grown, on a mat let alone on the bare ground – and outside in Warmsun. She tried to look away, but couldn't. Rok hung her last piece of fish and waited while Ch`e finished, then they walked back to the river's edge. Moon hollered, looking into the brush.

"I found another one, Ma!"

Fem'ma leaped to her feet drawing her knife from its sheath. Kia also leaped into action, not knowing what, exactly, the upstart mem had found. Fem'ma pushed into the bushes and reappeared carrying a long, very thin sapling.

"I'll help with that," Kia offered and began stripping branches and bark from the little tree.

With a nod, Fem'ma scooped up the rope and headed for the drying rack. Before Kia could move or speak, Moon was already searching for another pole.

A mem working. No one would believe it if I told them. Strange. I hope he can sing. Silly, all mems sing, it's the fems who only croak the words.

She held the pole in place on the drying rack while Fem'ma tied it.

Fem'ma tied her last knot. "I'll need much more rope before we're finished today."

"I need to drink water and bring some to my bond sisters," Kia said. "Will you come with me?"

"I can if you wish, but it's only a few paces to the water, and Rok and Ch`e have been up and down so many times a predator can't possibly be in the area. Wait here." Fem'ma dove into the den and returned with two drinking skins. "Fill these and we will all share."

Jogging down the trail, Kia kept a sharp eye to the brush and sky. At the riverbank she stopped in awe. The monstrous fish appeared even larger in the light than it had been in the dark. The carcass still lay on its belly, but the black hide had been stripped away exposing the pinkish meat. In spite of the amount hanging on the drying rack, it didn't look like much had been cut from the fish. Rok sliced thick strips and laid them in Ch`e's arms. Kia shook her head.

"I don't know how you two are still at this. Ch`e you must be about to drop in place."

74

"I thought we were forbidden to walk alone," Ch`e grumbled.

"Fem'ma asked me to get water." Kia made an attempt to sound angry, but it didn't show for the admiration she suddenly felt for Ch`e. She dipped the water then held her arm out to receive part of the load. We'll get finished quicker with extra hands."

Rok piled strips of meat in her arms.

Ch`e looked as if she would collapse at any moment. Kia told her, "Our sister, Stix, is in pain again. Will you make her a tea?"

"Ugh. Everyone needs me. All I do is work. Yes, of course I'll take care of your sister."

"I said 'our' sister. You've been awake all night. You should take your rest."

"And leave all this good meat? It's my kill, and I'll see to putting it up." She huffed.

Kia's admiration flared into anger. "So it is your meat? Do you intend to share, or barter your meat?"

"The meat belongs to all of us!" Ch`e glared.

Rok bent double, coughing. "Ch`e, if you make more of that tea, please make some for me."

Ch`e touched Rok's cheek. "Of course. I'll take care of that nasty sore throat for you."

Kia felt her own throat tighten.

Before Warmsun had reached her zenith, nothing was left of the fish but scraps. The skin had been rolled tight, the gut washed clean and stretched between trees. Three spines had been hacked off and the flesh removed, exposing weapons deadlier than any stone point Kia could put on a spear. And flat, hard plates had been cut loose from around its head to be used for serving dishes. Small black birds and bleeding jays zipped back and forth scooping up insects and even sampled the shreds of meat still hanging from some bones. All of the entrails had been returned to the water with respect and gratitude.

"Too bad it didn't have eggs," Ch`e mumbled as she lowered her tired body into the water to scrub the filth away. "That's my favorite food – fish eggs." Even in the cold water her head drooped. Kia scooped her up.

"This is no place to sleep. I'll help you back to the den."

Ch`e submitted and Kia held her close as they walked back up the trail.

Stix sat on the ground outside the den weaving a container for the dried meat. She already had two made from the thick, strong targus grass stems. They would protect the meat and be strong enough to carry when the troupe moved.

Ch`e stumbled past Stix, brushing a hand across her forehead. "I hope you didn't stand up on that leg. Wake me when you have pain." She slumped into the sleeping place beside Rok.

*****

Song swept flying insects away from the drying racks with a leafy branch and added wood to the smoky fire when needed, but she kept her head low, refusing to look at anyone. Kia sat beside Stix. Warmsun had brought heat to the boulder at the door of the den and Kia stretched and leaned back to enjoy it.

"Where's Fem'ma and Moon?" Kia asked.

Stix nodded. "Just over in the trees, walking around. I think I heard Moon singing before. I guess he's preparing his talk."

"I hope we get to hear it. The way our luck has been, we're about to be attacked again." Kia sighed and covered her face with her hands.

"Not what I want to hear right now. I think my leg is healing and the way it hurt when we ran before, I'd rather be eaten by a short tailed lion than run again." Stix tied off the last blade on the basket and stacked it with the rest. "Ch`e said I have to sit for the changing of the moon. I may lose my senses by the time Moonlight only shows half of his face."

"We'll keep you busy making baskets."

Fem'ma returned from the woods. Moon was sleeping in the sling. She sat on the ground near Stix and Kia.

"This camp will only be safe for a handful of days. It is one of the things Moon wants to talk about." Fem'ma spoke softly and Moon didn't stir, but snored peacefully. "This is all quite strange to us as well as for you. Ch`e courted only one fem in our village, but her skills are few and no one ever called on her. Then this happened. I had no choice but to befriend her."

"So, she's mad at all of Terah. But she has sisters here if she will accept us," Kia said softly.

"Trust takes time, child."

"How did you escape?" Stix reached for another stack of reeds and started a new basket.

"I am not only this mem's arms and legs, I am also his birth mother. When he was born I labored for days. Then when he came, my sisters were frightened. They asked me to leave."

"How horrible for you to be cast out from your bond sisters."

"Yes, it hurt my heart. Worse, I had to leave my two young daughters. The village refused to cast me out, so I became an elder. But many of the other elders also fear Moon. Most of our clan thinks he is both fem and mem."

"All of your clan has seen him walk on the ground?"

"Yes. When he was still too young to go into training he was determined to move around and play with the other babes. It didn't take long for all the fems in the village to know about him. We were both treated badly until Moon went into training. He works harder than all the other young mems and already knows as much as our wisest elders. Still they don't trust him. It was a difficult day, before the attack, and we were walking in the valley between the high mountain and the green mountain where our village is… was. Dirt, broken rocks, even dead targus beasts fell everywhere. The village vanished. We don't know if anyone else escaped. We found Ch`e just before dark."

Stix finally spoke, a tear rolled down her cheek. "He was rejected because of his deformity, and for that he was spared. Ch`e was rejected for lack of skills, but she saved me. We were spared because of love. But we lost the one member who represented love."

"With all this chatter, how's a mem supposed to get any sleep? Is there anything to eat?" Moon shifted in his sling and peered out at Stix and Kia.

"Lots and lots of fish." Kia retrieved a small strip hanging close to the heat. "I hope it's your favorite, if not, I can get you, um, some fish." She took another piece for herself and broke off a chunk for Stix.

"I'll take the fish, then. Ma?"

Fem'ma broke the meat into chunks and Moon rolled a piece at a time into his mouth.

"How about a sip of water?" Moon asked through a mouthful.

Kia hopped up and retrieved the water skin.

"Ah, a mem should be so lucky. Call the others. We will talk."

He looked up at Fem'ma. "Will you set me on the stone by our shelter?" Fem'ma lifted him, but Kia stopped her.

"He can't just sit on the bare Terah. Especially not to speak to us. I'll make him a proper place to sit, but for now please use my blanket."

Rok and Ch`e emerged from sleep in less than happy spirits. Ch`e lifted a chunk of barely cooked meat from the rack and tore it in half, offering part to Rok. Kia smiled inside.

Moon cleared his throat when the six fems were seated and comfortable. Song sat a little farther away, her head still low.

Without speaking Moon began a song. His voice was clear and rang through the clearing. And Kia felt a stirring in her heart like nothing she'd ever experienced before.

False words from our leaders
Don't kill but lay waste
Our bodies and children
The world lies defaced

13 Pieces Falling Into Place

As if transported to a time long lost, Moon felt his heart carried away. The words of an ancient song came to him. He knew it was a gift from the Most High.

A trespasser comes
And sets down the seed
Chaffing and growing
Its heart filled with greed

Beware of the light
Hide from the night

Disguised with perfection
The tumor will grow
Polished and perfect
Death soon will follow

Look to the light
Come out in the night

In silence and dark
The message awaits
Lifted and shining
The world celebrates

Follow the light
Fear not the night

With eyes closed and face pointed skyward, he paused. The intense faces he looked into filled him with a joy he never knew existed. The dreams he'd kept secret for so long were true. As impossible as it seemed, he knew he had been chosen for something great. But he never once had the courage to speak about such things. His heart pounded so hard he was sure he'd fly from the top of the boulder at any moment.

Will they believe me? Or will they wish me dead for my blasphemy?

Taking the biggest chance of his life he began. "Fems, beautiful fems. I should receive punishment for my thoughts. The hope of being chosen is something I never had. But not one of you is repulsed by my oddness. I know Veenah brought us to this place and she will lead us to fulfill the prophecy. As the song says, now is the time to seek the light."

Kia sucked in air.

Rok shook her head slowly and covered her face with her hands.

But Ch`e laughed. "How can you still believe the old stories? Songs mems sing to put babes to sleep. Fables to tell each other while your matrons feed you grapes and wine. The only thing we can do right now is travel down the river and find a village and safety." She stopped and glared at the five sets of eyes drilling into her.

Rok moved closer to her, and Moon feared there would be a fight. No one had ever spoken with that sort of disrespect to an elder or a mem, and if anyone tried they were punished. And Moon knew well the temper boiling inside both of these fems. He held his breath, knowing he had no right to interfere. To his surprise, Rok took Ch`e's hand.

"You know," the warrior spoke softly, "he's right on at least one point. We have been brought together. Apart we were weak, but now we are strong. Each of us has a skill to lend, and at least we can continue on our bonding quest. Ch`e, you have done what none of us could do. You brought food and leather strong enough to protect a warrior, and you bring the skill of healing. And even though I tried to refuse, you gave me medicine and healed me. I...I..."

"It was my pleasure, my strong warrior."

"I know I speak for my sisters and if we were in a village, I...we, would court you. But now, out here in the wild, I ask you to join me. I am warrior and hunter, Song is spiritual strength and cook, Stix is hunter, but more than that, she makes leather and beads, and many other things, she is creator. Kia is the bridge which binds us, strong, brave, and wise. Bond with us and be our sister. Stand in the place of love and heal our broken hearts."

Moon trembled, struggling not to topple. He almost wished he'd remained in his mother's sling, safe and secure. His ears rang with the spinning of his mind. This was yet another ancient song unfolding before his eyes. *The broken becomes one.*

Ch`e threw her hair back with a toss of her head. "So far, I have done everything for your sisters and you, Rok. I've had nothing in return. But I don't have anywhere else to go. If we bond, we bond, if not, when we find a village, we separate. But I haven't chosen any of you as a leader. I can make decisions, too. Maybe I'm to be your leader. Would you follow me, Warrior?"

"You've proven yourself healer and hunter. The rest will come in time. I'm curious about what Moon wants to tell us. Already I know he believes and you don't. Kia believes, and Stix, but I'm not so sure. It almost came between us, but I loved Song, and so I stayed with her. You are not alone in your suspicion."

"Okay, I'll listen, but I've heard it all my life." Ch`e clamped her mouth shut, crossed her arms, and glued her eyes on Moon.

Moon released his breath and steadied himself, rising almost to his toes. He couldn't hold back a chuckle. "We know how two of you feel, and soon we will know how the rest feel. Do you know why we call the ruler of the day sky 'Warmsun'?" He waited for an answer, then continued. "Because she gives us heat to live and light to show us the way. And Moonlight reflects this great light, the way a mem reflects the love of his wives. I know you've seen the coldsun. She shines day and night for a turning of the seasons, but gives no heat and very little light. If you look at your hands together, the fingers of your own two hands, this is the number of cold seasons she sleeps and now she is returning from far beyond the stars. The Zid celebrate this lifeless thing that hangs in Veenah and blocks our view of the sky. I think this is why the Zid came to our world and attacked us."

Kia spoke, interrupting Moon's speech. "Don't you mean it is why the Zid attacked our plain? They have always been here. We just have to stay away from them while they dig."

"This is where I disagree with the teachings. Because I was so often shunned by the others, I spent much time walking alone with Fem'ma and practicing the old songs. I observed the birds and animals and discussed my thoughts with Ma." He saw a dreamy look lighten Song's face and nearly forgot what he'd plan to say. *If they choose me, she will be the one to carry me.* Clearing his throat, he continued. "Allow me to teach you further. Haven't you ever wondered why the boar targus has four legs just as the sow? And the cock bird has wings and legs just as the hen? I believe mems once had legs and arms just as fems."

Song shook her head. "But that goes against the great plan of Veenah. How can a perfect family be formed if a mem had arms and legs? He would have no need of fems." She trembled as if about to burst into tears.

"I can assure you, sweet Song. A mem has much need of a fem other than for walking and eating."

Kia's face instantly turned bright red and Moon was sure he heard a low chuckle bubble up from Rok. The look on Fem'ma's face made him flinch.

"Son, this is not the time for such talk. You do not have the right."

"Forgive me. But as I said, I believe that when the Zid first came here, I mean to our world, in the belly of Coldsun, they did something which caused mems to lose their arms and legs."

Ch'e again laughed. "We will pretend for a moment that these hideous lizards floated down from the stars in your so-called coldsun just as Terians float across a lake in a boat. Then what? They went around chopping off arms and legs and soon mems were just born that way? Not possible. None of it is possible. I don't know how you could think such a thing."

"I can't explain, but clues can be found in the old songs, and I am proof that mems should have arms and legs. And that my dear fems is the reason the prophecy was written." Moon smiled triumphantly.

Kia let out a gasp. "Just to grant you the pleasure of arms and legs? There must be more to it than that."

Stix leaned in. "I know something of signs and symbols, patterns. I've solved the language of birds. Tell us the clues. I might be able to solve those as well."

"The prophecy says that after life is torn from its place, the innocent will find the stone, and we'll all know the truth." Grunts and nods of agreement rippled through the group of fems. "According to ancient songs, life was stripped away long ago. I know a song which talks about leaders covering up the truth while bodies were laid waist. Not killed, but ruined. Like mems born with no arms and legs. It was then that the old ones prayed for deliverance. Veenah promised to help us when the time was right. Those who understood The Great One's words prophesied these end times.

"I don't understand all of it. Not just yet. But I see signs opening before my very eyes. And the signs are here, believe me. Tell me, fems, think about what you know, and tell me if you have ever seen yourself in one of the verses of the old songs." He waited, searching their faces, hoping that they would recognize this amazing truth – and praying that they wouldn't strike him dead for his bold words. He nearly jumped off the boulder when Rok spoke first.

"I've always been different. My blood mother is even fairer skinned than I. She is almost pure white, but the strongest of our entire village. She was cast out of her first village because of her whiteness, and then she wandered in darkness. I often think I'm the one who drinks strength from the white breast for some great fight."

Kia spoke next. "I've been afraid to leave my mother's side for as long as I can remember. The only time I ever went out hunting was with her. I think I knew I would be torn from her but come back from the edge of death."

Stix choked back a sob and took a breath, but remained silent.

Kia swiped at a tear sliding down her cheek. "My beloved hearth sister, who joined us for this bonding, was killed in the attack. She used to sing, well, she tried to sing the verse that starts *Walk forward my beauty*. I can't remember the words exactly, but there is something about not being afraid."

Moon nodded. "I know the verse. The rest of it is *Fear not what is gone. New life is given at breaking of dawn.* You can take comfort that her loss was part of Veenah's great plan."

"I am the hunter who sits alone." Stix spoke through silent sobs. "When I sat under the precipice with my leg bleeding, watching those falling rocks crush the life out of Vee, I could only repeat to myself *Feed me, heal me, teach and guide me. Give me strength to face tomorrow."*

Ch`e stood to face the group. For a breath of a moment, Moon's skin tingled with anger at her disrespect of turning her back on him, but he remembered another song which gave him hope for this one. He strained to hear her words.

"I suppose you are all guessing that little Song is the one who heals the rift, since she stitched the rift in Stix's leg. But it is I. From my earliest memory I knew my gift of healing came from Veenah. I knew I was set apart for great things, but I could never get anyone to understand. That's why…" She stopped suddenly and turned away, stuttering. "That's why, um, I'm the one who heals the rift." She finished quickly and sat down in the grass.

Moon saw her face bloom red blotches and beads of sweat. He was sure the others also noticed when the cloud of anger and distrust swept across Rok and Kia. Ch`e was hiding something else, and the others knew it, too.

An uncomfortable silence covered the area and Moon felt it difficult to breath. He hoped against hope, but he knew that Song would not be able to speak. *How do I know such things?* Would the beautiful child forever hate him if he betrayed her by revealing her secret? He continued his talk, his heart beating so hard it hurt.

"I have seen these things and more in each of you. I hope you understand what I want to explain. The Zid have come back to this plain, and coldsun is returning. Life has been torn away, and love has been lost. But the one sign that gives me hope, the last piece of the puzzle, is the innocent we have among us."

All eyes turned to Song. She scooted backward, eyes wide. "No! It's impossible! None of that is true! Rok? Help me."

Rok jumped to her side. "You're okay, sister. No one is going to hurt you and all of us are staying together. I don't care what he says."

Moon wished he had longer arms so he could embrace Song as well. "I believe I can explain much of the cause of Song's grief. Aside from her sadness over losing a sister, she is indeed guilty of sin. You are on a bonding quest. Am I right?"

"You already know that." Kia spoke barely above a whisper. She put an arm around Song's shoulder. Rok stood strong on the other side. "I will not allow you to punish her for this sin. You are neither our syr, nor chief. I will protect my sister above all."

"Dear Kia, punishment is the farthest thing from my mind. I'm actually pleased. Your young sister has never experienced her first moonflow." Kia gasped and Song cried out as if she'd been struck by a hard stick. "I'm surprised your village allowed her to go on this quest with you. She is much too young. However, my heart flies to Veenah each time I look at her."

Rok backed away, trembling, her eyes wide in shock.

"How can you know a thing like that, mem?" Kia demanded.

"I knew the first time I laid eyes on her. She is innocent. However, because of her sin, she is alive."

Song sobbed into Kia's shoulder. "I'm sorry. For my lies we are all punished."

Kia held the young fem's face in her hands. "I don't care what he says. I forgive you. And I'm glad you're here with us." She looked up at Rok. "Join me, sister, show your love."

"I suspected," Stix said. "But I didn't care. Song, you passed every test. You have nothing to be ashamed of. Some fems don't have their moonflow until many seasons past their growth and some never do. It doesn't mean you don't have the right to bond."

Rok looped her arms around Song, kissing her on top of her head. "That explains why you've been so annoyed by your tooth for the past few days. Your last molars haven't fallen out yet. But I'll never stop loving you. We are all in this together, and none of us should ever hide anything. If we are to be one bonded unit, we can't have secrets. I, too, broke a rule. It filled me with guilt for a time." She pulled the necklace from under her tunic. "We're forbidden to take anything with us on our bonding quest, but Lona made this for me as a bonding gift. I didn't want to leave it behind."

Gleaming beads of red, blue, amber, and shades of pink and white contrasted against Rok's buckskin tunic. The pearlescent inner surface of the five river clams seemed to shimmer in the sunlight with their own life.

Ch`e yelped and ran forward grasping the necklace with both hands. "It's the Jewel! We have the Jewel! I knew when I left the village I would find it. Now we can go into the next village with pride and be heroes. Everyone in Terah will follow us with this! Oh, yes, Rok. I will gladly and happily bond with you."

Rok pushed her away. "Lona's beads are not the Jewel of the Prophecy. And, what do you mean, 'When I left...', Ch`e? You told me you were out practicing with the bow, then you told Song you were collecting herbs. Now you say you left. And we know you have more than one dress. Speak the truth, fem, or you will be cast out."

Ch`e glared, balling her fists. "You are all so smart, aren't you? Figure it out." She spun on her heel and stomped toward the river, grabbing her spear on the way.

The stranger is the enemy
The enemy is the friend
The hiding place a trap disguised
The light falls down but truth ascends

14 Seekers

"I'm staying up to stand watch," Stix announced. "I've been treated like a newborn long enough and I couldn't sleep if I had to."

She considered the days which had passed since the morning of Moon's speech. The excitement had passed with few words, but the atmosphere was still tense, like a rope about to break under a heavy strain. Fem'ma had kept Moon busy walking at the river's edge or tucked away in his sleeping quarters. Ch`e slept or searched for medicines, by day, and hunted for fish at night – and avoided contact with everyone – except Rok. Something needed to change.

"Let me check your wound first," Ch`e said, removing the dressing. "This is no good. The cut is not yet closed. The one on duty needs to keep the fire hot. One wrong step and you will tear out your stitches."

"I'll use my spear as a walking stick and move carefully."

"You will have pain, and I don't have any more herbs."

Stix groaned. "Right now I don't care."

Ch`e grunted and nodded once to the cluster of fems then picked up her spear, and slipped away into the woods. Fem'ma followed with Moon standing on her shoulder.

"That was rude of her to just leave," Song sighed, sweeping the scraps of the old poultice into the fire.

"She's probably going for more medicines," Rok picked up a stone and slid it along her knife, honing the blade until it was sharp enough to scrape the hair from her legs.

"If I can't take my turn at the watch, what can I do?" Stix complained. "If I make one more basket, my fingers will fall off. I just don't want to feel useless anymore." She kicked the ground in frustration. Then winced in pain.

"My love," Kia said, "You are not useless. Because of you we have all of our meat stored safely in good containers, and each of us have tree dog fur head pieces to keep us warm when the cold comes."

Rok looked up from sharpening her knife. "You've worked the water cat skin so that it's soft enough to dress a newborn mem. When Warmsun awakens, we will cut tunics for all of us."

"I'll see if I can find shells or stones by the river and we can make beads," Song offered. "We can adorn our new clothes."

Stix warmed at the love and concern of her sisters. "Thank you. I guess I'm just tired of watching all of you go off to hunt or scout. Even Moon gets to walk around and that's just weird."

"It's settled," Kia announced. "We will all stay in camp tomorrow and cut tunics. There should be enough. I'd love a belt from the straps Song made from that gut. And maybe we can use some of the white belly skin to make a covering for Moon."

"We have to find a way to reach Ch'e," Song whispered. "It's true, together we are strong, but she won't even speak to us now."

"I can reach her," Rok said. "When Moonlight rises at the second watch, she will teach me to hunt the water cat. We spoke about it in the sleeping place before Warmsun rose yesterday."

"Good," Kia said.

"At least she doesn't wander alone anymore," Song said. "But I think it's wrong to make Moon go out every day so we can be alone, and I know Fem'ma gets tired."

"So, young love," Stix said, "does that mean you'd like to carry our mem?"

The fems shared a chuckle at Song's expense when her cheeks turned red.

Stix leaned back against the boulder and closed her eyes, basking in the warmth, both from Warmsun, and from the love of her sisters.

Warmsun traveled closer to the Forbidden Mountains

Kia sighed in the rare moment of peace. *Almost perfect. If only….*

A shadow flashed across Warmsun an instant before the fems heard the whir of a Zid skimmer. Kia and Rok leaped to their feet, weapons drawn. Rok nocked a new arrow, tipped with the deadly spine of the water cat. Song backed into the shelter, dragging Stix to safety.

"Get under cover," Kia whispered.

"It's too late for that, they've already spotted us. Did you hear one or two? Usually they hunt in pairs." Rok crouched near a boulder and scanned the sky.

"Only one, but I didn't see it. I wish the others would get back here. I don't like us separated and Moon has to be protected."

Kia edged to the woods where Ch`e had disappeared earlier. The whirring returned, moving slower. A single Zid lay on the airborne vehicle and twisted its murky green snout to better view the river's edge. It circled again then dipped out of sight for a moment before regaining altitude and racing away.

"We have to go – now," Rok whispered.

"I don't know why we're being so quiet. It's not like those things can hear us from so far up," Kia snapped.

"Never underestimate your enemy, especially the Zid. We don't know what they can do with those skimmers."

Bushes and dry grass crackled beside them, sending them both into battle stance. Ch`e burst into the clearing with Fem'ma hunched over her precious cargo. Moon complained, and not too quietly, about the jostling he was receiving and the fact that he couldn't breathe.

"We've been spotted!" Ch`e panted. "We don't have much time before it brings others to hunt us. I knew we needed to go sooner!"

Moon finally pushed his way out of the tight bundle Fem'ma had wrapped him in. "It was so close to us I could see its tongue flicking as it went by. It had orange eyes! It looked straight at me." He struggled to escape Fem'ma's clutch, but she held him tighter. "Why didn't it fire on us? It knows we're helpless and I know it had weapons. Why?"

With one hand, Fem'ma cut down the food cashes. Stix and Song bundled blankets and packs and Ch`e covered the small fire and scattered the stacked wood.

89

The skimmer returned, moving even slower, nearly hovering over the camp. Rok took aim, but knew the Zid was out of range of her arrow. She waited behind the shelter of a tree for it to come closer.

By the shimmering scales of the being, Kia guessed it to be young, possibly a juvenile out playing on its new skimmer, but the deadly cold, orange eyes showed no play. It pulled a hand from the controls and pointed its crooked finger toward the camp. A yellowish-green blob zipped from its palm. The Zid waited until the thing made its way to the camp and landed at the door of the shelter then the skimmer was gone.

Song screamed from inside the shelter. "Get it away!"

Fem'ma ducked behind a boulder, hunched over Moon.

Rok edged up to the thing and poked it with an arrow.

"Don't kill it!" Moon hollered. "Ma! Set me down!"

"No! You stay right where you are!" Fem'ma yelled just as loud.

"Well, someone bring it to me! Ma! Let me out!"

Kia saw him struggling in the protective sling Fem'ma had wrapped around him and considered that the first tunics to be made from the water cat skin would be for them. Moon had to be protected. She remained combat ready between Fem'ma and the fleshy thing pulsing in their doorway.

"Rok!" Moon shouted. "Pick it up with your hand. It's harmless."

The warrior backed away, shaking her head.

Kia hollered back to him. "How do you know that, Moon? How do you know? When we first saw you, we thought you could be Zid spies. Tell me how you know about this thing!"

"Because the hunters of our village captured a Zid," Ch'e said. "And kept it alive. I'll get the bio-message. It's slimy and just looking at it makes me want to vomit, but safe enough." She reached for the thing, but Song stopped her.

"No!" Song shook with fear. "No, Ch'e. You are our healer. We cannot risk your safety. Let me–." The instant her fingers touched it, the mass crawled up her hand to her arm. She staggered, and pressed the fingers of her other hand into her temple, shuddering. "My head hurts! Stay back! No one touch me!" Rok and Kia stopped just short of grabbing her. "Clicks and Squeals are in my head!"

"That's part of their language," Moon said, excitement rising in his voice. "Set it on my head. Careful. Don't drop it."

"Are you kidding? The think is stuck to me! I can't shake it off, and it's killing my head."

"Touch it to me, it will move."

"Is it alive?" Kia breathed, ready to spear the thing and throw it into what was left of their cooking fire.

"Partly. It knows where to go and it can carry messages back and forth between two beings. But it is made by the Zid, not grown or hatched." Moon pushed farther out of the pouch and when Song touched the thing to him, it oozed off her arm and wrapped itself around his head like a hat. She shuddered again and scrubbed her arm with a handful of sand.

Fem'ma sat down with a thump, clutching her temples with both hands.

Moon hummed a wordless song. His eyes were clenched shut and his shapely mouth was nothing more than a thin line in his squnched up face. After what seemed like an entire day, Moon opened one eye and whispered for Song to remove it and send it back.

"Where am I supposed to send it?" She reached for the goo, but this time Rok held her other arm for support.

"I've given it directions to return to the Zid that sent it. I hope."

Song waited for the thing to slither onto her hand, then pointed to the sky. It detached itself with a snap, and flapped, almost like a bird, into the sky.

"Ugh," Rok groaned. "I felt that horrible thing all the way through your arm. I don't think I ever want to do that again."

"You?" Song whimpered. "I'm the one who had to touch it – twice."

"Fems," Moon said. "First will one of you bring food and water for Fem'ma. She is weak, and I'm hungry as well. Then gather close. We'll sit by the door so Stix won't be injured moving."

Song held meat and berries on a bone plate for Moon, and Rok helped Fem'ma.

Fem'ma tried to lift the water skin, but dropped it. The warrior knelt to hold it for her. "I'm worried about you, elder. Will you recover from this?"

"In a while," she answered. "I don't know how the mems can do this, but fems can't. If the mems could hold those things alone, it would be easier."

"I am able to stand, Ma, why don't you ever trust me?"

It's hard enough to allow you to stand on the ground. I can't stand to think of that thing touching you without my help."

"Next time, I insist you let me try."

"Next time?" All fems chorused together.

"How long have you been doing this in your village?" Rok growled. "You have been working with them all along, haven't you? Did you call these things to kill us?"

"Of course not, fem, you need to remember your place," Moon shouted. "All of you! Ch`e spoke the truth when she said we captured one of them. Hunters snared it in a trap, but one was wise enough to bring it back alive. It was more afraid of us than we were of it. Eventually we learned from it."

Ch`e shook her head. "Why didn't the rest of village know you kept it so long? I know it happened when I was young. I only knew about it because my hearth mothers were needed to heal matrons. And you likely hadn't even lost your milk teeth. Most of the village, if they even knew about it, thought the thing was killed. The rest figure it was just a story made up to scare the young fems.

"Our elders are sworn to secrecy and the mems who knew this thing never spoke about it even to other mems. I was lucky to be chosen to learn from it. I was the first one allowed to touch it. Only three of us ever understood it. And yes, I was quite young when the Zid was brought to us."

"They were likely afraid of the blob," Ch`e said. "They probably chose you so they would be safe if it killed you."

Kia crossed her arms, scowling. "Why was Fem'ma afraid of that thing when it first landed? If she's been with you while you learned, she would know it was harmless."

"You ask good questions, wise leader. The truth is, sometimes these things shoot poison fluid in all directions, but they do it soon after they land. They wait long enough for a few fems to come close then they explode. I felt the message of this one as it flew past and I knew it was safe."

"Well, I didn't get that message, and I'll never trust them," Fem'ma finally had the strength to sit without support.

"If we are ready," Moon said. "I will tell you the message. At least I hope I understood it. This young Zid tells me he is a seeker. His message is that he grieves for our losses. That's the part which confuses me the most because Zid only want us dead, even the one we captured so long ago. But this one says many like him are trying to save us before we are all gone from the world. I don't understand that either, but I can usually tell if the message is un-true."

"How can you know all this if you only studied one Zid? Was that thing still in your village at the time of the attack?"

"No, we released that one long ago, and I got the feeling this one who saw us today is its offspring or relative. I only understood in pictures and feelings. It communicated too fast and I couldn't get the messenger to slow down. I don't know if that meant it was urgent, or that's just the way they speak. I think it wants us to go up the river, not down."

"That's toward the Forbidden Mountains," Kia said. "They have been calling to me since our quest began. But now I fear it could be a trap. I – I don't know what to think."

As she gazed at the faraway peaks, glowing red in the evening sun, a brilliant shooting star, rarely seen in the light, flashed orange and blue across the sky. Kia's heart raced. *A message.*

Rok and Stix each raised a hand. Rok said, "We're with you either way, Kia. But, a good hunter, or a soldier, will lay an ambush while convincing you it's the safest trail."

Song spoke boldly. "I believe Moon. If we don't go to the Forbidden Mountains we probably will be killed."

"You'll never make it," Ch'e growled. "The only safe thing to do is go the opposite way. Down the river to find a village."

Everyone looked Fem'ma. "I have to choose the way the mem tells me, but I won't vote until we all agree."

"Moon," Kia started, but hesitated. "Moon, what did the message mean, or what exactly did it say about 'seekers'? That could mean so many things. And how did you know that thing didn't mean to lead us to our deaths?"

"It was how I felt when the messenger touched me. I felt – love."

Gifts are offered
Promises made
A contract for blood
The debt never paid

15 Medicine Or Poison

Warmsun slid behind the mountains and darkness covered the camp.
Fem'ma and Moon disappeared into their corner of the den. Moments
later Song stored their food in a tree-cache and ducked into the sleeping
place. Kia followed her.

Ch`e sighed and glanced around the clearing and the sky. "I don't
know if I'll be able to sleep. We should have left tonight, but Kia's right,
as usual. I should be out here instead of you."

"I'll be okay, healer." Stix grinned. "And after today, I'm not a bit
sleepy either."

"If anything happens," Ch`e said waggling her finger, "you stay
where you are. Use the spears like you did with that nightbird. Scream
and holler and we will all be here to help you. Don't hurt your leg this
close to healing. If my herbs are dry when I wake up, I'll make you a
pain-relieving tea." She ducked into the shelter, her hand on Rok's back.

*****

Stix lowered the amber stone she'd been working on and scanned
the sky looking for anything unusual. Moon had said that Coldsun was
returning. She hardly remembered it from her childhood, other than the
elders were unsettled about it. Many new songs were chanted by all the
mems during that time.

Pondering, she found the summer constellation she called Serpent, a
string of stars following the horizon. The great slitherbeast in the sky
forever carried a spear through its head. Some days she pitied the beast,

94

others she was grateful it had been slain. Tonight it would simply tell her when to wake Rok and Ch`e for their watch.

A movement caught her attention and she watched Kia duck out of the den, stretch, and throw more wood on the fire.

"You don't have to do that," Stix said in a low voice. "But since you're up, would you bring me a drink of water?"

"Anything, my love. And I told you I'd sit up with you, but I wanted to make sure Song fell asleep. She's wrapped up in Rok's arms. I can't rest without you next to me anyway. It's funny how we got used to each other's company so quickly."

After a couple of gulps from the drinking skin, Stix hugged her sister's arm. "I know. It's like we were born to be together. But what surprises me is that I feel comfortable with Ch`e, as well." Tears suddenly stung her eyes and trickled down her cheek. "I'm glad we found her – and Moon and Fem'ma. But, do you ever think of Kine?"

Kia brushed the tear from Stix's face. "I think of him all the time, as well as the others."

"I wonder if anyone got away like we did." Unashamed of her grief, she searched the face of the fem she'd loved all her life.

"We may never know. Sometimes I wish we'd gone back. But it wouldn't have been safe. You know they'd want us to do anything we could to survive."

Stix took a deep breath and smiled. "You made the right choice to get us out of there. And if we do survive this, we'll be the strongest femtog ever." After a moment, she added, "Are you afraid the Zid will return to this place and attack?"

"Yes. Terrified. But, Moon said we are safe." Kia leaned back against the warmed boulder and closed her eyes. Stix watched her rest, feeling a rush of love and admiration. Then she quietly riffled through the flint drills she'd knapped earlier and went back to work on her amber bead.

A long-ear hopped into the clearing, rattling the dried grasses and both fems jumped, startled out of their thoughts. Kia stood, looking all around, then put another branch on the fire before settling back down.

Stix scanned the sky and tree line, rubbing the amber bead between her fingers. Her thumping heart slowed and the adrenalin cleared from her veins calming her shaking hands. She fitted the drill back into the hole, twisting it gently in the soft stone.

Her thoughts drifted to Ch`e. The healer had returned from hunting herbs that day with a flint nodule and dropped it into the fire, waiting for it to shatter. When the flint stopped popping and splitting, Ch`e had raked the pieces into a heap and left them beside Stix without saying a word What made her so angry? Was it just her way of covering her grief? Stix peered at the hole in the amber in the light of the fire and blew the dust from it.

"Pretty," Kia said. "You do nice work."

"Thank you. These will be for Moon, for his new cloak. I was just thinking of Ch`e. I think she's so angry because she's been badly treated. She doesn't know how to love because she's never been loved. She thinks she's worthless, but she healed my leg and saved my life. How can I ever equal that?"

"Hmph. She doesn't think she's worthless. She thinks she's better than everyone else."

"No. Ch`e is covering up a horrible pain the only way she can. We just have to show her more love."

Stix set the bead beside her and selected another piece of amber. A star cut a brilliant path through the dark sky and disappeared in a flash.

A message from Veenah.

She prayed for safety and glanced around the dark clearing then hunched over her bead.

Song had given her four stones. Moon would be pleased with the beads she was making. She would sew two to each side of the opening in the front of his cover. Her heart warmed again.

I think I will love this mem. She glanced up at Kia again. "Hey, what do you see out there, sister?"

"Only the stars. Have you noticed that all the falling stars go into the Forbidden Mountains? Veenah is telling us something. It's so dark tonight. I don't like it." She slid down from her perch and put more wood on the fire. It flared up and she sat next to Stix. "How's the bead-making?"

"Three so far, one to go." Stix held up a stone so the firelight shown through the amber.

"Nice. It's hard to believe you can do this in the dark."

"Not so dark with the fire. I should have this one done before you wake Rok. Do you think we should leave tomorrow?"

"We'll stay for at least one more day to cut our tunics and make a new carrier for you. We have too much work to do."

"Work. You're right." Stix examined her last stone for the best spot to place the hole She only had three unbroken flint drills left. Her hand was beginning to ache, but she pushed to finish her project.

*****

The spear in the head of the star serpent touched the far mountain. Stix had strung the four beads on a strip of willa bark and was admiring them in the firelight. Kia stood and stretched then crawled into the shelter to awaken Rok.

"Do you want me to carry you to the bushes to take care of nature?" Kia said.

"I thought you'd never ask." Stix tied the strand of beads in a loop and slipped it over her wrist, reaching for Kia's neck. "I'll be so glad when our healer releases me to walk. This is embarrassing."

Rok emerged from the den and helped carry Stix to the bushes and the three of them relieved themselves.

Just as Ch'e stepped into the firelight, a Zid skimmer whirred into the clearing without lights or warning. The fems crouched by the door and Kia shoved Stix inside, tossing her a spear.

The whir stopped and Kia's blood ran cold. The sticky slurping sound of a Zid tongue testing the air ripped into the silence sending chills up Kia's arms. A movement in the clearing marked the sound of something dragging toward them. All three fems raised their spears and gripped their knives, but still could not see anything in the dark.

A sharp squeal followed by two pops sounded in the night.

Kia knew the creature stood just outside the light of the fire. It's yellow eyes, with the vertical pupils spread wide, glowed in the darkness. Another pop, this time softer. The Zid inched into the light, walking on all four legs. Kia knew the beings were able to walk on their hind legs and use their front legs and feet as arms and hands. But if there was danger, they always crawled on their bellies to protect the only vulnerable part of their bodies, the soft abdomen.

Trembling, Kia leaned against Rok. Three sharp knives and three deadly spear points waited for the Zid to come closer. It didn't. It popped its mouth again and Kia had the impression the thing wanted to tell her something.

"Don't move," Kia whispered. "I don't think this is the same one we saw before. This one looks older."

It crept closer to the fire and slowly raised itself to stand on its hind legs, balancing on its heavy tail. By exposing its abdomen, Kia felt it must be friendly, but these things were crafty and it could be waiting for the Terians to lower their weapons so it could strike.

The Zid opened one clawed hand and curled a finger in a gesture meaning one of the fems should come to it. Kia shook her head 'no' and stood firm with Rok and Ch`e. The thing gestured again, stronger, and popped its mouth. It opened its other hand and a small package dangled from its fingers. It made a motion as if to offer the package to the fems. Finally, it pointed to the package, then to its leg, then to the den.

Kia whispered, "I think it wants to give us something for Stix to help her leg."

The Zid cocked its head and popped its mouth twice.

Rok whispered back, "I think it wants us to come closer so it can capture us. This is the way Ch`e catches her fish." She raised her spear, ready to cast it and the Zid dropped to all four feet again, letting out a soft hiss. With its belly sliding along the ground it inched forward, still holding the package out to the fems. Almost within range of the spears, it set the package down and pointed to the den, making a light whistling sound. Rok raised her spear higher, and the Zid whirled and raced out of the firelight, flicking its tail in a serpentine motion. The skimmer took flight and was gone.

"What just happened?" Rok whispered. All three fems leaped into the air and yelped when Moon cleared his throat behind them.

"It brought a gift," Moon said.

He was standing on the ground with his feet bare and only a loose woolen tunic covering him. Kia resisted the urge to lift him from the dirt.

"Why do you stand, Moon, you should never touch the ground!" Kia had to force herself not to shout.

"You'll have to get use to this. In the meantime, I think it came here because of the message I returned. I told them we had an injury and could not travel. I didn't even know if I communicated the right way or if the bio-messenger would carry it to the right place."

"It must have because we are all still alive. Do you think it was the same one that came here earlier?"

"I think this was a different one. They must patrol in shifts. I have only been close to one in my life, but it almost sounded like a fem."

"I'm glad you could tell," Rok growled and poked at the package with her spear. "But don't call that thing a fem, or a mem. They are horrible killers. Do you really think this is safe? It pointed to its leg."

"I believe it is medicine for Stix," Moon said. "I don't know for sure. One of you can look at it. Touch it and see if it burns."

Ch`e nudged the package with her toe then lifted it by the cord. She opened it in the light of the fire. A glistening gel wiggled in the small bag. With one finger, she gingerly tapped it. "It's warm and tingly, feels good." She smeared a small bit on a scratch and it fizzed. "It still doesn't hurt. Kia, let me put some on your head. Maybe it will take the bruise away and lower the lump, and even cure your head pain."

"My head pain is not so bad. I don't want any of that touching me. It could be poison."

"I don't think so. Look at the scratches I had on my arm from capturing the water cat. They're all gone. Bring a torch from the fire. I'll put some on Stix."

A blood curdling scream emitted from Stix when Ch`e spread a gob of the gel on her cut. What felt warm and tingly on Ch`e's small scratch burned and boiled on Stix. Ch`e scooped up a drinking skin and poured water over the fizzing mess, but it only bubbled harder. Out of her mind with pain, Stix screamed then fainted. Kia fell down beside her, holding her head.

"It killed her! It's poison! I told you not to trust that slimy spawn of Perg!" Kia cried uncontrollably. Rok and Song knelt beside her, holding her tight. Bloody foam, bits of crusty scab, and particles of the sinew stitching boiled from the wound and dribbled down her leg to the dirt, where it bubbled up once again.

Ch`e looked on, mouth gaping. "What have I done? They will never follow me now." Grief and guilt boiled up in her like the bubbling mass in front of her. She studied the remainder of the gel, shimmering in the bag, seeming harmless. "I couldn't possibly have been wrong."

A bruise on her shin bone had been bothering her for days. When she'd first cracked it against a fallen branch, she'd thought it was broken.

She could barely walk. The spot was now a sore, purple knot with a crust over the small cut. Dipping her finger into the gel again, she spread a bit over the bump and around the entire sore place.

Heat radiated into her leg bone, causing intense throbbing. She sat on the floor, covering her face with her hands, waiting for the strange pain to stop. But it wasn't really pain, just heat; more and more heat. How could she have considered that Zid medicine would be safe for a Terian's fragile body? She slumped into the dried grass in the den, hugging her knees to her chest.

Kia cried until she fell asleep, still holding Stix. Rok cradled Kia's head, and despite knowing it was her watch, she also dozed. Song slept, leaning against Rok. Moon watched silently while he sat in Fem'ma's lap. In the fading firelight he saw Ch`e also slump, snoring softly. He grinned.

"Looks like we are on watch, Ma. And I think the fire needs feeding. How 'bout it? I've always wanted to stand guard."

Terah's heart holds tight the sign
Lifeless are the tears divine
Brilliant light now lies confined
High above the timberline

16 A Rebel With A Weapon

"You are worse than a rebel. I'll never be accepted back into a village for allowing you to be outside in the dark." Yet Fem'ma gathered her carrying sling and a blanket and hoisted herself and Moon into the firelight.

"I may be a rebel, but I know our world is changing. I know Terians are changing. When I sleep, sometimes I dream – more like I have a vision – I remember what it's like to walk on long leg and hold tools in my hands. I know mems once had arms and legs. Don't ask me how I know, but I do."

"You have always been so full of strange ideas, my shining Moon, maybe it's my fault. I allowed you to have your way far too often instead of keeping your training strict. That's why we were both rejected by so many. The dreams you have about walking are simply because you and I walk so often you know how it feels through me. I don't know why Veenah chose to curse you with hands and feet when no mem has ever had them. I suppose it's simply our burden to bear."

"You'll never understand. But you watch, when I make children, they will all have arms and legs mems and fems alike, I know it."

Fem'ma laid a handful of branches on the fire and gazed into the flames while it flared up, sending sparks into the sky. She watched them fade before moving.

"Are you sending prayers to Veenah with the firebrands again?"

"Always. It has been so long since I've stood watch, I don't

101

know if I remember what to do." She picked up one of the spears leaning against a tree and strolled around the clearing.

"Ma, why don't you set me down so I can really stand guard? I want to sit on top of the shelter where Kia likes to sit. And I want to hold a spear, too."

"I'll be struck down by a bolt from Veenah if I do such a thing."

"You'll choose to break my heart rather than break a stupid rule made up by some fem at the beginning of time? Those rules are old. I am new."

"You are full of unrealistic dreams, and a spear is far too heavy. It would be like me trying to lift a tree."

"Then make me a shorter spear."

"You'll tip over and skewer yourself and I'll be sent to Perg for allowing you to be harmed."

"Make it a little longer than me, so I won't stick myself with it. And. Put. Me. Down!"

"Okay, but not on top where a nightbird can pick you up like a mountain rat." She eased him out of the sling and held his shoulders until he gained his own balance.

"This is better. Now I feel like I am contributing to our clan instead of only taking. Don't forget my spear. Make it twice my size. I have a plan."

Fem'ma selected a pole from the disassembled drying rack and hefted it for balance and size. With her knife and a heavy chunk of firewood, she hacked off the thicker end to a more appropriate length and shaved off a few ragged knots and left over bark until it was smooth and straight. She kept a wary eye on the skies, but kept a constant watch on Moon, who waddled back and forth in front of the den. Finally satisfied with the condition of the short spear, she held the narrow end in the fire for sharpening. As it charred, she trimmed and shaved the coals off until the point was sharp enough to pierce the toughest hide.

Moon breathed in the night air and gazed at the stars. Only on the most rare occasions were mems taken outside at night to study and learn from the stars. He would change the practice. A mem was not helpless simply for lack of hands and feet. But he didn't lack these.

The thought brought an ache deep within him. He simply

couldn't be the only one, but his village didn't trade with many others, and no word had ever come to his clan of another born like him. Of course other clans would likely be as ashamed of their malformed mem as his had been. They would never share such a thing. He would lead his femtog to the ends of the world to find these other mems and prove that they once walked.

Another scowl dented his forehead. This was not his femtog. This was not even close to becoming a femtog. And a mem could never be a leader. He could influence the leader, if this femtog would ever start working together. But this was only the start of a bonding quest. As he waddled across the opening of the den he glanced inside. He should have felt shame or guilt at observing fems sleeping, but it was dark and he could only hear their breathing. A low moan told him that one was also dreaming – likely something horrible.

He already loved them, all of them. When had he realized it? Of course Song, like a breeze in summer, an innocent summer. He smiled. Kia. She could be loud and angry or soft and understanding.

The others look to her often, but the responsibility seems to weigh her down. The mark of a leader.

Rok, she brought strange feelings to him. His face flushed. She was the strongest fem he'd ever known, though he didn't know many. Still, he hoped she could bear children; his children. His burning cheeks were evident of a deeper fire kindling inside his body. He shook his head and hobbled away from the doorway.

Ch`e frightened him a little, but not as much since they met this wounded femtog. Then he'd seen a different side of the angry fem. He didn't even know she was a healer while they wandered alone for those terrible days. He didn't know her femtog very well, either, other than the healer who came to the mem's lodge. But that didn't matter, what mattered now was surviving each day and looking toward a new future.

Stix, the brave. He'd been to funeral pyres of fems who'd died from lesser wounds. She would certainly pass this quality to her children. That is – if she… Grief passed through him, driving out the flutterings of joy.

She simply couldn't be gone. But she was. He'd seen her fall.

He turned at the end of his little pathway, a little too quickly, and caught a tender toe on a sharp rock. He stifled a yelp and glanced at

Fem'ma, who had already leaped to her feet, rushing toward him.

"What happened? Are you injured?" she plopped him on her lap and examined him head to foot, front and back. A drip of blood formed on his toe. "I knew you were going to hurt yourself. A mem shouldn't be on the ground. Not even you." She proceeded to wrestle him back into the sling.

"No! I don't want to be carried right now. Let me go!" He struggled and spread his feet wide so Fem'ma couldn't tuck him into the carrier. "I want foot coverings!"

"You can't dress like a fem."

"I have feet like a fem, I should have foot coverings like one. Maybe like a warrior's foot protectors."

Fem'ma finally gave up and pulled the sling from around her shoulders. She smoothed it out and lifted Moon onto it. "If you won't get in it, please at least stand on it."

"Thank you. If you won't make me foot coverings, I'll ask Kia. I know she will, or maybe Song." Moon settled onto the soft leather. "Watch, I've learned how to pick items up. He wobbled to the edge of the blanket and bent his torso. The fingers of his left hand were longer and better formed and he twisted just enough to curl those fingers around a stick. He straightened and held up the stick. He adjusted his grip and turned his abbreviated hand so he could use the stick as a walking cane. "How's that?"

"Very good, Moon. But, I've seen it before. I just want to know when you learned that little trick."

"Sometimes I wake in the night and I practice while you sleep."

"Impossible. How do you stand up when you are on your back?"

"Easy." He dropped the stick and again bent nearly double. This time he twisted to lean on his right hand then he rolled onto his back. "That's how I lay back down, and I never even wake you. Now comes the tricky part. I figured this out when I was sick of lying on my back and wanted to lay on my stomach."

He curled up and wiggled himself to his side, then to his belly. He tucked his chin and pushed himself up with his forehead. One by one, he wiggled his feet so his toes pointed forward and he uncurled into a standing position.

"Now do you believe me? I want to try something I never could do while you were sleeping." He reached for the ground, curling his fingers around a stone. Drawing his shoulder back, he used his entire body to fling the stone into the clearing. "Ha! Just like I imagined. I want to learn how to throw a spear. Are you finished with it?"

"If you think I'm going to give that thing to you now, you're wrong."

"Have it your way. I'll do it myself." He wobbled to the fire where Fem'ma had dropped the short spear. Fem'ma hovered to catch him if he tumbled toward the fire. He maneuvered into place and picked up the spear. Balancing was more of a chore with the heavy weapon, but he finally hefted it.

"Now what are you going to do with it?"

"I don't know."

He padded back to the soft, leather sling, and sat, balanced on his feet and muscular hind end. Sliding the fingers of his left hand down the shaft of his spear, he tilted it toward his other hand. Grinning, he feigned a jab – to the side, then frowned. He twisted his torso and attempted a jab to the front. The tip swung but the back end caught on the ground and he nearly lost his balance. With a quick glance toward Fem'ma, he righted himself and practiced moving the spear from his left hand to his right, and then back again. Remembering the stories of Stix's miraculous kill of Nightbird, he lowered the spear almost to touch the ground then raised the tip, leaving the heel on the ground. He smiled.

The twinkling stars beckoned to him. The Serpent on one side, the Cooking Ladle on the other; both pointing to the Forbidden mountain. And the Hunter also marched toward the mountain to take her rest there.

What do the old songs say about the jewel? High above the timberline. What is timberline? A mystery, but it's high. And that song is about tears. What about a wide open mouth in the dark, or a heart made of stone which is laid open with a knife? How does one cut a stone with a knife?

"What are you thinking about, my son?"

Moon leaped out of his thoughts. "We'll find it, you know."

"Find what? A new home?"

"The Jewel."

"That is not something you should be concerned about. Finding the jewel is the duty of a fem."

"But it is the duty of a mem to teach and explain the prophecy." Moon thumped his spear for emphasis. "And tomorrow I will discuss this with our fems."

"You push them too hard and they will reject you. You have no right to teach them until they choose you and ask you for knowledge. You know the law."

Moon leaned down and picked up another stone and threw it into the clearing. He stood on his toes as tall as he could.

"I only know the new laws I will teach in the new world."

Shattered are the dreams and hopes
Of mother, father, daughter, son
While anger strives, the promise bides
Until the broken becomes one

17 Together We Work

Rok burst from the den and crouched in battle stance, her knife ready. There was no danger that she could see. Warmsun had not yet lifted, but the darkness was falling away from the horizon. Panic captured her.

Who is on watch?

A stone launched from the shadows beside her and landed next to the fire. Like a cat, she spun toward the movement, ready to defend her family.

"Moon? What are you doing? Why are you out here?"

Fem'ma chuckled from her perch on top of the den in the lookout seat. "Our mem believes he is a warrior, or a hunter. He has a spear and stones. If we come across a nest of baby water birds by the river, he will surely bring home dinner."

"Not nice, Ma," Moon huffed. He smiled up at Rok. "I insisted we allow you to grieve and sleep with your sister. Fem'ma and I stood watch."

"But, you can't stand watch! You're a mem!"

"I can, I did, and I will again, warrior. Just because I'm a mem, doesn't mean I'm helpless." He thumped the short spear for emphasis.

"Forgive me. It's just…just different." Rok sheathed her knife, her heartbeat slowly returning to normal. "It was kind of you both to let us be together."

In a quiet voice Moon added, "I know the death ceremony if you want a proper funeral pyre."

"Who's dead? I'm healed," Stix said emerging from the den. "At least mostly. It's still a little sore, but the poison is gone and the cut is closed. Not even bruised or red anymore. But I think I'd rather heal slower next time. That Zid medicine really hurt."

Kia came out of the den carrying the heavy mass of water cat skin. "When you screamed and sleep took you, I thought you died. I was ready to kill every Zid in the world."

"As long as I don't start growing green scales I think we're good. Hey, can we eat something before we get to work on our tunics?"

Fem'ma pointed to the cooking bag hanging over the fire. "I took a small long-ear last night and it's been boiling. It's only water and about a mouthful of meat for each of us."

"Fem'ma," Moon said. "Are you forgetting something about that story of yours?"

"Okay, Moon saw the longear before I did."

"My stomach is grateful," Stix said. "I feel like I haven't eaten in a moon-phase. And I won't even question how you learned to hunt."

She dipped the broth with the only utensil they had, the spine plant cup. One by one her sisters joined her. In moments nothing was left but a few bones which were added to the fire.

"Fems," Ch`e announced rising to her feet. "We have work to do and Warmsun is already high."

Song ducked into the den and re-emerged with the water cat tail. "It's not right that a mem be touching the dirt, especially while he teaches. If you will not sit in your proper place with your matron, Moon, will you accept this gift? It is a seat fit for one such as you."

Moon chortled as he inspected the seat. "Nothing like this has ever been created and so it is perfect. I accept your gift, dear Song, and thank you." He tested the softness of the leather with a toe then collected his short spear and settled down. The pointed tips of the tail-fins were fastened together, curving his backrest and providing shade. He tapped his roof with the spear.

"You are clever, my dear Song. Tell me, does this mean you might be courting me?"

Her face instantly went crimson and she dashed away toward the river with Rok and Ch`e following.

Fem'ma growled deep in her throat and plunked down beside him. "Moon, you must watch your manners. What you just said is improper and unlawful. These fems have high values and haven't even completed their bonding quest. You will get us cast out right here in the wilderness."

Moon only grinned and began singing.

"Stix," Kia grunted, tugging at the heavy skin. "Since you've regained your health and strength, you can help me stretch this leather."

The tough water cat hide was coarse on the outside, and strong enough to deflect most weapons. The inner skin, scraped and rubbed with fatty tissues of the fish, was as soft as a tree dog's fur.

Rok and Ch`e returned to the clearing, with Song staying safely behind them. They went straight to the water cat skin. Working together the leather was quickly ready to cut.

"We'll cut simple tunics," Kia directed. "Make them as long as we are tall, then cut the openings in the center for our heads and close it with a belt." Suddenly the giant piece of leather didn't seem so big. Any direction Kia measured there didn't seem to be enough.

"We'll have to make our coverings smaller," Ch`e suggested.

"What good is the armor if it doesn't cover our bellies?" Stix said.

Rok added her comment, "They really should be longer to cover the tops of our legs. Like Stix said, it won't do for any of us to be only partially protected."

Fem'ma said, "I don't really need an armored tunic."

"You need it more than any of us if you are to protect our mem," Kia said.

Moon spoke up. "Fems, if you will permit, listen while I tell you what I see from my wonderful high place. Some of you are taller, one of you is thicker."

Fem'ma chuckled.

"Go ahead," Kia said. "What is your suggestion."

"Lay yourselves side by side in different directions until you all fit. I believe you will have enough left for my foot coverings. I hope you didn't forget that Ma."

"Why do you need foot covers?" Stix said.

"Maybe I want my feet warm, or maybe I want to walk and not step on something sharp, or maybe I just want them."

"Too strange," Kia and Stix said together. With Moon's coaching, six tunics were cut. Kia, Rok, and Song worked the leather until the head openings were soft while Stix, Ch`e, and Fem'ma worked on the white belly leather.

"Fem'ma?" Song said softly. "I dare not approach him, but if you will measure Moon's…um…feet against these scraps, I will make his foot coverings and line them with the long ear fur he hunted."

Rok finally stood and stretched her back. "If we're leaving at first light, we need a way to carry our food and blankets easier. I'm going to cut two poles to make a carrier like we had before."

"I'll go with you," Ch`e said. "But I think we should leave as soon as possible."

They hung their new tunics over the smoky fire to finish curing and walked together into the woods.

"Fem'ma?" Kia said, "I've been listening to Moon singing the prophesy song. What do you think it means?"

"If any of us knew that," the elder sighed, "I don't think we would be here in this place. Why do you ask?"

"Remember the part that says when the innocent finds the jewel a battle will begin? I think the battle has already been going. The Zid destroy us along with the land. They started the fight." Kia sat down to sharpen her knife, worn dull by the tough water cat leather.

"I've never thought about it that way. It makes me wonder what sort of new battle will begin when the jewel is found."

Kia continued to hone her blade. "I watched the sky last night and I saw a streak of light fly across it."

"Veenah sending messengers to Terah."

"Veenah sends many messages these days." Kia gazed into the sky. "And they nearly all go straight to those mountains." She shivered remembering the streak of multicolored light she'd seen the evening before. Why did that one light call to her? What did it mean?

Fem'ma rose to join Moon by the den. She spread her blanket and laid down. Moon was sleeping soundly, sitting up in his seat.

"You look like you're on a faraway journey," Stix said plopping onto the ground next to Kia.

"I think I am far from here, but I don't know where."

"You've been standing on your head cutting leather too long. Tell me what you're thinking instead of speaking in riddles like a mem. It seems like everything is upside down now. Mems wanting to do fem work, and fems trying to understand prophesy."

"Isn't a bonding quest supposed to be a chance to figure it out? Aren't we supposed to be searching for a way to heal Terah?"

"I didn't know she was sick." Stix cocked at eyebrow at her bond sister. "I mean, this is how we live; stay away from the Zid and praise Veenah for what we have."

"You're probably right."

"Right about what?" Song said. She handed each of them a chunk of dried meat. "It's too bad we don't have any grain. A little bit of bread would be good with this."

"Thanks, sister. I was hungry. I suppose we'll be that way a lot before we find a village."

"We can look for roots and greens when we travel tomorrow," Song said. "Hand me your sharpening stone. My knife is ruined."

Brush rustled and the three of them gripped their weapons. Kia saw the look of surprise on Song's face. She turned to see Rok and Ch'e step into the clearing laughing and dragging poles, and holding hands. Rok had never been one to express affection and Kia wondered if this was her bond sister's way of courting this newcomer.

Something inside her tightened. At least Moon was out of sight, it would be completely unacceptable for any of the fems to show affection in his presence. She blocked the thought from her head.

"It took you two long enough to find a couple of poles. Did you have to go all the way across the territory for those?" Kia said.

Rok laughed, but her cheeks turned pink all the way to her ears.

Ch'e pointed to the river. "We went down to the place where I caught the water cat, I mean, water lion."

"She showed me exactly how she caught it, shoving a stick tied with a rope down its throat. I don't know why the thing didn't eat her. We're going to try it again the next time we stop near a river."

Kia stared at their hands. "Hey, let's not do anything like that when Moon's around. It's not proper and I've been taught that it actually hurts a mem to see it."

"You're kidding." Ch`e held Rok's hand even tighter and lifted both their hands over her head. "You're all supposed to be bonding out here, this is part of it. You say you would all court me if we were in a village. Ha! You probably don't even want me here. But Rok does. I love her and it's time we bonded. It doesn't matter if we have a mem here or not."

"Whether you believe me or not, Ch`e, I do want you here. I just…" Kia turned her head.

Stix nodded. "She has a point, Kia. We should have been able to bond, learn to work together and love each other, but we can't because of the mem. What can we do?"

Rok, still gripping Ch`e's hand, said, "Moon will probably be our syr soon enough, especially if we don't find another village."

Kia stood, waving her arms in exasperation. "Don't you all realize what can happen if we don't control ourselves? If he demands attention from one of us out here – and one of us does become pregnant––"

"Then," Ch`e's voice raised as if presenting a message to an entire clan, "we will prove ourselves to be a good femtog able to give him children. I say we act like we're on a bonding quest and let Fem'ma keep him out of sight if it's so important. And I also say we need to leave this place now. We follow the river. I feel deep in my bones we'll find a village there."

Kia took a deep breath. She knew Ch`e would challenge her, just not so soon. Her heart led her a different way, toward the mountain, not away from it. But she couldn't force her fems to follow her. If they were not all willing to follow, she couldn't lead.

"I've thought about the way we should travel. The bio-messenger told Moon we go toward the Forbidden Mountains." Grumbles and mutterings of 'No' rippled through the little group. "Hear me out. Have you ever seen the flashes of light that travel across Veenah in the darkness? They all go toward those mountains."

"That's exactly why I say we go the other way," Ch`e said, her voice growing deeper. She squared her shoulders, facing Kia. "Don't you think it's odd that the Zid want us to go there, *and* those lights go there. It's forbidden for a reason."

Kia suppressed a tremble, she couldn't afford to fight openly with this fem – but she couldn't argue with the facts. She knew how dangerous this voyage could be.

"Ch`e, I understand, and you're right, but think of the words of the prophesy. It's a light from above and a stone from below. I think the reason those mountains are taboo is to protect some secret." She waited for her words to sink in. "The secret we have been spared for. It is not by chance we are all here, with a mem who knows the prophecy better than any elder of our old village."

An uneasy silence draped over the fems. Kia watched her beloved Stix take a deep breath and step toward Rok and Ch`e.

Stix held her hands toward Ch`e. "Today we worked together as a complete femtog. It made me happy. I choose you, healer and fish hunter," Stix said. "You saved my life and I ask you to join me and be my bond sister."

"Thank you." Ch`e took Stix's hand and Rok laid her hand on theirs. "I warn you, though. I have a temper."

Stix giggled. "A wicked temper, but so does Rok. And I fear neither of you."

All eyes turned again to Song. Tears flooded the young fem's eyes. She tried to clear her throat, but couldn't speak. Kia and Stix both wrapped their arms around her.

"We all miss her, sweet Song, but she doesn't want us to grieve," Kia whispered.

Stix added, "She wants us to be happy and to be complete, let's give Ch`e a chance."

Song wiped her face. "The one I loved most from the time I took my first steps, stood in the place of the heart finger. She stood for love. She was love. But Veenah took her."

"You mean, the Zid took her," Ch`e said.

Song stifled a sob. "My heart is so empty without her, but I can make room for you. If you can forgive me for lying about my moonflow."

Ch`e laughed. "You didn't lie to me sister, and I doubt you lied to anyone standing here. I think you need to ask yourself for forgiveness. We will travel down the river and be united by the Memlore in the first village we find. Then we can do anything we want in front of Moon because he will be our syr."

Song added her hand and their fingers entwined. "Let's bond, then, and go find that jewel." She managed a weak smile.

Trembling over her entire body, Kia slipped her fingers into the ring of hands. She glanced at the faces filled with love. A piece of her feared the new future. The rest of her was happy. She knew that Moon and Fem'ma were watching from the den, but she didn't think they could hear what the fems were saying. Her eyes locked with Ch`e's and began the ceremony.

"I bond myself to you, Ch`e, and pledge my love and loyalty for life."

Toil in darkness
Strain in silence
The one is many and one together
Growing in your heart, defiance

18 Together We Rest

"I have a bad feeling about this." Song whispered to Kia while they tied the last of the food into place on the drag, which was Ch`e's name for the carrier. "Ch`e is meaner than ever this evening. And I am really afraid of the dark. Moonlight won't shine for much of the night and we won't be able to see the nightbird or wolf before they attack."

"I know, sister. Worse, there is no way we can find shelter as good as this before Warmsun goes to rest. We are not leaving before light comes tomorrow. I know Fem'ma won't put Moon in danger, so we will simply lie down when she says to go."

"She'll be angry."

"Oh, well. A leader shouldn't have to get mad to make her fems follow her. Fems stay together because of love. That's what we're going to show her. Love."

Stix, Rock, and Ch`e suddenly exploded in a game of tag. They dashed in circles around the clearing, laughing and squealing. Rock caught Stix and Ch`e tackled both of them. Together they rolled in the grass and stopped with Ch`e on top. Rock's arms went around the newcomer in an embrace, but Stix rolled away, still laughing. She turned on her knees and lunged back into the other two and the three of them wrestled, each trying to stay on top.

Kia's heart surged and part of her wanted to join the fun, but Song had turned away, another tear rolling down her cheek. She draped an arm over Song's shoulder and they relaxed watching the game. Three of these fems Kia loved with all her heart. But something in the eyes and sassy behavior of this new sister stirred her in a way which had never even been touched by Stix. How could the danger loving, headstrong beauty cause her to feel this way? She shook her head and drew Song closer.

Maybe they could bond, but she wasn't going to leave the den today.

A chill ran down Kia's spine and she glanced over her shoulder, feeling as if she were being watched. Moon stood in the door of the den wearing his new sandals and holding his small spear. His cloak was barely closed. Kia's face burned red to the back of her neck and a stone formed in her stomach. This game her sisters played in the grass was sure to excite the mem as much as it excited her. It was so very wrong to play this way in front of a mem. Guilt flowed up into her throat.

Where is Fem'ma?

She should be keeping him away from all this. The wise matron surely knew better than to put him in this sort of danger. As if summoned by Kia's frantic mind Fem'ma scooped Moon into her sling and hurried into the woods where he liked to walk. Kia knew they wouldn't go far, but she kept an eye on Fem'ma's retreating form anyway. Her mood darkened.

Laughter in the clearing increased and suddenly Ch`e sat up and shouted to the sky, "I love these fems! Do you hear me Terah? I love these fems!"

Kia smiled. Song buried her face in Kia's shoulder, sobbing softly.

"Will it ever stop hurting?"

"It's okay, sweet Song. The pain will leave one day, I promise."

"I miss Vee. I just want her back." Song let her heart out, crying without shame.

"Vee will be with us as long as we remember her. But think of this. If you had died and she lived, would you want her to hurt? Or would you want her to find happiness and joy in life?"

"I know, Kia. I'll be alright. It was nice having Rok so close to me, but now she's more interested in Ch`e. Who wouldn't, she can do anything."

"Enough of that. You are the one who can do anything. She

knows medicines and she catches big fish."

Ch`e stood and brushed the grass and dust from her buckskin dress. She skipped over to Song. "Hey little sister, no more crying. This is our bonding time. Be happy. We have a long adventure in front of us and we need joy, not sorrow. C'mon fems, let's finish loading the drag. It's a long walk to the next shelter."

Kia kept her arm over Song's shoulder. "You are impatient as the river beautiful Ch`e. But we face dangers the river doesn't have to fear. We will leave in the morning. Besides, Fem'ma and Moon are off on one of their walks."

"Well, go get them. You *have* been watching them, I hope." Ch`e hooked her fists on her hips.

"Yes, but Moon likes his long walks. I think he misses the company of other mems and they talk wisdom and stuff on those walks. Fem'ma will bring him back when he's ready. Besides, Song has prepared food."

"No, we're running out of time, go get them so we can leave."

Rok and Stix looked at each other, then at Ch`e and Kia. A shadow of sadness crossed Stix's face, but Kia looked away. She stretched and yawned.

"Song, I'm tired, aren't you? Why don't we lie down for a while? We can eat your wonderful stew when Moon gets back." In the corner of her eye Kia saw Stix take a step toward her. Rok looked confused.

Ch`e kicked a stone. "Wait right there. We talked about this. In case you forgot, the Zid know where we are right now, and I'm not interested in being here when they come back. We go now."

"The Zid who saw us was friendly. I don't understand it, but it was. Stix is proof of that. And I notice your leg is well, too. We don't need to be afraid of that Zid as much as we need to be afraid of things like nightbirds, slitherbeasts, wolves, and lions. I'm going to sleep. Stix, you could use some rest, too."

Kia turned, her hand still locked in Song's and offered her other hand to Stix as she headed for the den. She called over her shoulder. "The drag will be safe until the dark, but we'll have to hoist it into a tree until morning." Her heart beat faster and faster but she resisted looking over her shoulder for Stix. She prayed to Veenah this would be peaceful."

"Fine," Ch`e growled. "I'll go find Moon myself. Rok, you're with me."

Kia froze, half in and half out of the den. She felt Stix's hand slip into hers. What would Rok decide? She couldn't force the young warrior, but her heart would break if Rok followed the newcomer. Another step and she would be inside the den and out of sight from Ch`e and Rok. Her ears strained for a response.

"Rok! I said, go with me to find Moon!"

"Ah, I'm a little tired after working that skin and cutting our tunics. If you don't mind, I think I'll lay down with our sisters. Come rest with us. Or, if you're not tired, you can stand watch."

Kia's eyes tingled with tears of love when she felt Rok's strong hand on her back. Together, they piled into the thick mat of grasses, spooning. Stix, Kia, Song, and Rok. Sounds of Stix snoring quickly filled the den. Kia grinned. Stix could sleep any time, any place. She closed her eyes, but her ears were alert.

Slowly, Kia felt the tension melt out of her muscles. Song had finally drifted off to sleep and she thought Rok had as well. The warmth of Stix peacefully sleeping in her arms rather than thrashing and groaning in pain, brought joy which drowned out the sting of quarreling with Ch`e. In her village fems rarely fought. They talked, or brought their argument to an elder. Leadership of a femtog was a natural evolution of companionship and working together in a bonding quest. Up until the attack, Kia had been leader. But what if Ch`e was right. How much easier would it be to allow someone else to make the decisions? She floated into a troubled sleep.

The watcher stands upon the tower
And guards a precious treasure
An oath is made
By blood and bone
Prepare the blade
Defend the home
Release the hidden light of power
A gift too great to measure.

19 A Leader's Burden

Coarse fingertips brushed across Rok's cheek and her eyes opened. She looked up into the gentle face of Fem'ma, and for a moment felt disoriented. Darkness surrounded her, interrupted only by the flickering of the fire. Song shifted comfortably in the sleeping mat, and she remembered following Kia into the den to sleep. A soft hand lay across her waist. Her back stiffened. No one ever slept at her back. Ch`e. Rok smiled and lifted her new sister's arm.

"It's time for your watch," Fem'ma whispered.

Rok lifted herself from her cozy nest, glancing around. "Who stood first?" She stepped out of the den and looked up at the watch-seat.

"Moon."

"What? No, not again!"

"Our rebellious mem demanded, so I stayed up with him. I just settled him on his sleeping mat."

"It is unnatural for a mem to stand guard. You should have taken him inside anyway. Either Kia or I could have done it."

"He threatened to yell and wake everyone if I didn't agree. He insisted Ch`e sleep with her sisters after I helped her hoist the drag into a tree. After all, this was her first official night with her femtog."

"I wish she had come in with us instead of being so angry. It's a poor way to start our family." Rok stared off into the heavy darkness. "I could have carried her into the sleeping place and we would have held her between us so she would know she's a true sister."

"She is no longer so angry. Moon had a long talk with her. She is better as healer and Kia is better as leader."

"That makes me happy. We should only have one job in a femtog, other than helping with hunting and building the hut. I even thought about leadership, but I'm a warrior and that makes me a dangerous leader. Kia has been a leader her whole life."

"You are worried about small things. Trust me when I tell you, a bonding quest can be difficult. Some fems never truly learn to work together." In a quieter, sadder voice, Fem'ma added, "Sometimes not even love is enough to keep a femtog together."

"I'm sorry. Is that why you became a matron?"

Fem'ma sighed. "I've been happy just raising my son. And the other matrons and elders are kind."

"But you miss your own sisters."

"And my husband. I most often carried him when I wasn't suckling a babe. I had three, you know." Fem'ma raked her hair back. "But all of that is behind us, and we have a new life in front of us. I'm sleepy. I'll see you when Warmsun returns."

Rok watched the wise fem disappear into the secluded section of the den. A generous stack of firewood indicated that Moon and Fem'ma hadn't just sat during their watch. A chill ran down her spine. This sort of behavior would never be understood or tolerated in any village – if they ever found one. The memory of her mother drifted around her like a ghost.

"Oh Lona, what will we do? I don't want us to wander homeless like you did before coming to our village." Rok pondered her blood mother's stories of traveling with the traders. Many tales had been told, traveling, as well as dangerous hunts, and even battles with raiders. But never once had Rok heard any of her hearth mothers discuss their bonding, or even mention the prophecy. "Were you truly bonded? Or were you only adopted? Or did Aga only allow you to stay because of your strength. I wish I could talk to you, my mother."

Taking her place in the watch seat with her bow and spear, Rok listened to the river and studied the horizon for the coming Moonlight.

The ruler of the night would be smaller and come a short time before his mate, Warmsun, arrived. Soon Moonlight would disappear for a span of nights. Then he would peek out of the sky in the place where Warmsun went to rest. Just over the top of the Forbidden Mountains.

Something inside Rok stirred. Why, indeed, are those mountains forbidden? Never in her life had she thought of traveling toward them, not until Kia said there may be a secret hidden there.

A flash of light darted across Veenah straight into those jagged peaks, just before Nightbird glided over the river and dipped into the brush. Far away in the badlands a pack of wolves howled.

Fully alert, Rok crouched closer to the twisted roots of the old tree and banished thoughts of the Forbidden Mountains to watch for danger. Did fems stand watch on a normal bonding quest? One which hadn't started with the destruction of the world? Maybe she would ask Fem'ma while they traveled. Up the river, or down? Not her worry, she was protector not leader.

However, the most dangerous part of the night was fast approaching. So far, every night had been the same. Just at the time of the last watch, something horrendous always occurred. Rok's eyes darted through the shadows. Her ears strained for every little sound. The dried grasses of the sleeping place rustled and a moment later, the brilliant yellow hair of Song glowed in the firelight.

"Can I come up and sit with you?" Song stretched and rubbed the sleep from her eyes.

"Always. Why are you awake? Is your sleep troubled?"

"I missed you." Song grinned and made her way up the fallen tree to settle beside Rok. "I thought maybe you didn't want to sleep near me anymore when I felt Ch`e so close."

"No one can take your place beside me. Especially not Ch`e. But I hope you won't be jealous, because I really do love her."

*****

Warmsun had barely pushed light over the edge of the world when Rok lifted the drag. She thought Kia looked more tired than when she'd gone to sleep, and their leader hadn't even taken her watch. *Leadership is so much harder than fighting enemies.* Rok felt her heart beat harder with emotions new to her. A love such as she'd never known before Kia came into her life.

Finally, the young leader scooped up her pack, slinging it over her shoulder, and hefted her spear, tipped with the deadly spine of the water cat. Rok held her breath. *This is it.* For the first time in her life she felt the need to send a prayer to Veenah.

"I've given this much thought," Kia said. "Until we got that message from the Zid I never would have considered going close to the Forbidden Mountains. They call to me, however, I know all of you fear that place, and it very easily could be a trap. So, I'm not going to force us to go there. We travel down the river to find another village. Do you want to vote, sisters?"

Rok answered first, letting out an audible breath. "I am starting to understand how you feel about this quest, and I'm with you." A chill settled over her. A trap could be waiting anyplace.

"Me too," Song and Stix spoke in unison.

Kia waited, then finally said, "Ch`e?"

"What's to say, leader? I knew you'd come around. You are wise and I'm happy for your decision."

All eyes turned toward Fem'ma.

"The mem and I are happy to follow you Kia," Fem'ma said.

Rok clearly saw Moon's expression cloud with anger and thought he actually pulled Fem'ma's hair a little, but he didn't speak. She didn't understand the tightness which formed in her stomach, knowing that Moon felt differently. She glanced around, paying attention to the shadows in the trees.

Ch`e put her hand over Rok's and lifted the pole. "Allow Stix and me to carry the drag, warrior. You are needed to watch for danger."

Rok shivered a little as she relinquished her hold on their supplies and felt Ch`e's fingertips trail along her arm.

"Lead on, fearless one!" Ch`e shouted.

The peaceful beauty of the riverbank belied the dangers lurking around every bend. Rok didn't know if she should be walking ahead of the group, preparing for ambush, or staying at the rear where she could watch for an attack from behind.

Where the land was wide and flat, Kia led the band near the water, but because the river was swollen with the snowmelt from the mountains, the rapids crashed angrily over boulders and broken trees. Where the river bank was steeper, they had to travel closer to the woods.

Often the small band had to follow narrow game trails, hacking their way through tangles of brush and branches. Far ahead loomed a narrow passage and they would have to trek through the woods even farther from the river.

I'll scout a safe trail while they rest.

Song poked and prodded into small animal dens and parted the branches of bushes with her spear as she walked along the narrow game trail. Something a few paces from the path caught her attention and she darted into the brush.

"Hey, look! I found mushrooms!"

Ch`e puffed under the loaded drag and called out, "Leave them. We don't have time to be gathering food."

Rok felt the hairs on the back of her neck rise as anger filled her. Fems never walked away from food. Especially not valuable food like mushrooms. Before she could do or say anything, Kia dropped back and lifted an empty basket from the carrier. Walking toward Song, Kia said loud enough for all to hear, "We'll gather only enough for a meal, because we don't have time to properly dry them. You have a good eye, sister."

Ch`e growled under her breath and stomped past the mushroom patch. She shifted her grip on her side of the drag and pulled Stix off balance. Rok jumped to help her sister but stopped. Stix was stronger than ever and quickly recovered.

"Take it easy," Stix said. "You don't have to take your anger out on me. I didn't do anything."

"No, but you could back me up sometimes. We don't need more food, but we do need to get down the trail."

Before Ch`e finished speaking, Kia was already taking her place back in front of the little caravan. Song followed, carrying the basket of mushrooms so they wouldn't get jostled and bruised on the drag.

Stix grinned at Ch`e. "See there, no time wasted and we will have a delicious addition to our next meal. Veenah provides for us, but she expects us to take what she offers."

"Oh, please spare me. She just wants to put me down."

"Who, Veenah? How could you say such a thing?" Stix nearly dropped the drag in shock.

"Of course not. Kia. She hates me."

"Then why did you promise to bond to her and why did you welcome her bonding promise to you?"

"Because I had to. I don't have anywhere else to go."

"Maybe so, but I think you're mad at her because you want to be leader."

Rok trembled as the fear of insulting the head-strong healer collided with the hurt she felt at Ch`e's jealousy and the new argument she knew was coming. She jogged to catch up and walk beside her newest sister. "We are one family, my sisters. No one is more important than another. Tonight, while we sit around our fire and feast on the mushrooms Song found, we will talk about your anger."

Stix smiled and nodded in agreement. "I can pretty much assure you that Kia doesn't hate you. We can talk honestly about our feelings for each other and what we really want."

The valley narrowed and the trail became rockier. Everywhere in the soft ground by the river's edge were tracks of animals, from the tiniest of grass rats to the big stripe-tail who could use his front feet like hands, to the massive two-toed impression of the targus beast. Upturned river stone and a rotted log torn to shreds indicated that the animal had used its deadly sharp tusks to dig for food. Rok yearned for a targus beast cloak with its soft black curls around the neck. It was the robe of the chief warrior in a clan and she always knew she'd wear one. She just never thought it would be because she was the last warrior in Terah. She spied the game trail leading into the forest.

"Kia," she called out. "I suggest we rest here and make sure we have plenty of water. We need to scout that trail for danger. This valley makes a perfect ambush place."

The words had barely left her lips. From out of nowhere, a blast from a Zid weapon hit the drag, sending the supplies flying. Suddenly the sky erupted with firing from every direction.

"Run!" Rok screamed a war cry as she let fly an arrow. It lodged in the body of a skimmer flying low. Smoke poured from the side of the skimmer and it careened into the ground. Rok smiled, grimly.

"I didn't know I could kill their flyers."

Crouching between two boulders, she sent an arrow into another flyer. Then she realized the Zid were no longer shooting at her family, they were shooting at each other.

A shriek split through the sky and a skimmer spiraled to the ground. Purple blood gushed from the side of the Zid riding it. The blast from a weapon had removed the thing's arm and laid open its side. Three more blasts focused on one point at the edge of the forest and a flaming Zid tumbled into sight just ahead of a smoky explosion that sent bits of a skimmer into the air.

The battle was over as quickly as it had begun. An eerie stillness hung over the forest.

Entombed within the stony walls,
It prays and waits for one strong hand.
A birthright stolen. A promise calls
To grant the courage and will to stand.

20 Captured

Stix bit her lip to keep from screaming, though she was certain the hunters knew exactly where she was hiding. She held Ch`e tight and wriggled deeper beneath the tangled branches. The last thing she'd seen was Kia and Song diving for cover, but she grew ill not knowing what happened to Fem'ma and Moon. One of the skimmers moved away from her hiding place and set down. The Zid jumped off and ran on two legs toward the place she'd last seen the rest of her family.

Kia!

With a spear in one hand and her long knife in the other, she rushed toward the creature. The Zid stood still with its hands high. Staring straight at the spear in Stix's hand, it turned its armor plated back to her. Slowly it dropped to all fours, spouting clicks and whistles. It circled her, keeping its back tilted in her direction. Between the flicks of its tongue, Stix heard a soft pop and several staccato clicks. A shock ran through her, she was sure there was a pattern to the sounds the beast made.

A rustling of leaves made Stix crouch and turn. Rok dropped down from a tree and grabbed her by the arm, trying to run to safety. The Zid scuttled in front of them, blocking the escape. It made a sharp squeal, then the pops and clicks again.

"I've got your back," Rok whispered. "They have us surrounded. Why aren't they attacking?"

"They're saving us for dinner, would be my guess," Stix said.

"You should have stayed hidden."

"I couldn't let you face that thing alone. Kia managed to get Moon and Fem'ma under cover, but I don't know where Song and Ch`e are."

"I never noticed how big they are before. I just wanted to kill them and get away. Standing up, my head only comes up to its arms."

Rok shifted her grip on her spear, waiting for a chance for a lethal thrust. "But on all fours, it's not as big as a targus beast. And we kill those easy enough. Easier now that we know your 'long-spear' tactics."

Circling, back to back Stix and Rok surveyed the area. Two skimmers scanned the tree line and small clearing. The Zid riding them flicked their tongues rapidly as they peered beneath and around the thick brush. Another monstrous lizard worked feverishly on a skimmer with an arrow protruding from its side.

"Nice shot," Stix said.

A shriek erupted from the bushes. Rok and Stix faced the new danger with weapons poised. Ch`e stumbled into the clearing in front of a skimmer. She rushed toward them. Stix drew back her spear, but the skimmer veered out of range. The Zid gazed at her with dead, yellow eyes and made a short squeal followed by a pop and the same clicks she'd heard before. She lowered her spear. A moment later the other Zid flushed out Song. Rok scooped her up in a tight embrace.

Song cried out, "You're alive! I don't understand! Why didn't they kill us?"

"I don't know, but something's not right," Rock breathed. "Where are the others?"

"I didn't see anything after the attack. What's that thing doing?"

"GET AWAY!" Ch`e slashed with her knife. "It's deciding which of us to eat first, can't you tell. Kia led us straight into an ambush! Some leader!"

The four fems pressed close, watching the Zid walk around them on all fours just out of reach of their spears. It gazed at them, never blinking, its vertical pupils barely a slit in the bright sun. It continued the sounds, but when Stix raised her spear or knife it made a short squeal. The other two Zid continued hunting.

Suddenly all the Zid set up a mournful keening and one of the hunters carried a dead Zid into the clearing and set it down. The one guarding Stix and her sisters, scuttled to join the other three, bending over the dead one.

"I guess one of their friends got what was intended for us.

The large creature that had been working on the broken skimmer pawed the dead one all over with its front feet, keening louder than the others. Then it looked straight at Rok and emitted a treacherous sounding rumble, baring its rows of sharp, jagged teeth. The smaller beasts cowered until the roar was spent. The smallest beast sat on its tail and pawed the big one, cooing and chattering. The other two just stared at the four fems.

Stix's mouth went dry. "I can't believe what I'm seeing, but I think they're upset over the death of their friend."

Song whispered, "It's almost like the big one is the dead one's mother or something. It's acting like our hearth mothers do when a babe dies."

"And I think that smaller one is trying to comfort it," Stix added.

"Look at the dark green one, the one that found me," Song said. "It has a wound on its back. That horrible smelling blood is oozing everywhere. Why aren't they helping it?"

Rok crouched lower. "I think we should make a run for it while they're busy grieving. Get ready. There's a pile of boulders up ahead near the riverbank with a cave behind it. They've put their weapons away, so they can't shoot us, and I don't think they can get through the tiny spaces between the boulders. Ready?"

Stix kept her eyes on the four Zid and made ready to run, but the creature which had been guarding them raised its head, and like lightening, it ran on all fours to block them again. This time it opened its mouth wide and made a loud hiss. The stench of its breath hit the fems like a cloud of heavy smoke.

"Oh! Perg's fires!" Stix coughed. "I can't breathe! If they do have a language, I think that thing just told us to stay where we are."

"I wouldn't have guessed!" Ch`e snapped. "But don't try to translate. Animals don't talk!" She slashed out at it with her long knife.

The thing ducked and leaped, trying to grab Ch`e by the arm. All four fems dodged its grasp, but the long, serpentine tail curled around and tripped them.

Rok scrambled to her feet and knocked an arrow. The Zid swiped at her, knocking her down again. It wrestled the bow from her grip, then scooped the remaining arrows from the quiver, while keeping Stix, Song, and Ch`e busy with its tail.

Ch`e had lost her knife when she fell, but Stix and Song hacked at the heavily plated beast trying to stay on their feet. Their knives hardly made a scratch.

The Zid swung its tail again, sweeping them off their feet. Song fell hard and clutched her stomach gasping for breath. Rok leaped on its back, bashing it with a large river stone, but it managed to disarm Song.

Stix raised her gleaming blade high to bring down on the thing's head while Rok hammered it. She didn't see the big one pounce behind her. Ch`e, Song, and Rok screamed as the big Zid opened its jaws right behind their sister.

The guard, now bleeding from the wounds Rok was dealing, curled its head and charged into Stix, knocking her away from the big one. Stix swung with all her might, but her knife only glanced off the thing's shoulder as she hit the ground. Before Stix could regain her footing, the guard had her knife and spear. It stood high on its hind legs and tail and Rok fell from its back.

The injured Zid shook its head and gathered the strewn weapons. It hissed and snapped its jaws at the big creature. Stix and Rok huddled together with Song and Ch`e between them. Stix trembled as if she was freezing.

"I feel sick," she said. "I don't know what just happened, but I think that thing just saved my life while I was trying to kill it."

The big one hissed and croaked and the other two left their dead member to scuttle back to their skimmers. Stix could see the injured one limping badly. The Zid resumed their search for Kia, Fem'ma, and Moon, but this time one of them carried a weapon which it peered through as it hovered over trees and bushes.

At the tree line, several paces from the river, one of the hunters squealed then fired its blaster into the forest. The smell of scorched wood filled the air.

Stix screamed and fell to her knees. "They've killed her! They killed Kia!" She pounded the ground with her fists. Her insides twisted in the agony of loss and fear. "Why don't they just kill us all and get it over with." She felt a thumping on her back and looked up.

Rok pulled Stix to her feet and the four of them once again huddled close. Kia and Fem'ma dashed out of the woods closely followed by the Zid with the weapon. It blocked them and pointed toward the rest of the captives. Stix rushed forward to meet Kia.

"It was a trap," Kia sobbed. "I was afraid of that, but none of us wanted anything to do with the Forbidden Mountains. I'm sorry I led you to this."

The Zid nudged them forward and the clan was once again together.

Fem'ma hunched over the sling she held tight to her chest.

The hunters set their skimmers down in a triangle and the guard took over. It began a cooing sound sprinkled with a few staccato clicks. It waved its hands in a downward motion, pointing toward the skimmers and bobbing its head.

"Come on," she whispered. "It wants us to move."

"I don't know why you're trying to whisper," Ch`e said. "They've got us and I don't think they intend to let us go. But I'm going to fight them to the death." She picked up a stone and slung it at the guard.

It only continued to coo, click, and point. As soon as the group was confined, the guard connected the skimmers with a metal rope. It made one last "coo" then returned to its own group. They all resumed keening over the dead Zid.

Stix stretched a finger toward the metal rope enclosing them.

"I wouldn't do that if I were you," warned Rok.

But it was too late. A sizzle which began at Stix's fingertips shot a jolt through her body. And because the family was crammed into the space, shoulder to shoulder, the shock went through all of them.

"Ouch!" Moon screamed inside his sling. "Whatever you did, don't do it again!"

Stix rubbed her fingers. "It's like poison and fire all in one place. I thought we could climb over these things and get away, but I won't touch that again. And what are you laughing about, Rok? That hurt!"

"I knew it was some sort of trick. Warriors always set alarms and traps to protect the village. It makes sense that they would do the same thing. We call it a booby-trap."

"Oh, for the love of Veenah. Look what they're doing now," Kia said in a low voice.

Stix tried to turn away, but the horror opening up on the other side of the clearing kept her eyes riveted. The big Zid that had been so angry now held a tool with a silvery beam of light shining from it, and sliced the dead one in half from nose to tail. When the two halves fell apart, it sliced those in half through the middle to make four pieces. What happened next made her gag. The creature opened its jaws wide and gulped down one of the front parts, jerking its head then snapping its teeth together in a resounding crack.

The guard began the same thing with the other front piece. A glimmer of the iridescent scales on the side of the dead creature's head flashed and Kia caught her breath. "Stix! I think that's the Zid that brought the medicine we used to heal your leg!"

"It can't be," Ch`e said. "How can you tell?"

Rok answered for her sister and leader. "The color on its head."

Song groaned. "We're really in trouble now. We killed one of those seekers, didn't we? Oh, I can't watch that."

A muffled grumble came inside Fem'ma's sling. "Let me out, Ma," Moon shouted. "I'm hot and you're crushing me. Let me see what they're doing."

Fem'ma loosened the laces and Moon stuck his head out gasping for fresh air.

One by one, the Zid gulped down their pieces, slurping and belching. They finished and one of them made a chirping grunt, then two of them went back to work on the skimmer and the injured one went to the river to drink. The guard returned, walking slowly on two feet.

"If I were to make a guess," Moon said. "Based on some of the songs the elders sing among themselves, I would say they ate their friend in order to take its power."

"Well," Stix said shuddering, "that was the most horrible thing I've ever seen and I don't care how strong a dead Terian is, I'm not eating her."

"That's good to know," Rok said.

The tension was temporarily broken by strained laughter.

Stix eyed the guard. She'd long studied the language of birds and other animals she came across. Every creature had a different sound for danger, safety, happiness, and even for mating. While hunting, she relied on these sounds to guide her to a successful kill. Now she studied the language of this creature.

"I'm going to try something," Stix said quietly. "I need a big rock."

Kia shuffled her feet and kneeled, careful not to touch the metal rope. "I've got one. It's not very big, though. Here."

Stix took the rock, about the size of her fist and acted like she was going to throw it.

The Zid's voice changed back to the first sound it had made; cooing and clicks.

She lowered the stone, and the thing made a soft pop and bowed its head.

Rok gouged her in the ribs. "What are you doing?" she mumbled.

"I'm going to try to talk to it. I think the coo and click means 'calm down'."

Stix laid the stone on the ground and listened to the creature. "That sound might mean 'good' or something like that." She tried to mimic the sound.

The guard tilted its head then spoke its words a little slower.

She repeated the sound then tapped herself on the chest. "Stix!" The Zid cocked its head farther. "Stix!" she repeated, then tapped Rok's chest "Rok!"

The creature stepped closer, drawing its head back, jaws snapping.

Step lightly my beauty
And dance while I sing.
Be happy and joyful
Let friendship take wing.

21 Allies

The guard snapped its jaws rapidly then whistled and clicked several times, and the two working on the skimmer scurried over on all fours then stood. Tapping on its own abdomen, the Zid made two clicks and popped its mouth, making a hollow sound like a stone striking a piece of dry wood.

Stix tilted her head slightly and the Zid repeated the sound. She mimicked the sound then added, "I'll call you Pop!" She pointed to it and said, "Pop!" Tapping herself, she said, "Stix."

The Zid waggled their heads and clicked. Pop tapped the large Zid and pointed out three stars carved into the pale scales below its neck. Then with crossed hands against its chest, it bowed and made a deep cluck. They looked at Stix, waiting for an answer.

She crossed her arms in front of her chest and bowed toward the decorated Zid, then said "Chuck." She pointed to each of them and said, "Chuck, Pop, Stix, Rok."

Chuck and Pop clapped their hands and chattered. Pop introduced the smallest member of their group with a hiss and click.

"Snap," Stix said.

The young Snap pounded its feet and chattered at Chuck. It dropped to all fours and scuttled into the bushes, reemerging holding a yellow flower. It stood and pointed to Song, then the flower, making a short, high whistle. Song huddled behind Fem'ma.

Rok laughed hard and took Song's hand. "I think Snap just

named you Flower!" She attempted the whistle.

Ch`e huffed. "Nice. Now they can call us by name to eat us. See if you can get them to let us out of here."

Stix rubbed her chin. "Pop cooed and clicked when it put us in here. I'll try that. Maybe I can convince it that we are calm and will stay." She pointed to the metal rope and imitated the coo, then waved her hand as if she wanted to brush the rope away.

Chuck clicked at Pop then went back to its skimmer. Snap appeared agitated and kept trying to get Song's attention. Finally, it set the flower on one of the skimmers and scampered after Chuck. Pop flicked its tongue out and stared at the prisoners, saying nothing.

Stix tried the movement again with sharp clicks. Pop flopped down on its belly, still staring.

Ch`e giggled. "You've taught it to lie down. Now teach it to let us go."

Stix tried a series of clicks and pops while she brushed at the rope. Pop got up and gathered the knives, spears, and the bow and arrows and secured them out of reach on one of the skimmers then ambled to the river.

Song peeked around Fem'ma. "Are they gone?" she squeaked.

"I don't think we need to be afraid of them," Kia said. "If they were going to do something to us, they would have already done it."

"So they're just going to leave us here to burn under Warmsun," Ch`e grumbled. "At least they could let us get our packs, or give us enough room to sit down."

"If we live through this," Song said, still trembling, "maybe Moon can sing a song about it. You could do that, couldn't you Moon?"

"Of course. I'll put my mind to it now, I hope we get the chance to share it with other Terians." He hummed a tune and mumbled to himself. "This could be an important time for us and my new song will be sung for great celebrations." He sang a soft melody.

Pop raised its head from sunning himself on the warm rocks of the riverbank and looked at the group of Terians.

Stix whispered, "Moon, sing louder. I think Pop likes it."

Moon raised his voice, watching the Zid, then said, "Ma, lift me up on your shoulder. I'll sing so they can really hear me." Once he was comfortable on his perch, he cleared his throat and clearly sang.

> Hand of the innocent,
> symbol of might,
> defender of honor,
> promise of life.
> Jewel of the Covenant,
> gift of the soul,
> waiting in secret
> until life is made whole.

Pop stood and walked over to them, swaying slightly with the music.

When Moon finished, he stared at Pop and nodded toward the metal rope. But the big lizard only sat on its tail cooing.

"Ma, put me back in my sling. If it wants another song, it will release us."

Pop stood up and swayed, cooing and holding its hands toward the group.

Kia grinned. "Okay, everyone point to that rope and turn your back. Since Pop obviously wants to sing and dance with us, she must know we need more room."

"You called it 'she'," Ch`e said as she turned her back. "How do you know? As far as I can tell, it's neither. And I certainly don't respect those creatures enough to give them Terian qualities."

"Sorry. I guess I slipped. It did sound weird, I guess." Kia crossed her arms and stamped a foot for emphasis.

Pop trotted around the enclosure to face them. Swaying again, it now chattered and clicked. When the group turned away, it hissed loudly and walked toward its leader.

"Hmph," Kia grunted. "We already know that means 'Stay here.' Like we can get out anyway. Rok, maybe you can throw me over the top of one of the skimmers and I can run to the tree line before Pop catches me again."

"I'm not about to risk it," Rok said. "They'll lose patience and kill us for sure."

Time wore on and Warmsun passed her zenith and began the descent toward the Forbidden Mountains. The three Zid still worked on the skimmer. Even though Stix's leg was completely healed and strong, she began to ache all over from standing in the heat. She knew the rest of her family was suffering as well.

Time to do something.

"Pop!" she shouted. "Pop! Come here!" She waited for the Zid to raise its head and look. She pointed to their ruined drag then to her open mouth. "Pop, come here. We're hungry and thirsty and need to rest!"

Pop chattered to Chuck. Finally, the huge lizard plodded toward them. Snap scooted ahead, chattering. It sat on its tail and whistled.

"Song," Ch`e said. "Your pet lizard wants you."

Stix whispered, "Step in front of me and put your hands toward it. Try to let it know we're friendly."

Song complied. "I'm too tired to even be afraid anymore." She reached out with her palms up, which made Snap coo and pat its feet on the ground.

Chuck arrived and sat on its haunches and tail.

Stix tried one more time. Brushing away at the metal rope, she said, "Chuck, let us go so we can eat and drink water." She pointed to their supplies, then to the river and to her mouth."

Chuck stood and hissed. But it touched something on the nearest skimmer and the metal rope dropped to the ground.

Gingerly, Stix stepped out of the trap. She crossed her arms over her chest and bowed her head. "Cluck." She made the same sound Pop had made when it introduced them. The rest of her family hurried to the river with Snap closely following Song.

After drinking their fill of water, Stix and Kia gathered their supplies and served dried water cat for a quick meal. Moon scraped bits of food into his mouth quickly and demanded more. Song broke several mushrooms for him.

"I'm going to try something." Stix got up and tore off a large chunk of dried fish for herself. She walked over and stood in front of Pop.

Kia watched her and Stix thought she might stop her. "Don't worry, dear sister. I'm not going to get us killed. I hope." She held the chunk of meat out to Pop and said, "Food." Taking a small bite first, she held it out to the Zid again and nodded her head. "Food."

Pop chattered a short cackle and stretched an inquisitive finger to touch the meat. It cackled again and lifted the meat from her hand. First it flicked its tongue out to test the chunk then it sniffed. Its jaws opened just a bit and it tossed the meat into its mouth. Suddenly Pop dropped to all fours shaking its head and backing up. The cooked and dried meat fell onto the ground and Pop tilted its head to inspect it closer.

The fems all giggled and Kia said, "I don't think Pop likes our food very much."

Pop stared at them and Stix was certain she could detect a bit of a challenge in the yellow eyes of the beast. She tried not to laugh with her sisters. Pop cackled at her again and picked up the meat with its front teeth and with one quick flip of its head, swallowed the chunk whole. It sat on its tail and burped, staring flatly at the group.

"Food," said Stix. She held up another chunk of meat and bit into it. "Food."

Pop cackled then slipped into the water, submerging near the middle where the river was deep and the current swift. Moments later, it surfaced and swam to shore with a fish caught in its teeth. Sitting on its tail in front of Stix, it tossed the fish back into its mouth and swallowed with a few quick head-jerks. Again Pop cackled.

Stix laughed and repeated the sound Pop had made. "Food!" She pointed to a large river rock, the only other thing close to her that she could identify with one word. "Rock."

Pop jerked its head toward Rok.

"Oh, no. That sounds just like your name," Stix said.

"I guess that's because I'm named for it," Rok answered, still giggling.

"Rok!" Stix pointed to her sister, then pointed to the river rock. "Rock, stone."

Pop pointed to the rock and made one click.

She clicked and said, "Stone." Walking around the little camp she pointed out different things, saying its name. In minutes she could discern their words for the skimmers, each of their weapons, food, water, and interpreted the third Zid's name as Sam because of the flat sounding whistle.

Snap, lying near Song, clapped its hands and pounded the ground with obvious excitement. It whistled her name and jumped up, motioning her to follow.

"I guess I'm going to learn to speak their language, too," Song said.

Moon had been watching with great interest. "Put me down, Ma! I want to talk to them, too!" he grumbled.

"You can talk just fine from where you are." Fem'ma held him tighter.

"I always figured their noises were like the animals," Stix said. "But they have a language just like ours. Pop wants to be friends and communicate with us. I'm going to try to introduce you. Listen to the sounds they make when I give your names. That's what they will call you."

Before introducing Kia, Stix crossed her arms and bowed, showing them that Kia was their leader. Pop and Chuck responded with three high pitched clicks. Moon was delighted that his name was a low pitched whistle.

Although now much more relaxed, the two groups stayed on alert. Stix could hardly keep from staring at the razor-sharp teeth, some pointing upward and some downward, on a head as long as a fem's arm. The thought of those jaws clamping down on her sent chills of terror through her.

Ch`e pointed to the injury on Sam's shoulder, a long burn which oozed purple blood. Streaks of blood stained its side.

"It's hurt and I'm a healer. If we're going to be friends with these things, I'd better take care of it." She motioned with her hand for Sam to follow her. "Sam, I will heal your wound, but I have to wash it first."

Sam seemed reluctant to move from its bed on the warm river rocks and skooched back a step, looking at its comrades. Chuck said something and pointed to Ch`e.

Stix didn't think it sounded happy. "I think Sam is afraid, but Chuck just told it to go with you," she said.

Sam took a hesitant step toward Ch`e, glancing at both Terians and Zid. Finally, at the river's edge, Ch`e scooped up a handful of water and splashed it on the dried blood, scrubbing him clean. Before she was finished, Sam slipped into the water and swam in the current. It flipped its tail back and forth to keep from being carried away.

"Okay, Sam," Ch`e said. "That's enough. Come here."

Sam lifted its head above the water and looked at her then glided back to the river bank. It followed her back to the scattered supplies and watched while she rummaged for her pack with the medicine. When Ch`e lifted the bag containing the Zid healing gel, Sam backed away, popping and clicking.

Stix laughed. "I think she just said she doesn't want the medicine. And I think I actually understood the word hurt. That stuff must hurt them as much as us. Put it on her."

"You called it 'she' again," Ch`e growled.

Sam must have comprehended the meaning of the laughter, because it lowered its head and looked away. It stood still on all fours while Ch`e approached with the bag.

Knowing how the gel reacted, Ch`e kept an eye on the Zid's teeth and prepared to apply the medicine as quickly as possible. The wound was still bleeding and she dipped two fingers into the salve and swiped it down the gash.

Sam shrieked and flinched violently, snapping his jaws shut just short of Ch`e's arm. Ch`e screamed and jumped away, but Sam just lashed its tail back and forth while the medicine bubbled and did its work. Finally, it lay down and just twitched.

Kia spoke, "Stix, see if you can find out who they are and why they killed their own, um, whatever they are, people, I guess. Ask them why they killed their own people to protect us."

Stix tried to voice the questions and had no idea if Pop understood her. But when Pop started clicking and chirping, Stix shook her head.

"I'm sorry, Pop. I don't know what you're saying." She pointed to her head and then shrugged her shoulders with her palms up.

Pop dashed to the nearest skimmer and returned with a shiny blob in its hand.

"Be careful of that thing!" Fem'ma shouted.

Stix stood her ground and Pop set the mass on her head. Instantly pain shot through her head and into her body. She screamed, clutching her stomach before falling to the ground. Pop snatched up the bio messenger and looked on helplessly while Stix writhed in agony.

Moon spoke loudly. "Give it to me. I understand them. Stix, tell it to give me the messenger."

Stix rolled, groaning, and pointed to Moon. Pop almost ran to him.

"Wait," Moon said. "Ma, put me on the ground. It's time I do this on my own and not cause you pain."

"No, it's not safe." Both Stix and Rok yelped in unison.

Song touched Snap on the shoulder and gave the sign for *wait*. She hurried to the pack on the drag. "He can sit in his place of honor." She set up the water cat tail seat where it wouldn't tilt and then crossed her arms and bowed while Fem'ma lowered Moon. Song handed him the short spear which she had decorated with feathers and bone beads and backed away.

Moon tilted his head forward and said, "Speak. I am ready."

The stranger is the enemy
The enemy is the friend
The hiding place a trap disguised
The light falls down but truth ascends

22 Home Is Not My Home

Moon braced himself as Pop set the blob on his head. He instantly felt the presence of another being in his mind and wished it to remain.

Why?

It was the first thing that came to him, and as pictures danced through his consciousness, he began to understand the grief felt by many of the Zid for the condition of Terah and especially for the Terians. He now wondered what it meant.

A great change comes and we fear. They are coming and we are not ready.

Moon struggled to understand the broken thoughts and images coming faster than he could grasp. How can this happen and when?

Must protect the leader. Struggle. Death. Sadness. Home. Go to the mountain. Protect. Cannot protect all. Go to the mountain now. Home.

Moon's mind was filled with the cacophony of battle.

Dizziness and exhaustion weakened Moon, but he wanted to know more. Home is gone, destroyed. Where is home?

Born here. Parents born here. Fathers of fathers born here.

He saw great stores of glistening silver and golden metal, and sparkling gems of great value. He saw the beings, their infants and children laughing and playing and experienced an intense love like he'd never felt before. Almost, but not quite, he recognized them and wanted

141

to be closer. But he couldn't go there. He saw sprawling landscapes in unnatural colors and knew a sadness he could not place.

Home. Not home. Must restore.

An image of a lodge as big as a mountain seemed to float in Veenah. It moved closer and closer.

They come and we are not ready. We are not finished.

A mixture of grief and sadness spread over Moon like the crushing weight of the biomessenger. As the Zid removed the blob, breaking the contact, Moon also understood the anger shared by Pop and his few friends.

No one cares.

I care.

*****

Moon lay in Fem'ma's lap contemplating the conversation he'd experienced with Pop.

A battle is coming and someone has to protect the leader. Who is the leader? Why does Pop say they aren't ready? Haven't they taken enough from Terah? Or does he mean something else? Did he show me the jewels of the Prophecy? Or is that what they took from Terah? This is going to take a lot of thought. I miss the elder-mems.

His body shook uncontrollably and pain welded his eyes shut. His head thumped like the drums at the harvest celebration and his stomach felt queasy. Fem'ma massaged his head, rocking gently. He became aware that one of the sisters – *Rok?* – supported his matron. He knew that Song sat close with a skin of water. He could sense the four Zid nearby.

"Should I make him some tea for the pain?" Ch`e whispered.

"I knew better than to allow him to do that alone," Fem'ma said.

Moon sensed her grief.

The Zid clicked quietly among themselves and finally Chuck got up and shuffled away. Moon assumed it was to again try to heal his skimmer.

Did I communicate our sorrow that we killed it? If we had understood...

"Will someone give me water?" Moon finally said, though his eyes remained closed.

Song held the skin for him to sip, but at the same time, Pop dashed for the river and scooped a mouthful then ran back. Song jumped back in fear of the huge reptile. Pop leaned over them and dribbled the water out of his mouth onto Moon's head.

"What are you doing!" Moon shouted. "Oh! That's cold!"

Rok pushed Fem'ma away from Pop and sheltered Moon from another dousing.

Kia giggled, then Stix and Ch`e joined her with full laughter.

"You asked for water," Stix snorted. "Pop was just trying to please you by bringing some. You should be honored by its gift."

"I'll be honored to get dry. But at least the pain is gone. Maybe that's what we need to do after a session like this; wash the head."

Fem'ma patted herself dry with the corner of a blanket then dried Moon. "Maybe you shouldn't try to do that again. It's dangerous. One day that blob will kill you."

"How long was I out?" Moon said. "It looks like Warmsun is getting ready to go behind the mountain."

Fem'ma answered, "Pop held the biomessenger on your head for most of the time. All the while, you kept moaning and saying things we couldn't understand, but Pop only clicked a few times."

"You just sort of fell over just a bit ago," Song said softly. "I almost caught you, but I remembered my manners and Fem'ma picked you up. You frightened me when you fell."

"My beautiful Song, it wouldn't have bothered me a bit if you caught me."

Rok reached for Song's hand. "Except that it is still forbidden. Come, sister. We need to pick up our things and repair the drag." They stood up together.

"And," Kia said quietly, "we need to prepare a shelter. Those Zid won't be able to protect us from Nightbird, and I've seen wolf tracks near the river. Fems, we have work to do."

"By the way," Moon called to them. "They are 'he' and 'she'. Chuck is their father. I get the impression he is called a bull. Snap is his daughter, a cow. Pop and the dead one are his sons, but Sam is, um, they say it strangely—"

"Moon, in case you never noticed, they say everything strangely," Ch`e said.

"You're right. I guess they are to be mated when Snap is old enough."

"That's good to know, I guess," Rok said, trying not to laugh. "Ch`e, will you stay near in case Moon needs medicine. Song and Stix can gather our supplies, and Kia and I will check those boulders for shelter."

As soon as Rok took a step, Pop jumped in front of her and hissed.

"Look, lizard," Rok growled. "We have to take shelter and make a fire. The dark is dangerous! Get out of my way!" She tried to brush past him, but the Zid restrained her and began pushing her back toward the wide, rocky area near the river.

Moon struggled to sit then pushed himself from Fem'ma's lap.

"Where do you think you're going?" Fem'ma wrestled him back to her lap and attempted to put him into her protective sling.

"Let go of me, Ma. Get my foot coverings. I want to sit in my seat and watch them. Pop is trying to tell us something important."

Pop gazed at Moon, then up and down the river. He glared straight at Rok and hissed.

Sam raised his head at the commotion, and trotted over to stand between Rok and Pop. After some fast chatter, Sam stood and looked down at Rok.

"Click coo, click hiss." He pointed to the ground and pushed Rok down to sit. Kia sat next to her.

Rok huffed. "I know the first sound is my name and I know the hiss means 'stay', but why is he telling us to be calm, unless that coo means 'safe'?"

"Well," Kia said quietly. "I don't feel very safe out here in the open. Especially after the ambush. Right now I wish we were still in the bear's den."

Pop held out both hands and hissed again, then dropped down to all fours, inspecting the rocky fringes of the riverbank. A moment later he chattered to Sam then walked toward his skimmer. Sam trotted past Chuck and into the woods.

"At least he didn't put us inside that metal rope again." Kia leaned against Rok. "I'm so tired of running and being afraid and fighting."

In a voice loud enough for everyone in the clearing to hear,

Moon began his song in a melody reminiscent of the giant mountain wolves howling at night.

> The darkness falls, I wander lonely
> Without hope, no home or hearth.
> Another has taken all you had to give.
> Your love is all I ever wanted
>
> Return to me the green and goodness
> Promised before the dawn of life.
> You turned away, the gift betrayed.
> Your love is all I ever wanted
>
> Too late, the stranger stripped you from my grasp.
> Alliance broken the jewel destroyed.
> Life still beats beneath your cold, hard crust.
> Your love is all I ever wanted
>
> Memory stirs of treasures lost
> Not gem, nor silver or gold.
> The treasure is you, your love the jewel.
> Your love is all I ever wanted
>
> Sons and daughters hear the call
> The splendid message sent in the night.
> A pure and perfect gift awaits
> The darkness soon to lift.
>
> Your love is all I ever wanted.
> My life and all I have I give
> To rip the stranger from your breast
> And grant you joy to live.

Moon sat in his seat with his eyes closed, still feeling the power of the words he'd sung. It was if Veenah Herself had spoken. His heart quickened. Veenah only spoke to the most devout priests and he was too young to even think about that training, but it felt real. The realization that the Ruler of the day and night may have spoken to him sent a shockwave through him and he wobbled.

His eyes flew open in time to see Snap, Song, and Fem'ma, all three reaching for him.

Pop sat on his tail with his nose pointed to the sky, softly keening.

Tears flowed from Song's eyes.

Holder of truth
Guard of the gate
Lift up my heart
And help me create
A bounty of love
Destroying the hate
Rebuilding the home
None will devastate.

23 The Map

Snap's tongue flicked, touching the wetness on Song's cheek. The motion startled Song, but the yellow eyes bulging from her new friend's head held a hint of softness, almost as if the huge reptile truly cared about her.

"It's okay, Snap. I cry for happiness." Knowing that her words probably made about as much sense to Snap as the clicking and chirping meant to her, Song touched her cheek and smiled. Then she held both hands over her heart and raised them to the sky. Snap seemed content, and since Moon was no longer singing, she resumed helping to repair the drag. With dexterity which surprised Song, Snap tied Zid ropes on the drag, creating a strong net in place of the grass ropes.

"Moon," Song said. "I have never heard that one before, but I think it's the first time I ever understood."

"Psht!" Ch`e hissed. "Fems don't understand such things. I could barely make out the words. I think you were just listening to the pretty sound. Which was indeed nice, Moon." She nodded toward him and half grinned.

Rok got up from the beach where Sam had set her and went to Song's side. She sat crossed legged and held Song's hand. "I at least heard the words, but they were all a riddle to me. If you understand, I'd like to know what message you heard."

"Yes," Moon said. "I want to know too. The words came to me so fast I didn't even have time to think about the message. Please tell us."

"With respect. I know it's not proper for a fem to interfere or give direction to mems, but we are fems on our quest. And I think I discovered the secret."

"Go ahead, child," Fem'ma said. "I wondered about the prophecy when I bonded with my sisters. We talked about it for days and even thought we might figure it out when we found brilliant red and blue stones where the river from the ice mountain flows through a narrow channel."

Moon smiled and goose bumps ran up Song's arms, sending a shiver through her.

She set her chin with resolve, pushing back all fear and shyness. "Terah herself is the jewel. It is the most precious thing we have. Our world. Terah is the one betrayed and broken. We always thought it was us, the Terians who live here, who needed healing. But it's the land."

Moon rocked in his seat, grinning. "If I understand what Song just said, I believe our 'innocent' has discovered the jewel of the prophecy."

"If that's true," Ch'e pondered, "then we're standing on the jewel. Why would we need to go to the mountain to find it?"

Song stared at the distant mountain. "Because there is still a message from Veenah to be found. She sends these messages every season when it's hot, which is when fems go out on their quests. She hopes that one day, one of us will discover them." She stopped and scratched her head. "But the only place Veenah sends Her messages is into the Forbidden Mountains – where we are not allowed to go."

Murmurs and nodding heads rippled through the group. Snap flicked her tongue and crept closer.

"I suppose it was one of those 'others' mentioned in the song who first made up that law. They take everything then hide the truth." Rok stretched out her hand. "Kia, Stix, Ch'e, come sit here in a circle and let's talk about this."

"I'm not sure I should leave the river," Kia said. "Pop and Sam were pretty serious when they told us to stay here. But I guess that's when we looked like we were going to leave." She got up and jogged to the others, watching Pop who was now bent over the injured flyer with Chuck."

"What's to talk about," Ch`e said lightly as she plopped between Kia and Rok. "We're going to the mountain. Anyone have an idea of how to get there?"

Snap nosed her way into the circle and lay next to Song, flicking her tongue rapidly. Sam sat on his tail right behind her.

Song trembled and gripped Rok's hand for courage. "I'm afraid. I'm afraid to go so far from home. I'm afraid of the Badlands. I'm afraid of never finding another Terian. But if this is the Will of Veenah, then we should just start walking toward the mountain."

Rok squeezed her hand. "Home is wherever we are, at least for now. We're together in this and that should give us a little courage. We'll have to leave the river because it flows a different path. I know my blood-mother wandered out here for many seasons before coming to our village, but she never described her path."

"We follow the path that Warmsun takes across the sky toward the mountains," Kia said. "And if there are times we're not sure, and can't see where we're going, one of us can climb to the top of a tree or one of the towering rocks to keep going the right direction."

Snap raised her head, screeching and chirping. She cleared a patch of sandy ground and drew a curved line, then pointed to the river. She waited until the fems nodded their understanding then pointed to the Forbidden Mountains. With the nail of her long, middle finger, she drew the jagged peaks in the sand opposite of the line for the river. She scattered a handful of pebbles in the area between and proceeded to draw out a trail, indicated by walking her fingers, from the river to the crest, weaving among the pebbles.

Pop wandered back to the cluster of Terians and Zid and studied the drawing in the sand. He dropped down to all fours and nosed between Rok and Song. With a few clicks and coos, he drew some small circles along Snap's line in the pebbles and sketched a second river. Then he re-drew part of the line to stay within the pebbles a bit farther before it followed the other river, and then on to the mountain. He sat on his tail with a quick chirp.

"I know what this is," Rok said jumping to her feet. She shielded her eyes from Warmsun and gazed across the Badlands. "Snap is drawing a map. Lona told me about this and taught the rest of the warriors how to draw and follow a map."

"Fine," Ch`e said. "We have scratches in the sand. But that walk is sure to take us at least a moonphase or more and I can't remember all those details. I suppose Snap will come along with us to show the way?" All eyes turned toward Snap.

Moon cleared his throat. "I believe our new friends have other work to do and we cannot expect them to protect us the whole way as they did today. But if this is Veenah's Will, then She will provide for us."

Kia nodded her head and let out a breath. "I agree with Moon. Song, this is your plan. Do you want to call for a vote? We can leave at first light."

Unseen untouched around us lies
Like smoke long gone from flame
The shield sent from up on high
To comfort, shade, and save.

24 Invisible And Invincible

Kia glanced at her sisters. A tingle of anticipation tickled up her spine and parked in her belly. The vote had been solemn and quick. Most of all, it had been unanimous, including Ch`e who would argue if someone said that Warmsun was smiling on Terah. The gravity of the journey settled into her.

Just then Sam burst from the woods hissing, clicking, and cackling. He carried a bundle of long, flexible willa branches and ran across the clearing on his hind legs. Kia scrambled to her feet and dashed for her former perch at the riverbank.

Sam cooed and clicked and patted his feet on the ground in front of her.

Song laughed for the first time that day. "I'm not as good at learning their sounds as Stix, but I'm sure Sam just said you are good for staying where he put you. I think the foot stomping means he's happy."

"At least he's not mad at me. What are you doing, Sam?" Kia waved her hand toward the willa branches.

Stix joined her sister and best friend. "I thought you might need some help over here."

Sam drew an arc over their heads with both hands and made a short screech-click-click sound.

"Shelter. Scree-click-click. Shelter. Thank you." Stix traced the arc through the air and patted her feet on the ground.

Pop selected two branches and shoved the wider ends into the rocky sand a fem's height apart. Then repeated the action, creating a crude circle. He demonstrated how to use a Zid rope, which was much finer, but stronger than a grass rope, to bend the four branches together and tie them at the top of the soon-to-be shelter. Kia judged it to be low enough that a Zid would have to walk on all fours, but the fems would hardly be able to sit up. This one would barely be large enough for the four present Zid to lay in. Then Sam untied his work. Pushing the rope into Kia's hand, he motioned for her to retie the branches.

Song walked up carrying the blankets and skins for sleeping places in the shelter. She raised an eyebrow. "Um, Kia? You two are *not* planning for us to actually sleep on those are you?" She nodded her head at the largest of the stones under the crude shelter. "And where is Moon supposed to sleep? He can't be in here with us."

"Uh-oh." Kia said. "Help me here, Stix. I have no idea how to tell him we can't sleep here.

"I got this love. Sam. Over here. Terians cannot sleep on rocks." Stix stepped onto the softer, grassy part of the clearing.

Sam pointed to the current spot. "Click-click-coo scree-click coo pop-pop."

"Hmmm, he said that this is the safest place for the shelter, and I think the last pop-pop means warm. I remember Sam saying it when he was lying on the rocks before. I'll have to show him what I mean." She lay down on the rocks under the branches. "Ow! Hurt!" Rubbing her head and whimpering, she walked over to the grass. She lifted a blanket from Song's arms on the way. Lying down on the grass, she covered herself and closed her eyes. "Click-click-coo scree-click coo pop-pop."

Kia swelled with pride and amazement listening to Stix perfectly imitate the language of the Zid. She joined her sister and spread the rest of the blankets on the ground. She tried the word she thought was for shelter. "Click-click-coo-squawk," She coughed as her voice cracked. "Don't laugh, at least I tried. She lay down next to Stix and closed her eyes.

Sam tilted his head and snorted. When the fems finally looked at him, he pushed his palms toward the shelter he'd built and waved toward the spot they had chosen. Then he sat on his tail and waited.

"I guess we do it ourselves," Song whispered. "I hope he doesn't get too mad at us."

"I'm afraid this is going to be a waste of time anyway. This isn't going to protect us." Kia gave a worried look at the sky. "Out here in the open anything can attack us, even if we did have enough blankets to cover it."

One by one Stix and Kia pulled the branches from the rocks and pushed them into the softer ground, setting them farther apart to fit the Terians a bit better. Song laid out blankets to help with the size.

"I love this rope," Kia mumbled as she tied the last branch into place. "I wonder if we can ask for more of it."

"Okay, now what?" Song put her fists on her hips.

"Maybe we're supposed to cover it with leafy branches," Stix said.

Sam remained seated on his tail and turned his snout toward the river.

Pop examined their work then sauntered to his skimmer. From under the seat, he produced a bundle of something rolled like a blanket. As he approached the stick-shelter, Song was sure he looked amused and pleased with himself. With a flourish, he shook out the roll.

Kia sucked in a breath. The blanket billowed out into something large enough to completely cover the shelter. It shimmered in the light and seemed to change color as a corner brushed the grass. She touched it.

"This is thinner than any skin I've ever seen. It's even thinner than the tunics we weave from the white fluffs that come out of the plants at the end of the growing season or the curly hair from the mountain woolies. And it has no weight!" She watched as Pop flipped the thing in the air and let it float down over the stick shelter. First it shimmered then it reflected the grass, brush, and stones around it like a very still pond of water. Then it was gone! Kia's knees buckled and she might have fallen except for Pop's arm which suddenly braced her.

"Pop, what is this? Where did it go? Where did it come from?"

The Zid took a step forward and swept open a door to the shelter. All Kia could see was the shaded inside through the slit in the hidden blanket. "Click! Whistle, Scraw-click," he waved for Ch`e to enter, then called Rok and Song again. "Click, Whistle."

Song took a short step and stopped, casting a worried look at Kia. But Ch`e scooped up her hand and led the way to the door. "I'm not afraid of this...stuff. I think it's great."

153

When the fems were inside, Pop let the door fall closed. Nothing could be seen of the shelter or of Song and Ch`e.

Kia sat down with a thump, her mouth hanging open.

Pop pounded his feet on the ground and waved for Rok to follow him. He unstrapped Rok's bow and arrows from his skimmer and started to hand them to her, then hesitated. "Click click click-coo!"

"Coo," Rok answered. "Don't worry Pop. I'm not going to shoot you." But she backed up a step when Pop retrieved his blaster from its case.

"Coo," Pop assured her, then motioned for her to follow him back to the shelter. On the way he clicked and chattered at Sam and Snap.

Kia had stiffened a bit when she saw the deadly weapon in the Zid's hands, but she nearly screamed when Sam and Snap escorted Fem'ma and Moon into the woods.

Pop tapped his feet, then curled his tail and sat on it. He called to Kia and pointed to a place at the back of the weapon. In the small circle, Kia saw Rok. As Pop swung the blaster around past the shelter, across the grass, and into the woods, she saw stones and dirt, the grass waving in the breeze and even a small black bug. She saw brush and trees, then suddenly she could see the two Zid far back in the woods standing near Fem'ma. She could even see Moon *and* his hands and feet, pressed against Fem'ma's chest in the sling.

"No wonder these beasts can kill us so easily. There's no way we can hide from them." Kia thought she would be sick. She put her hand on Pop's scaly arm and swung the blaster back to where she knew the shelter stood. All she could see were the bushes and a few boulders and the rough ground. She struggled to take a breath.

Pop thumped his feet and Kia was certain he was laughing at her. He trotted to Rok and motioned for her to send an arrow toward the shelter.

"No. I'm not shooting at them."

"Coo!" Pop insisted.

"No!"

Pop snorted and touched something on the blaster. It made a sound like a mosquito buzzing and a tiny red spot shined beside the circle that showed the boulder behind the shelter.

Rok and Kia both screamed at the same time Pop took aim and fired. The boulder exploded in a shower of splintered stone.

"SONG!" Rok dropped her bow and rushed toward the shelter, fumbling to find the door. "Song! Where are you? Ch`e! Talk to me!"

A shimmer appeared then a dark slit as the door opened.

Ch`e choked on her voice. "Perg's Fires! That scared me so bad I lost my water. And the look on your faces was something I'll never forget!"

Kia still couldn't make her legs work, but she saw Fem'ma running as hard as she could back through the clearing. "I never even heard them scream." Kia's voice was so shaky she hardly recognized her own words. "Rok. I want you to shoot at it. Shoot as hard as you can." The instant Pop dropped the door flap, the structure and her sisters disappeared.

The warrior stepped back a few strides and drew the arrow back. Her elbow shook as she released the string. The deadly bolt sped harmlessly into the brush.

"That was too high, Rok. Shoot again. Lower. Try to hit it." Kia thought her heart was beating more normally now, but she still couldn't stand. Fem'ma dropped to the ground next to her, panting so hard she couldn't speak.

"Let me see! Let me out of here!" Moon's muffled voice came from under Fem'ma's water-cat tunic. Kia raised a shaking hand to loosen the thongs that held him secure. Moon's head popped out. "Where is it? Where are Song and Ch`e?"

"Right in front of you, Moon." It was all Kia could say.

Rok knocked another arrow and drew the bow back so far that Kia could hear the tension on the string. The arrow left the bow silently, but wobbled and ploughed into the ground. She threw a rock. It rolled to a stop when it hit the grass.

"I'll find it with a club!"

Kia thought Rok might be getting angry. She grinned.

Rok found a piece of drift wood, the remnants of a tree root, and swung it savagely in front of her as she stepped forward. She slashed the air from one side to the other, walking back and forth around the clearing. "I know it's here somewhere! Pop! Where is it!"

The door-flap swung open and the structure shimmered into

view ten paces behind her. Ch`e stepped out laughing. "Didn't you hear us calling you?" She said. "You were nearly on top of us, waving that stick like you were fighting off wolves. Then you just walked past!"

"No, I didn't hear you. I didn't see you. I didn't see anything but grass, brush, and trees. What is that thing?" Rok roared. She stared at Pop waiting for an answer of some sort.

Pop pointed to the sky. He stood up and Kia thought he pointed to a very specific place in the sky.

Moon let out an audible breath. "It's the blanket of Veenah. I once heard a song about it. I thought it spoke of the fog and the clouds."

Pop walked back to his skimmer and returned the weapon to its case. Then he unfastened the rest of the weapons he'd taken from the fems. He hesitated before walking slowly back. Chuck also finally joined them, riding his repaired skimmer. He landed on the beach near the spot where Sam had lain, then lumbered close and dropped the broken arrow in front of Rok. He held the flint point out to her with a click and a chirp.

"I'm sorry I hurt your flyer," Rok said. She bowed her head a little and accepted her arrowhead.

Snap flew her skimmer and landed it near her father's. Then Pop parked his with them. Snap was last, placing his flyer to close a circle. Snap chattered to Chuck then hurried back to Song. Sitting on her tail, she offered Song a tool.

"What is this?" Song asked.

Snap demonstrated how to make the tool shine like a flaming torch without the fire. Then she taught Song how to use it to heat a flat stone hot enough to cook food, or keep the shelter warm. With a flick of her thumb, a line appeared which pointed straight to the shelter door-flap.

Kia considered that the tool could probably do much more than what Snap was teaching.

"Moon," Kia said. "Our friends have done much for us today. They saved our lives and given us gifts for which we can never repay. Pop loves your songs, and Sam was gathering our lodge poles when you sang before. Can you sing again to show them how much we value these gifts?"

Who sees the stars
That guide the way
And pierce the dark
With sharp-edged ray?
A window into Veenah's soul,
Her promise, her love
'Till life is made whole.
Our life will be made whole.

25 Star Watcher

Fem'ma squeezed her eyes shut and tried taking deep, slow breaths. But sleep wouldn't come. The dome above her head was distracting enough by itself, but viewing the stars as if she was sitting outside on watch unnerved her. She rolled to her side and tucked her blanket under her chin. It would be a long day tomorrow and Moon would be sleepy and cranky because he stayed awake all night, gazing at the stars.

Hmph, he better be ready for cranky because he's keeping me awake too, and he can sleep all day in the sling while I'm walking.

"Ma! Ma, do you see those stars? I can see the chair where Veenah sits. Ma, look."

"Go to sleep!" Fem'ma whispered. "Or keep quiet. You'll wake everyone. I'm tired."

What she truly feared was the monsters, sleeping under another dome just like this one only a few paces away. Sure, they'd protected her and the others and had shared their valuable gifts, but those creatures were dangerous. Too many times she'd seen the results of their brutal attacks. She rolled over again, trying to block the visions from her mind. Monsters flying through the village blasting fems into dust or running after a child and in one snap, the child is gone.

My poor little sister.

She shook the horror from her mind and rolled to her stomach, covering her head completely.

The images returned. The attack when her malformed son was born. The same time hunters had captured the lone Zid. Why the eldermems decided to keep that horrible creature was the greatest puzzle she'd ever faced. It was so wrong. So dangerous. And it had caused her so much pain while her son learned to communicate with it.

And to lose all her daughters in this last attack was too much to bear. She had to hold onto the hope that maybe one had escaped. They had been due to return in just a few days. Maybe she and her bond sisters were far enough away on their bonding quest to escape when...

She'd only watched their beautiful ceremony from afar, not as a blood-mother. Her daughter must have felt abandoned. *Clara and her bond sisters must be alive.*

The memory of her life with her own femtog invaded her mind. She missed the warmth of her sisters' love around her and even more she missed the love of her husband, who always slept in her arms. The pain of their separation still tore her heart into pieces. So much love they'd shared. Their bonding quest so successful. The brilliant red gems they'd found...the Prophecy fulfilled...but nothing ever came of it.

I always knew I was chosen to fulfil the prophecy. Maybe now. But as an elder.

She flopped to her back again and threw off her blanket.

I'm no elder. I'm a cast-away. The birth mother of an abnormal child I didn't have the heart to return to Veenah. I should insist they all call me by my given name, Eve. Yes, I'm nothing more than the shadows which come before the darkness. Eve.

Tears rolled from her eyes and dribbled into her ears.

"Ma! Ma, look! Veenah sent another message!"

"Hush! Or I will insist we never sleep inside this dreadful enemy covering ever again. This is not natural."

"The message has gone into the Forbidden Mountains just like all the others! I know now, we must go there. I do hope Kia leads us well."

"Moon! Why are you out of your sleeping place and standing on the bare ground? You will injure yourself!" Fem'ma scrambled to pick

Moon up and return him to his blankets.

"What's going on?" Rok called from the other side of the partition. "Fem'ma, are you all right?"

Another voice. "Go to sleep, Moon. We all know Kia will lead us well." Ch`e sounded annoyed, as usual.

"Do we need to post a watch?" Kia mumbled.

"No," Fem'ma said. "Our star-watcher mem is happy with the view, but he's going to sleep now. I'm sorry we woke you."

"The stars are pretty tonight. Goodnight, Fem'ma."

The soft voice of Song the Innocent nearly broke the old fem's heart.

The trespasser comes
And sets down the seed
Chaffing and growing
Its heart filled with greed

26 The Badlands

Kia rubbed the sleep from her eyes. Warmsun had not yet stepped onto the edge of Terah, but her light filled the shelter. For a moment, she huddled in fear under her blankets, heart nearly beating out of her chest, thinking she'd fallen asleep out in the open.

"How to you get out of this thing?" Song said. "I have needed to relieve myself since Moon woke us up. I'm about to dig a hole and go right here."

Stix rolled over and stretched. "Remember, we put a flat cooking-stone by the door-flap. Just brush your hand above it and you'll find the door."

The dome shimmered and the clear view of the outside blurred. Kia rolled her blanket and tied it with her pack. "We survived. And without posting a watch. No. We did have someone stand watch, Moon! But usually we don't talk all night!" Laughter rippled through the shelter. Kia's gut wrenched in shame.

I sound like Ch`e. I've never been disrespectful to anyone before. She followed Song into the bushes.

"They're gone," Song said. "We didn't even say goodbye."

"Maybe. They covered themselves with a hiding blanket. They're probably still here and we can't see them."

"No, it just feels empty. I wonder if we'll ever see them again. Snap was interesting."

"I don't wonder anything anymore. Too much has happened."

160

Kia studied the faraway mountain. "Let's eat and figure out a way to cross this river. We're going to fulfil this prophecy – like a proper femtog."

Rok handed out dried fish. Through a full mouth she mumbled, "The river is not a problem. We only have to swim across. Then we face the badlands."

Ch`e licked the last crumbs of fish from her fingers. "You *are* making a joke, Rok. I'm not sure any of us can swim, and that river is swift and wide."

"We use the Zid rope," Rok said, hefting the coil to her side. "They left a piece long enough to reach from one side to the other. I go first with our supplies. The wood on the drag floats well. You all will hold the line until I get across, then you'll follow one at a time. It's a warrior drill. But I've never forded a river this wide before."

"I think that will work," Ch`e said. She put an arm around Rok's waist, smiling. "Next to a clan's healer, the warrior is the cleverest."

Rok gave her a one-armed hug. "But neither of us can go anywhere without someone to cook for us, or make tools, or decide which way to go. Remember, sister, we are only whole if we are together."

After checking every knot and every pack on the wooden drag, with all five fems gripping the slender line, Rok shoved the drag into the water and plunged in after it. Kia's skin crawled with dread and exhilaration at the task before her. She never took her eyes off Rok.

Angling into the current, Rok quickly reached the middle of the river, but began to struggle in the current.

Kia tied the end of the rope around her waist and shouted, "Move closer to the water! Give her some slack to get across!" The action of the waves and eddies pulled on the drag and nearly yanked the anchoring fems from their feet.

"Hold on, Ma! Don't let go! You're the strongest one here!" Moon shouted from the small opening Fem'ma had left for him to breathe. In his fingers he gripped a hollow reed. Rok had warned him he could be pulled under and by holding the reed in his mouth he would be able to reach air and not drown.

Rok pulled herself onto the opposite bank and slumped beside the soggy drag. Kia's heart froze until Rok lifted her head. Kia waited until her sister found the strength to wedge the strong poles between some immovable boulders to create a safe mooring for the rest of the crossing.

"I want to go next," Moon shouted.

"No, Moon," Ch`e said. "I'm going next to show you how to do this. Watch me carefully. She hopped into the river, gripping the rope and screeched. "Oh! It's too cold!"

Kia nearly lost her footing trying not to laugh. But they all had to keep the rope tight because as Ch`e waded farther out, the swirling river kept pulling her down. She finally reached the other side, sputtering, coughing, and totally exhausted.

Song stepped into the river and with a weak smile to Kia, she gripped the rope with both hands and floated onto her back. With one foot over the life-line, she pulled herself, hand over hand, across faster than Rok or Ch`e had been able.

"That's how we'll go, Ma! On your back. Let's go now!"

Moon struggled to push his head out of the sling. He almost sat upright as Fem'ma glided onto her back in the cold water. Her weight was considerably more than Ch`e or Song, and now only Stix and Kia held the rope. Kia leaned back as hard as she could. She heard Moon's shouts of glee over the roar of the waves.

Stix was next. Kia trembled and felt a lump come up in her throat when Stix hugged her tight.

"I love you, Kia, more than anything, so please don't let go!"

"Never. Now go, before I cry."

Kia sat and braced herself in the rocky riverbank. Stix sped across, then waved her over. Kia shuddered. With no one anchoring the end of the rope, she would be like fishing bait flung between the whirlpools and eddies of the river. And she'd never been in water deeper than her waist. She stepped in and barely had time to gasp for air when the current took her legs out from under her.

After what felt like a lifetime, bouncing from one deep river boulder to the next, head under the water as much as out, Kia felt solid ground under her. She released the rope to grab for the bank and clawed her way to safety.

"We did it!" The entire clan whooped and danced.

"At least we don't smell so bad now," Song said, laughing.

"Let's go find that jewel!" Stix sang out.

"We're standing on the Jewel, sister," Song said. "Remember Moon's song?"

"Well, there's something secret and very likely shining in those mountains, and I say we go get it."

The lifetimes since the Zid had mined the wide plain had softened the scars. Wind and rain had smoothed the jagged edges of layers of rock turned on end, and deposited rich soil in the low places where everything green had found a place to take root. Even berry vines and fruit bearing trees dwelled among the ruined ridges.

"I never knew it was so beautiful on this side of the river," Stix said. "All anyone could ever see were the broken rocks."

"And the old songs only tell of the destruction," Moon added. Perched on Fem'ma's shoulder, he began singing, recounting the history of the world as the fems trudged along.

"Moon?" Song called at the end of a song. "We already know the enemy Zid did all this horrible destruction in the badlands, but what is the ci-cit the cita-thing?"

"The citadel? I believe it is a place where great numbers of Terians once lived."

"All in one place?"

"According to the songs, yes. Terians as far as the eye could see."

"How did they find food? It would take many hunters and many working the fields to feed such a large village. I don't know why they would all want to live in the same place. There wouldn't even be enough targus beasts to feed them all."

"It is one of the mysteries we hope to discover on this journey."

The group ambled on, following beneath the path Warmsun walked in the sky.

Stix said, "With this good trail, we'll be to the mountain in two days."

"I only hope the trail stays this good," Song said. "Why don't I take the drag for a while so you can walk with Kia.

Kia heard a deep-throated 'whoof' from somewhere in the distance. She crouched against the side of a ragged stone outcrop and signaled danger. In a breath, Rok was beside her.

A great brown bear stood twice as high as a fem, snuffling and smacking. Purple berry juice dribbled from his sagging lips. It woofed again and swatted the air with a paw wider than the length of Kia's forearm. The animal reeked and Kia gasped at the heavy, rotten scent. She glanced back down the trail, but her sisters and Fem'ma had taken cover. With her hand on Rok's arm, she backed silently away from the bear. It dropped down on all four legs and Kia breathed a sigh of relief.

Rok tugged at her and they crept along the broken ground to find a safer trail. Kia's stomach curdled in terror and she tried not to run or make a sound that would attract the beast.

An ear splitting roar blasted behind her. She stumbled and fell to her knees, kicking backward into a jumble of rocks. The bear swiped the rubble away and roared again, snapping its jaws and just missing Kia's foot. She jabbed at it with her spear, aiming for its eye or nose, but the beast's leg was longer than her weapon. She thrust the tip of the water-cat spine into its paw and the thing simply shook it loose. Kia scrambled backward and dove for cover under a twisted tree which was bent around a layer of rock the size a lodge. She didn't see Rok.

The bear, infuriated by the sticks and pokes from its prey, raked at the roots of the tree, nearly tearing it out of the ground. Kia was trapped against the outcrop, still barely out of reach of the hideous claws. An arrow settled itself in the thick fur of the bear's back. It roared again. Thick saliva dribbled from its fangs in long strings. She drew her knife and swung.

Another arrow stuck into the back of the beast and it turned with renewed rage. Kia scrambled from her trap. Rok and Stix were on top of the ridge, pelting the bear with stones and arrows. She scooped up her spear and swung up the climbing vines to join her sisters.

The more they jabbed the bear's face and paws, the angrier it became. Blood flowed from a gash in its black nose and an arrow dangled from its lip. Suddenly it bellowed and fell to all fours, spinning. One hind foot spewed blood.

Song screamed, "I got it! Get out of there!"

Hand in hand, Kia, Stix, Rok, and Song raced back down the trail, searching for Ch`e and Fem'ma.

They were nearly knocked flat by a second bear, even bigger than the one they'd fought, charging into the melee. Kia couldn't hear her own screams as she rolled away from the trail. But the beast bypassed the now-helpless fems and plowed into the injured bear. Kia hugged her sisters close and watched in awe as the two behemoths battled.

"What just happened?" Stix choked. "I knew it was the end for us. I prayed for it to be fast. I didn't want us to suffer. How is it that another bear came to fight for us?"

"Bears never travel together," Rok said. "They defend their territory to the death. The only way this happened was by the hand of Veenah." She ended in a whisper.

"I think it's safe to move," Kia said. "It sounds like they're moving away from us. I don't think I'll ever forget the sound of that roaring."

"I-I lost my knife," Song said, still trembling. "I tried to chop its foot off and when it jumped at me I could only try to get away."

Rok hugged Song tight. "My sweet, brave, Song. You could have been killed, so close to that thing. You saved our lives. I lost my arrows and also my spear. Let's go find our weapons while Veenah keeps those monsters busy."

Kia rose to her feet and held her hands to assist her sisters. She pulled Rok closer and spoke quietly. "You've never said anything like that about Veenah before."

"I've been told that a warrior knows the truth when faced with death. If her heart is true…" Rok cleared her throat and turned away. "C'mon, Song. We need to find our weapons."

"Hurry back, Stix and I will find Ch`e and Fem'ma." A few paces apart, Kia and Stix started back, cautiously poking around each clump of brush or rocky heap.

Suddenly a bush sprang to life and Kia faced the sharp end of a spear.

"Perg's fires!" Ch`e screamed from beneath the branches. "I thought you were the bear come back to kill us!" She dropped the spear and leaped into Kia's and Stix's arms. "I'm so glad to see you!" She drew back, gasping. The color drained from her face. "Where's—."

"Safe and unharmed. They went to collect the spears and arrows they shot at the bear."

"But how? The noise was worse than any animal I've ever

heard."

Kia and Stix took turns recounting the battle. Song and Rok joined them.

Song held up a curved, black claw longer than her hand and still attached to the ragged stump of the bear's toe. "I charged him a toll for disturbing our travels," she said giggling.

Stix admired the trophy. "I think you meant to say you charged him a toe. I'll be happy to drill a hole in this so you can wear it around your neck."

"But people will think I killed the bear and give me honors I didn't earn."

"No," Rok said. "You will only be wearing one claw and not the teeth. They'll know you didn't kill it. You counted coup on the bear. You touched him without killing him, which is the greatest honor. Veenah truly had her hand over you for you to survive this."

"Oh no!" Ch`e yelped, dashing away. "I forgot Fem'ma and Moon." Kia and the others followed her to a high ridge. "I hid them in a cave and knocked some rocks across the entrance."

"You buried them?"

Fem'ma was shoving the last of the rubble from the mouth of the cave when they arrived at the ridge. She cried with joy and waved. "Ch`e! You're safe! I thought you were right behind me, then a cave in closed us in. I've been digging to find your body. How did you get away?"

"I'm sorry. I should have told you. I went to help fight the bear. I was going to kill it like Stix did the nightbird, in case it ran back this way." Ch`e fell into Fem'ma's arms, shaking like a leaf. She added with a weak laugh, "But I nearly speared Kia instead."

Kia stared at her newest sister, wondering at this newfound bravery.

The mother will labor
The daughter will run
The father sings glory
The struggle begun

27 The Citadel

"Are we ready to go?" Kia said. She washed down her dried-fish
breakfast with a sip of water, glancing at the warming horizon where
Warmsun would begin his journey. Sleep had not come easily, and her
head thumped like a drum. Kia couldn't shake the memory of the bear
from her mind. And the howls of hunting wolves seemed closer than
ever.

Ch'e had taken final watch. Thankfully Moon hadn't demanded
the so-called honor. But then, they'd slept in a small rocky overhang, not
under the blanket of Veenah with a clear view of the stars. Kia listened
for argument or comment from Ch'e, but none came.

What are you thinking, Ch'e? Are you still undermining me?
Will you choose to follow me? Will you learn to trust me?

Stix hoisted the drag using a thick grass rope she'd woven during
her watch. It went over her shoulders and around her waist so that now
one fem could bear the weight easily. Kia smiled at her beloved's ability
to create new things from the raw materials she found around her.

Silently, the clan lined out with Warmsun peeking over the
horizon at their backs and the mountain in front, alert for movement or
sound of danger. Kia hoped their second day in the badlands would be
better than the first. The mountain appeared higher than ever. She
shuddered and pushed on.

As Warmsun reached his zenith, the forest of up-turned stone
gave way to the flanks of a hill, blazing with a myriad of colorful

flowers. In the open, Kia breathed easier, free of the claustrophobic, bear-filled maze. She almost wanted to run, or shout for joy. The trek to the top dampened some of those urges.

"We'll rest and have something to eat on the ridge," Kia said.

"Watch out for stingers," Ch`e puffed. "They are thick among the flowers."

"Watch for honey trees," Rok added. "Where there's stingers, we'll find the food of Veenah."

Stix laughed. "You'd be the one looking for honey. It's your favorite food. I've seen you eat a slab the size of both your hands and look for more."

"It was your best courting gift, and I still thank you." Rok caught up to Stix and lifted the drag. "Let me take this for a while so you can rest."

A wide plain spread out as they reached the crest of the hill. A braided river feeding into marshes, and a band of trees taller than calipsa, filled Kia's view. A movement and smoke curling from an enormous square lodge caught her attention. Smaller lodges lay scattered along the edges of the marsh and riverbanks – as far as she could see. Kia shrank back, crouching in the brush.

"A village," she whispered. "The biggest I've ever seen."

"A citadel!" Moon cried out from Fem'ma's shoulder. "Let me see!"

"I don't think so. Get down. Hide!" Kia waved her family back.

Rok slid into the grasses next to her and together they crawled on their elbows and bellies to the ridge. Kia shaded her eyes to see better. She pointed toward a splash in the water near a cluster of the boxy lodges. Something which looked like logs floating, swirled, moving to and from the banks.

A skimmer weaved among the lodges to land by the riverbank.

"Zid!" Rok and Kia breathed in unison. They backed away from the ridge.

"We're in danger," Rok said when they reached the others. "The village is not Terian. It's Zid!"

"I must see it," Moon said.

"No!"

"You don't understand. I saw something like this in my mind

while I communicated with Pop. I must see if this is the same. We may be among friends here." Moon struggled to free himself from the confines of Fem'ma's sling. "Ma, take me to the ridge. *Please!"*

Kia inched forward in the grass once again, but this time Fem'ma was between her and Rok. Beads of sweat formed on her forehead, and not from the heat of Warmsun. Stix, Song, and Ch`e waited with the blanket of Veenah, ready to cover them all in case they were discovered. "We're going to be killed up here!" Kia whispered.

"I see the lodge where the Zid work," Moon said. "They make things from the materials they take from Terah."

"Be quiet," Fem'ma whispered. "You'll give us away."

The chatters and squeals of several young Zid drifted on the wind toward the Terians.

"They're throwing something back and forth," Moon whispered. "Can you tell what it is?"

"Looks like a rolled up piece of Targus skin," Rok said, squinting her eyes. "I think this is a competition. They're trying to throw the skin into one of those circles on the ground."

Kia scooted backward down the hill. "We need to get under cover."

The Zid galloped on all fours up and down the hill, hefting the wadded skin into the air with their snouts or batting it with their tails. The game brought them closer and closer – and faster than Kia could get her group hidden. Two of the creatures tumbled to the top of the ridge, wrestling and snapping at each other. They halted in their tracks, staring at Kia, Fem'ma, and Rok.

"RUN!" Kia screamed.

The Zid screeched and dove after them. The rest of the mob poured over the ridge.

"HURRY!" Screamed Song. The hiding blanket shimmered in the bushes where she and Stix had unfurled it.

Dragging Fem'ma by the arm, Kia scrambled into the shelter. She glanced behind her just in time to see Rok launch a spear.

"Hold still," Rok whispered. She tugged the blanket to the ground and the dusky shimmer turned clear. "We haven't tried this thing like this, with it touching us. I don't know how well it will work."

"It's dark under here, but we can see clearly," Song said. "Just like the first time we tried it. So it must be working."

The Zid scampered back and forth testing the air with their tongues and standing high on their hind legs. Kia listened to their chatter, knowing that Stix was trying to interpret the noise. The largest suddenly hissed at two smaller ones and waved a clawed paw over the hillside.

"It just told the others to stay and watch," Stix whispered. "Look, some of them are going back to the village."

Fem'ma shifted to give Moon a bit of room to breathe and see out. "Did the village look like anything Pop told you about?" she asked.

"No. His was much smaller. This is a citadel where adults work. We are not safe here, I'm afraid."

"I wouldn't have guessed," Ch`e grumbled under her breath. She pillowed her head on her crossed arms and closed her eyes. "Wake me up when it's over."

Moon dragged himself free of the protective sling. "I must see what is happening. So much of what we've been through is fulfilment of prophesy and I need to record this event in song."

"You need to be still, Moon." Rok said. "We know they can't hear us under this thing, but we don't know what will happen if we move it. I'd hate for this cover to suddenly start sparkling."

"I only see four of them," Moon said, twisting his head in every direction. "Where did the rest go?"

Song choked back a whimper. "The others went for help, I think. Look! One of them found Rok's spear."

A skimmer zoomed over the ridge, followed by several more. The herd of youngsters galloped behind them. An adult stopped suddenly and snatched the spear from the youngster.

"Oh, listen to him," Stix whispered. "I heard him say 'weapon' and 'danger'. I'd hate to be that cub right now. It looks like she's in trouble."

The bull swung his tail, knocking several youngsters tumbling end over end. The leader of the herd screeched and chattered, whereupon the bull sent that one flying as well. The young Zid all scampered away.

"They're gone," Stix said. "The bull must have told them to stay out of the way, or out of danger."

Kia spoke low. "The adults are still here, and they're hunting us with those weapons that can see through anything." She pointed to four skimmers zipping around the entire hillside and over the forest of turned-up stones.

The bull studied Rok's spear. At length he threw it to the ground and returned to his skimmer. The four hunters joined him, and after exchanging harsh words, they disappeared down the hill. All except one.

"They've left a guard. We're trapped," Kia whispered. She shuddered. A gruesome scar ran from the thing's muzzle to its eye and along its side. One hind foot was missing.

"We'll move in darkness when it can't see."

"I wonder why Snap and Sam didn't warn us about this ci... What did you call it, Moon?" Stix said.

"Citadel."

"Whatever. I memorized that map, and I listened to Snap's words. She didn't warn us."

"I think Sam did," Rok said thoughtfully. "He placed some markers along what I understood to be a river–"

"This river?"

"I don't think so. But the trail he drew stayed in the jumble of stones he scattered. He made three marks along the way before the trail leaves the forest of broken Terah. We needed to stay in the badlands for three sleeps."

"I was so glad to get out of that place and into the open," Ch'e mumbled. "What a mistake."

Moon spoke. "If I remember the old songs, a citadel is a very large village filled with trained workers. Likely they don't hunt or gather their food here. It must be brought in. This place is more dangerous than I first thought. There will be many traders coming and going." He began humming and mumbling the words of a new song.

"Gee, thanks for the lesson," Stix said. "So if everyone is working in that big lodge, why don't we sneak down there and break something. We can stop up their smoke-hole. Maybe they'll leave."

"That's just like you," Kia said. "Always setting traps and picking fights–.

"Hey, I was just playing when we were children!"

"Like I said. But why don't we pass on that and try to get away from here alive?"

Rok pointed to the Zid standing guard. It hobbled along slowly, testing the air and ground with its tongue, coming closer. Then it flopped on its belly – and stared almost straight at the hiding blanket. Its head lowered as if to rest, but the dull, yellow eyes remained open.

Wide open the mouth
Prisoner of dark
From weakness comes power
And fire from spark

28 An Army Rescued

Stix snored softly and Kia hadn't seen Song or Ch`e move for some time, so she guessed they were asleep as well. She jumped when Rok spoke.

"That thing just moved closer. I think he suspects we are hiding here."

"Not possible." Kia stretched to relieve her stiffening muscles. "Don't you remember how hard you tried to find this shelter? Warmsun is going to rest. I think it only moved to lay on the rocks where it's warmer."

Darkness spread across the wide valley and suddenly the guard snapped his head to attention. Kia followed his gaze. She bit her lip to keep from shouting. A long line of ragged looking fems stumbled along a trail, all tied to a long rope and led by a single Zid. Another Zid followed, carrying a blaster.

"Slaves!" Rok breathed, trembling.

"We can't just leave them. We have to do something."

The Zid who had been hunting them took one more look around the area, slurping his forked tongue in the air, then limped on three legs to join the procession.

"I have to see where they're taking those fems." Kia whispered.

"It's too dangerous." Rok grabbed her leg and tried to haul her back.

"Either let go, or come with me!"

"You need a plan," Stix said, tugging on Kia's arm. "We all do. While you look for the captives, we will retreat to the badlands and find a safer place to hide."

"How will we find you?"

"Take this." Song held out the tool Snap had given her. "It points the way to this shelter, like this." She pushed a green button and a line lit up on the screen. It pulsed in all directions. This red button shoots a light that is hotter than fire, and this yellow one gives light like a torch."

Stix tugged on Kia's arm. "Promise me you won't do anything stupid. Come back to me."

Kia and Rok rolled out from under the shelter. It shimmered only a moment and was gone again. At the top of the hill, Kia could barely see the last of the line of enslaved fems herded into one of the smaller lodges. A dim light glowed in two small windows.

"Let's go," Kia whispered.

"Wait until all of those monsters have gone inside. I hope they are too stupid to post a watch."

Stars lit up as Warmsun rested. Kia nudged Rok and pointed toward the prison lodge. Together they inched down the hill on their elbows. The darkness nearly suffocated Kia. The glimmering light in the two small windows, went out.

"I can't see anything," Kia whispered. "Can you tell where they are?"

"Ahead of us. If we don't stray, we should be able to see something soon."

"But if we do stray, we could run into the lodge of a Zid." Kia turned the tool over in her hand, thinking of Pop's blaster and the spot that could see anything. Song hadn't mentioned it when she demonstrated how to use this thing, but maybe...

She felt around the haft, where she gripped it, then studied the end. Another button. She pressed it and, through the green lens, saw the ground as clear as day. Sweeping it back and forth in front of her, the fem's prison came into view.

"There! I really love this thing Snap gave us."

Rok reached the wall and tested its strength.

"We won't be able to break this down, and the windows are too small for even a child to crawl through." Rok whispered into Kia's ear.

"I'll stand watch, you try and signal the fems inside. Be careful."

Kia pulled herself up against the wall and used the tool to peer inside the low-roofed building. A few lean, filthy fems sat in the center, ripping scraps of barely-cooked meat from a few targus beast bones. Many more lay in clusters on the bare floor. She made the sound of a night songbird and two of the fems looked up from their bones and stared at the window. One cried out and scrambled backward, falling over fems on the floor. In an instant they were all huddled in a corner, some crying.

"Sshhh, you're safe." Kia reached inside the window to show them she was Terian. "We're going to get you out."

A thin-boned, gray-haired fem stood pressed against the far wall. She clicked and whistled, shaking her head 'no'. Kia guessed she'd been a slave for a very long time. A fem not nearly as thin as the others rushed toward the window.

"You can't get us out. We'll all be killed. Get away. You're in danger."

"Where is the door?"

The fem pointed to the next wall. Kia dropped down and grabbed at Rok, pointing around the corner. Inside she heard more fems crying and others shushing them. Kia hoped they would still be able to run.

She almost missed it. A heavy metal object hung from a metal strap, holding the door shut. Kia pulled on it then Rok tried to twist it.

"It's no use. If we try to break this, it will wake the whole village."

"I have an idea." Kia pointed Song's tool toward the object and pressed the red button. A beam of light hit the metal. It grew hotter and turned red then began to melt. A moment later it clattered to the ground. Kia and Rok ducked away from the noise waiting for guards to jump out from everywhere and kill them.

Nothing stirred.

Rok inched her way back to the door and pulled it open. She yanked her hand back, shaking it violently.

"Careful! It's hot!" she whispered.

Kia followed, keeping a look out for enemies through the green screen. Rok stepped inside the lodge, whispering to fems she couldn't see. "I am called Rok. Kia and I are here to rescue you. Come quickly."

One by one they moved to the door, most holding each other's hands. Rok pointed to the hill. They began running, falling over each other in the dark.

Kia held a spear in one hand and the tool in the other, her thumb on the red button. She didn't know how far the thing would shoot, but she knew it would do some damage. She couldn't help but grin, looking at the ruined door fastener on the ground, still red from the heat which melted it.

Rok felt around the empty lodge for anyone too frightened or weak to move, then motioned for Kia to follow. Together they backed away from the buildings and ran up the hill. The darkness pressed down on them and Kia only had an idea of where the fems were by distant whimpers. Nearing the crest, she finally dared to try the torch. She touched the yellow button gently and a dim light glowed.

"That's not going to help much," Rok whispered.

Kia pushed the button a little harder and the light brightened.

"Good." Rok whistled the song of a water bird and immediately Kia heard the footsteps of the fems.

"Everyone stay quiet," Rok said. "We will take you to safety. Is everyone here?"

Murmurs rippled through the group and someone whispered. "We're all here, even the elder."

"Stay close. Hold hands and don't lose anyone." Kia pushed the button to guide them to the blanket of Veenah. She checked their back-trail often, but they were not followed. They were in the badlands again before the line began to pulse. Suddenly she worried there would be no place to hide this many fems. She shined the light through the frightened group. "How many are you?"

"We are three tens and two," said one of the healthier fems.

A few more steps and the pulsing line swung toward a jagged and broken cliff face. The stone shimmered and Stix burst through the door.

"You're back! You made it!" Her eager embrace nearly knocked both of them to the ground. "I was so scared. It was so dark. I prayed to Veenah for your protection." Seeing the fem standing close to Kia, she stretched her hands out in a greeting. "I'm happy to see you. I am called Stix."

"I am called Daylin. We were on our bonding quest and ready to return home when we were captured only a few days ago. Only three of us remain, two were killed. How did you find us? Where did you come from?"

The shelter shimmered and Fem'ma pushed out. She shook all over and tears rimmed her eyes. "You are Daylin? One of your bond sisters is Clara?"

The press of fems shifted and one took Daylin's hand.

A third fem stepped up behind them. "Do I know you, elder?"

Song pulled back the door of the hiding blanket and held up a burning torch for light. "Kia! Bring them in. This cave is big enough for an entire village. Water runs through the back of it and we have built a fire."

"Do you have food?" Daylin asked.

The captives flooded into the cave, following Song.

Kia grabbed Fem'ma by the arm. "Where's Moon?" she whispered.

"Safe!" Fem'ma pushed away. "Clara, wait. Yes, you do know me." The young fem stopped and faced Fem'ma. "I am your blood-mother."

"My mother died when I was a small child. She abandoned me and was cast out. I have no mother."

"Yes, I was cast out, but the elders...the elders had need of me. I went into service and could no longer contact you."

"You must have committed a huge sin to be cast out, *if* you really are my mother. But because of it, you are dead to me." Clara ducked into the cave, following her bond sisters.

"I did not abandon you! Do you remember your brother?"

"There was no brother, fem. Only my sister. We had to take care of ourselves all these seasons, because our hearth mothers were suspicious of us. Likely they feared we would commit the same sin which our mother had." She disappeared into the depths of the cave.

Kia embraced her friend and elder. Stix joined them. "Don't worry," Kia said. "Clara has been through too much. She'll remember you and love you the way we do. Come, show me our cave." She let down the hiding blanket and waited for the view of the night sky to clear, assuring her that their hiding place could not be found. Before she'd gone a few paces, Ch`e crashed into her.

"What have you done to us?" Ch`e shouted. "You've ruined us! Song is handing out all our meat! That was supposed to sustain us until we reached safety! It's ours! No, it's mine and I did not give her permission to give it all away."

"Calm yourself, sister." Kia extracted her arms from Ch`e's grip. "Veenah shares with us as much as we share with others in need. I wondered why we carried so much heavy meat when we could take whatever game we needed each day. Now I know why. Nothing is by accident."

Ch`e shrieked through gritted teeth and stomped away.

Stix leaned close to Kia's ear. "It may take a little more love, my love. Be patient."

Kia slipped on the wet, stone floor as the narrow passage dipped sharply then opened into a wide cavern. Angry voices echoed across the space and she feared for Ch`e and the rest of her little band. A fire turned the walls orange and cast dancing shadows. Rok pressed ahead of her, and Fem'ma ran to a darkened corner. The angry echoes cleared as Kia reached the fire.

A voice echoed through the cavern.

"I say we go back tonight and kill every one of them in their sleep!"

"Lei`on, you are out of your senses. We have no weapons and we are weak."

"Some of us haven't had food in days." The fem who said this had both hands full of dried fish and her cheeks bulged. She forced what was in her mouth down her throat and ripped off another bite.

A frail fem spoke up. "I say we stay hidden until those monsters stop searching for us, then we return to our own villages"

Lei`on shouted, waving her hands in the air. "If we go back now, we will take them by surprise! And it's a cold night, they will move slow. I'm going back alone if I must! They killed my entire hunting party – my sisters. Now, I will kill them."

"You can't kill the pups. Some of them were kind enough to bring us food."

"You are only going to anger them more and they will follow your scent back to the rest of us."

"Does anyone have a weapon? I'm going back! Now."

Kia finally spotted the angry fem who wanted revenge. She moved through the crowd, hoping to convince the hunter to rest first.

Song stepped up on a mound near the fire, holding a spear and the knife which had belonged to Vee. "I have a weapon. I'll go with you."

War
Cruel Grim
Sickening Horrifying Suffering
Advent of death
Betrayal

The blade will render
We'll never surrender

29 First Blood

"No!" Rok lunged for Song and pulled her from the mound in a tight embrace. "You can't. You're too precious and I – I – we can't lose you."

Lei`on snatched at the knife. "Give me the weapon!"

Song shrugged out of Rok's arms. "Then come with us and protect me. I gave my word and I can't back down."

"I'll go, too," Stix said. "I know how to set traps that kill the beasts we hunt."

Kia squeezed her beloved's hand. "That means I'm going. And I have this thing to see in the night."

A fem whose tunic hung in shreds, stepped up. "Lei`on, you've protected me since I was captured. I've seen how they use their weapons. I'll help."

Only a handful of others took their place beside Lei`on. Kia's heart tightened with trepidation as she gazed at these ruined but not beaten fems.

"Oh, rot it all!" Ch`e got up from her seat on the carrier and what remained of the food cache and grabbed her pack. "Some of you are bound to get hurt and you will need a healer."

Kia nearly choked with surprise but remained silent as her bond sister joined the growing circle. Many of the other fems had slumped into each other, sleeping soundly. The rest kept their eyes averted. Kia guessed they were too terrified to join the battle.

The gray haired elder raised herself from the mass and stepped over sleeping bodies.

"I know every corner of this place and where every master lives. I know their language. Probably better than I know my own. I've been here since I was a child. I nearly forgot my own name because everyone called me Elder. The masters call me 'Scree-th'k-pah'. It means 'Old Slave'. I was once called Bird."

Kia thought she heard Fem'ma yelp in the darkness behind her.

"We must have a plan before we go," Song said in a soft voice. "The war has started."

Silently the small army crept into the citadel, crawling on their bellies and elbows. Many more of the refugees rallied to join them, armed with only stones and clubs hastily constructed. *So much hate and revenge fills the air*. Adrenalin set Kia's blood on fire. She could make out the shapes of the lodges against the stars in the sky, but beyond that, she couldn't see the ground in front of her without the aid of her tool. She felt a tap on her arm.

"Fem'ma!" Kia whispered. "What are you doing?"

"This must be remembered. Moon will record the war in song."

"No! Get back to the cave. He must be protected. Who knows what those fems we left back there will do if they discover him."

"They won't discover him. He is here."

Kia groaned.

"Worry not, my dear Kia." Moon's muffled voice came from under Fem'ma where his sling was tucked inside her water-cat skin tunic. "Only I fear I won't see anything to record."

"Veenah, have mercy on me for not sending you back." Dread shot through Kia's heart and nausea curdled her stomach. She rested her forehead on her arms until the shock passed. She shoved the Zid tool into Fem'ma's hand. "Here. Use this. The red button sends out fire like an arrow, but I don't know how far. Stay under cover."

Rok tugged at her. "Come, sister, we need to go. Bird will signal with the call of Nightbird when we are all in place.

Kia could hardly take in air and sweat flowed down her face despite the chilly night air. One of the freed captives stood by her side. Rok and two others were poised to attack the leaders. Bird, Stix, and one other captive would attack the lodge which held many of the Zid weapons.

How can we survive this battle against so many? Veenah help us.
Kia felt morning would come before the signal.
'Hoo-hoo-hoot-hoo.'
'Hoot-hoo.'
Kia brought her blade down on the vulnerable head of a sleeping bull. In the same instant, she heard a spear find its mark in the cow by its side along with the unmistakable crushing thump of a stone-tipped club.

Lights glowed throughout the village. Screeches and hideous roars mixed with the war-cries of fighting fems, and the brilliant orange flames of Zid blasters flashed through the air. The sound of two skimmers taking off was immediately followed by a crash and explosion, illuminating a metal rope which had tethered the vehicles to a tree.

Brilliant green scaled skin flashed past and Kia gasped in horror as a young Zid swept a fem off her feet, and then jumped on her, ripping her almost in half with its snapping jaws. With red blood dripping from its teeth, it leaped at the back of another fem.

Kia could only swing her blade as scaled, green bodies dashed past her in the chaos. She experienced a dizzying power overwhelm her as she was enveloped by the musky stench of purple blood. Despite their great size, many fell under her knife. The enormous square lodge spewed smoke, which flickered gold from the fires within. As if in slow motion, the walls of the structure began to expand and Kia dove for cover as a brilliant light and the force of the explosion robbed her of sight and changed the sounds of battle to a dull ring.

She slid behind a lodge and crashed head-long into a scaly body. Bracing herself with one hand, she grasped the footless stump of a hind leg. She swung her blade toward the putrid breath of the beast. Her vision cleared long enough to see the scar running up the thing's muzzle to its flat, yellow eye. Rolling under it as the deadly jaws snapped a hair's breadth away, she sunk her blade into its throat. It stumbled and fell, pinning her to the ground under its crushing weight.

War cries filled the air and the sickening sound of the blasters went silent. Kia struggled to get free of the dead beast and sobbed her fear for her sisters. Someone kneeled beside her.

"Over here!"

Kia didn't know the fem who'd discovered her, but she reached out to embrace her.

Stix and Rok appeared, and together they shoved the beast from Kia. They fell into each other's arms. Kia hardly had the strength to speak. Through sobs she asked, "Did Song…?"

"We haven't found her yet. Ch`e is treating the wounded. Lei`on is dead."

"Many are dead," Stix moaned.

"What are you carrying?" Kia lifted the thing from Stix's shoulder.

"It's a Zid weapon. One of the fems showed me how to use it. The blasters are too big for us, but we have enough of these to win the whole war. Here, take this torch-light. It's like the one Snap gave Song. This blue button shoots a killing blast."

"C'mon," urged the other fem. "Let's find the others."

Glowing lanterns swung from the fronts of several lodges, shedding enough light for Kia and her sisters to pick their way through the rubble. Dead Zid lay everywhere. More than Kia could count. Tears flowed down her face and she thought her heart was ripping into shreds. She knew war would be horrible, but she didn't realize how much it would hurt.

The yellow hair of a fem shimmered from under pieces of the lodge which had exploded. Kia tore away the rubble, screaming. The dead fem was not Song, but Kia still held her, rocking in her sorrow.

"Leave her," someone commanded. "We must find the living."

"No! We will honor those who have lost their lives here today." Kia lifted the body and carried her to a well-lit, open space. "Find every dead fem and bring her here. Especially Lei`on. We will have a burial ceremony and erect a monument."

Bird stumbled into the circle of light, bleeding from several wounds. "Some of them got away."

"Are you sure you didn't let them go, elder?" The fem who'd

found Kia sounded threatening.

"Remember your place, child! I killed the only pup who ever brought us food, even while she begged for her life!"

"You killed Shrr-cop? Why?"

"I begged her many times to release us and she only laughed."

A younger fem carried her injured friend into the light. Kia shined her light into the darkness and heard the unmistakable voice of Ch`e.

"Hold still. This will only hurt a moment." Her voice was followed by a shriek of pain.

Kia gripped Stix's hand and drew her closer.

"I know how that poor fem feels," Stix said.

Suddenly, broken pieces of a wooden table erupted and a Zid scampered through the village. Rok drew her weapon and fired an orange blast. The beast's side opened up and splashed purple blood in every direction.

Kia bent double and retched.

She heard a whimper.

"Can someone help me?" A small, fair-skinned hand waved from under a wall, destroyed by a fallen tree.

"Song!" Rok dropped the weapon and attacked the adobe with her knife.

Kia grabbed a piece of wood and helped pry their sister loose."

"My beautiful Song. Are you okay? Are you hurt?" Rok hugged her then held her at arm's length.

"No. I've been stuck under that mess the whole time. I didn't get to help with the battle at all. I didn't even see anything."

Stix and Kia joined the embrace.

Stix said, "It's a better thing that you didn't see this, my love."

"Rok," Kia said, "take her to the top of the hill. Don't let her look at this horror. You'll find Fem'ma up there – I hope."

"What?"

"The battle…oh, I'll let Fem'ma explain. Just get her out of here." Kia kissed Song on the cheek. "Go, both of you."

Kia and Stix found another dead fem. She was the one who'd volunteered to go with Lei`on. They carried her to the center of the citadel.

The promise seems forgotten
As I lay you down to rest
You charged the line with grace and pride
Called to give your last and best
The world has lost her hope and glory
And mourns the fallen crest

30 Fallen Heroes

Kia led the procession back to the edge of the badlands, carrying the thin, ragged fem. Two others carried Lei`on. Nearly every survivor held one who'd not survived. Ch`e assisted two fems still weak from their injuries. Kia counted nine dead. Her insides twisted in grief.

Daylin walked nearby. "You said we would have a death ceremony, leader. How can we do this without a Loresinger?"

"We will choose a site for the burial and monument before we concern ourselves with the ceremony." Kia feared what may happen when the presence of a mem was announced. He was not only young and un-united; he was not an appointed eldermem or lore. She only hoped he would keep his hands and feet hidden. If they didn't take him by force for his seed, they would destroy him for his deformity.

At the edge of the badlands, a flat-faced, pale sheet of stone stood higher than the other pieces of broken Terah. A gnarled nut tree twisted around its base and over the top like a crown.

"This is the place of the monument," Kia said, puffing with exhaustion. "Lay these brave fems here and take your rest. We will gather the others and prepare for the ceremony."

"I am Warrior. I'll stand with the fallen until you return. Go. Eat and wash in the river at the back of the cave." Rok stood tall, holding the battle-stained watercat spine spear.

One by one, the dead were laid in front of the monument. The horizon warmed with the coming of Warmsun. Kia looked back at Rok, still standing guard, and brought two fingers to her lips, then held her hand in the air. Rok nodded. The battle-weary fems trudged on into the badlands in the direction of the cave. Kia dropped back to walk with Fem'ma.

"Give me the torch-tool I gave you before the battle. It will show us the way to the blanket of Veenah. She heard Moon humming a sad tune beneath the watercat tunic. She pressed the button on the tool, but the line didn't light up.

"Hmmm." Kia shook the device. "Did you drop it?"

Stix caught up with her. "Maybe it needs to be in Warmsun for a time in order to work. Lei`on said all the weapons must sit for part of the day in the light so they will work. They grow weak if they are overused."

"That must be it. Strange, though. The torch still works." The remainders of the slaves-turned-warriors trudged through the tangle of brush and rocks as if they'd been on this trail every day of their lives. "We'll follow them. They've been here a long time and look like they know where they are going."

A jagged ridge came into view. The dark crevasse of a cave entrance shown in the dusk of early morning. The volunteer warriors began to file into the cave without hesitation. Ch`e pushed in with the first of them.

Kia rushed forward, still checking to see if the line would pulse on her tool. "I'm not sure this is the right place."

"Of course it is," Daylin answered her. "Don't you remember this black line running through the pale rock and this berry bush by the entrance? I saw it clearly even in the dark. Your sisters found a great shelter." Daylin shoved a fistful of berries into her mouth before disappearing into the dark cavern.

Kia pulled Stix and Song close to her and cast a worried look at Fem'ma. "Where's the blanket of Veenah?" she whispered.

Ch`e screamed inside the cave and Kia rushed down the trail holding the Zid torch in front of her for light. The fire had gone out, but none of the fems who'd stayed behind were in the cave. Neither were their supplies.

"I told you, Kia! We're ruined!" Ch`e ranted and kicked stones in every direction. "They've taken everything! The cowards." She sat down with a force that shook her whole body and bawled into her hands. "All our beautiful furs. My white dress. Gone!"

"It's not worth all this shouting, healer." Clara tried to calm Ch`e.

"Why do you act like you care? You wouldn't speak to me in our village and you shunned me when I wanted to court you! And look where it got you, slave. If you'd stayed with me, you would have remained free and safe, like me. Where did your friends take our supplies? Tell me! I know you know where they went."

Clara backed away without saying anything else. Ch`e slumped to the ground sobbing.

"We'll rest and wash ourselves." Kia stood on a mound and shouted for all to hear. "We can find berries and nuts for now. We will bury our dead and then we will hunt. Bears roam these badlands."

"And a large herd of targus beasts comes through here every few days," someone added.

Several fems lowered themselves into the dark pool of water and scrubbed the stench of death from their bodies and tunics. Kia joined them, glancing around for Fem'ma. The two elders sat at the edge of the pool. Fem'ma was speaking in a low voice, so Kia moved closer.

"…Bird, I have never spent a day without thinking of you and the horrible attack when you were taken. I always believed you had been killed."

"In a way, I did die. I hardly thought of home after a few seasons here. I don't know why Veenah protected me. I have outlived so very many captives."

"How did you survive?"

"I eat insects and worms, sometimes I'm able to grab berries and find nuts. Most of the captives can't eat such things. When a fem dies, one of us takes her dress." Bird lifted the hem of her buckskin tunic and sighed. "We don't ever get to bury our dead."

"It's a miracle they allowed you to live so long. The hand of Veenah is strong and merciful. Every time I thought of you, I prayed."

"Thank you, Eve. I know it helped, but I survived because I obey them and I'm good at my job."

A shock ran through Kia when she heard Fem'ma's birth name

187

and she forgot her manners. "What do they make you do?" She covered her mouth with her hands. "Forgive me for interrupting."

"It's okay, child. Their claws are clumsy with the jewels they mine. Of course they take many things from Terah, but our work in this place is to find the colored gems which reflect the light of Warmsun like a rainbow. We sift them from the piles of dirt dug up by the rock harvesters. Some fems have learned to break these stones into beautiful jewels. It's like knapping flint arrow points, but the gems break flat instead of curved and sharp. Other workers melt gold and silver metals and shape adornments for the leaders. Often the gems are set into the gold."

Bird finished cleaning herself and walked over to Clara and her sister. The only thing Kia heard of their conversation was, "Your mother is blessed…"

Fems stepped out of the pool, squeezing water from their tunics and hair. Whispers of better clothing rippled through the cave. Kia thought of what Bird had said about using the dresses of the dead and shuddered. "I had hoped to bring Rok her clean dress, the one she wore for our bonding. But it's gone."

"I wear two," said a young fem, stripping a wet dress over her head. "This was my mother's. She lost her life when our hunting party was attacked. It was my first hunt. She gave it to me with her last breath and said it might help protect me. It will fit your sister better than it fits me. And it's clean."

They emerged from the cave into the brilliant light of Warmsun. Song and Ch`e and a few others had gone ahead to start digging a single grave for the fems who'd died. The troop stumbled along the rocky trail toward the monument. Kia felt hot tears burning her eyes and she leaned on Stix for support."

"We did this to them," Kia sobbed. "We could have all escaped alive, but they had to die. I don't even know their names."

Bird stroked her head. "It was the only way for some of them. They were too filled with grief and hate to do anything else. They would have fought even if they knew for sure they would not come back."

Three fems standing near the monument hoisted a fourth to stand on the tallest one's shoulders. The fem on top began to chisel the stone with a torch-tool. She drew three fem faces; one looking toward Veenah, another looking toward the rising of Warmsun, and the third looking toward the Forbidden Mountains where Warmsun went to rest. As bits of stone fell away, the images seemed to come to life, glowing with love. Beneath them she carved a sunburst, with nine more faces around it, one for each of the fallen. Then she carved a Zid standing on all fours with its head bowed and tail tucked in fear.

"This marks the day Terians take back the world from their enemies." The carver called out so all could hear. "Let every Terian who walks this way know that these brave fems gave their lives to free them!"

Reverently, Rok lifted the first body and laid her at the bottom of the grave. As the others were lowered, Moon's song rang out.

"Who carries a Loresinger out here?" someone shouted. Fems stumbled backward, falling over themselves in surprise and confusion.

"Where is the mem?"

"How did he get out here?"

Moon continued singing. All eyes turned toward him to find Fem'ma standing in a high place and Moon sitting in his matron's arms. He wore his white watercat cloak with the amber beads reflecting the light.

One of the older fems began to drum on a hollow log with a stout branch. The elder, Bird, stood next to Fem'ma, witnessing the ceremony. The murmuring quieted again to reverence.

The burial chant continued until the dirt had been packed down into the grave and stones piled high over the site.

The drum stopped.

Moon spoke out in his clear tenor voice. "We praise you Veenah and thank you for the time we shared with our beloved sisters. Take them into your arms and give them rest and peace. And grant your children the courage to continue what they started. Remember their names and let their sacrifice never be forgotten."

Fem'ma stepped down and Bird took her place. "Fems we have declared war upon our enemies. The battle of the prophesy has begun. Veenah has promised us victory, though we be few and the enemy is vast."

Murmurs growing almost into a shout rippled through the fems.

"There is no prophesy."

"Blasphemy!"

Fem'ma took her place beside Bird, and Moon shouted above the ruckus. "The prophesy unfolds before you. The jewel has been discovered. The innocent hand stands with you today. In many battles since Warmsun and Moonlight exchanged places in the sky, this innocent has been untouched, see for yourself."

Gasps filled the air and one fem fainted while another cried with silent tears.

"Innocent One, come forward and declare your discovery!"

Song leaned on Rok for support. "I…I can't," she croaked.

Kia wrapped an arm around Song's waist. "We're here for you. You're safe."

Stix stood by Kia, and Ch`e went to Rok. "Go ahead, love," said Rok. "Tell them."

As Song made her way to the high place, Moon sang his song of discovery which had been given to him in the Badlands.

Encouraged, Song spoke clear and loud. "The Jewel of Veenah is the ground you stand on. Terah is the jewel. I am with my sisters on our bonding quest and with love in our hearts we understood the words of the prophesy. Terah lies in the darkness of oppression from our common enemy and she must be freed. A message from Veenah waits in the Forbidden Mou—"

"Get under cover!" Rok bellowed a war cry as a swarm of skimmers shot through the treetops toward them. "Arm yourselves!"

Children of Terah
From the place of your birth
Answer the call
And cast out the curse

31 The Enemy Cannot Stand

Rok led a charge away from the monument and took shelter in the stone forest of the badlands. Kia followed, dodging around rocky outcroppings and giant cone trees. A skimmer dipped down from the sky and Rok fired her weapon at it. The vessel burst into flame and blasts from three other fems killed the Zid before it hit the ground.

"Stay under cover and only shoot when they fly over!" Rok commanded. "Their weapons see through trees, but not rock!"

Two more skimmers dashed by. Bursts of flame shattered boulders, but the fems returned fire and both skimmers crashed. A shower of orange streaks reduced a tree to splinters and the shrieks of a fem was cut short by another blast.

"Run!" Rok screamed a war cry. "Move away every time you shoot so they can't find you. Here they come!"

Huddling close to a mound, Kia waited for the next wave. Someone shot too soon and the more powerful weapon of the enemy disintegrated the rock pile she was hiding behind. The suddenly unprotected fem exploded with the next shot. Kia couldn't even scream for the terror ripping through her.

The Zid fired through the stone forest tearing chunks out of boulders and sending shards of broken rock in all directions. Kia aimed at a skimmer coming directly at her and fired at the exact moment two other fems shot. The crashing flier nearly rolled over the top of Kia, but its rider leaped from the vehicle and tried to escape. Five shots ended its life.

"Keep moving!" Rok screamed another war cry and Kia dashed toward her voice. The ground exploded beside her and she leaped to the side and aimed. The skimmer veered away.

As suddenly as it had begun, it was over. The sky became quiet. Kia thought the ground was moving, but her legs were shaking so bad that she fell. Both of her arms carried new cuts and blood stained her face from where shards of stone struck her forehead.

"Call out!" Rok's voice echoed through the boulders. "I said call out! Fems! Call your names so I know you live!"

"Kia!"

"Song."

"Bird."

"Clara."

One by one, Kia heard every name but two. Silently, she thanked Veenah for protecting the rest.

Stix plopped to the ground beside Kia. "We made it! Our second battle! Oh, I have some water in my drinking skin. Let me wash your wounds. Then we can find the others."

They followed the sound of a bird call and found Rok with nearly the whole band. Song and Ch`e were nested under her arms.

Bird choked back a sob, searching through the faces. "Where's Bela?"

"She was killed," Kia said softly. "It happened close by me. I'm afraid there isn't even enough of her left to bury. And I saw Flora fall when the fighting started."

Several of the refugees gathered around their elder in a tearful huddle. Bird moaned, "How can we stand against an enemy so strong and cruel?"

Moon's voice rang out in song.

> The enemy cannot stand
> Against the One most Righteous
> When fems together fight as one
> To free the Jewel of Veenah"

"Oh brave fems," Moon called out from the safety of his sling.

"Blessings on you for your courage. Your battle in the night was indeed terrifying and I felt the fear from the hill, far above you. But now I can say I know the feel of war and I will never think lightly of it again."

Fem'ma took Bird's arm. "Come, friend elder. We must find shelter for our clan." They stumbled around the boulder and into the clearing arm in arm and both carrying weapons.

Fems struggled to their feet, looking to Kia and Rok.

Kia spoke. "We stay in the badlands. Remember, their weapons cannot see through stone. We also need to move toward the mountain. But we must move faster."

Deeper and deeper into the badlands they ran until exhaustion made them slow. A ravine spread out in front of them and Kia slid down the side to the bottom where she and Six collapsed, panting.

The brush erupted with a flash of fur and snarls. Kia palmed her knife with Rok, Stix and several other fems beside her. A mountain wolf glowered over the remains of a young deer, teeth bared. Daylin and Clara inched forward, crude spears held ready.

"Leave her," Rok said softly. "Don't you see how thin she is? She is feeding cubs. I don't think she means us any harm. She's only protecting her food."

"I'm hungrier than she is. I think we can use that meat better than that animal."

Ch'e huffed. "I don't think so. That meat has likely gone sour, and even if we tried to cook it, we would still get sick. Our great hunters can find something better, I'm sure."

Clara snorted and turned away, glaring, and the wolf dragged her kill deeper into the brush before she bounded out of sight.

The rest of their small army straggled in, sliding, stumbling, and falling. Kia felt a moment of panic until she saw Fem'ma and Bird, bolstered by Stix and two other fems at the rim of the ravine. Kia rallied to assist them.

"We need to rest and find food," Kia said. "Rok, do you think there is an overhang or a cave in here?"

"Let me catch my breath, and I'll scout." She raised her voice to address the clan. "Who will go with me?"

"Thank you," Kia said. "Stix, I know you're tired, but we need meat. Are you strong enough to find a game trail?"

Stix leaned on the broken stump of an old, dead tree, still shaking from the encounter with the wolf. She stood and called out, "Any skilled hunters who can walk, come with me." She set out for a wide place in the ravine. Two fems followed her.

"Song, you and Ch`e have a talent for finding water—"

"I can't move," Ch`e whined.

"I think I know where water flows," a young fem said. She took Song's hand. They walked toward a bright green stand of trees farther up the ravine.

"Thank you. Now, is there one among us who can hide in the leaves and is able to climb that tree and keep watch for the enemy?"

A dark-skinned fem pushed herself from her grassy resting place and walked to Kia. "I used to climb the tallest trees, and I could see better than any in my village."

"What are you called?"

"Siena." She scaled the embankment and gracefully climbed the tree. "I see their flyers circling the citadel and ranging over the river, but nothing coming this way. At least not yet. I think we really surprised them back there. Wow, I've never been so close to the Forbidden Mountain before. It looks like it could fall on us from here."

A chill ran through Kia thinking about the message waiting there and wondering how she'd find it. She knelt beside Fem'ma. "Are you okay?"

"I'll live, child. I should say, leader. Only days ago the thought of leadership was a difficult burden for you. Now you show the heart of a village leader." Fem'ma raised a shaky hand to stroke Kia's face.

"Thank you, elder."

"Ma." Moon's struggling shape bulged under Fem'ma's watercat tunic. Kia wondered how she'd cashed him there so quickly, and then remembered the elder wore her buckskin dress and carried the tunic during the ceremony.

"Ma, I can't breathe in here. And your heartbeat is going to destroy my ears. Please put me down so you can rest."

Fem'ma loosened the thongs which kept Moon tucked safely inside the sling and he gasped for fresh air.

"Oh, Kia, I'm so happy to see you. I've never been so afraid in all my life. I didn't know a Terian could feel that much fear. But the best part is that we killed one! Ma fired and it fell from its flier and I saw it. I wish I could hold a weapon."

"I'm just happy you're safe. I had no time to think about anyone back there." Kia couldn't help smiling. Suddenly she wanted to lift him, to carry him so that his cheek brushed hers, the way her mother had carried Trog. Her face burned and she turned away.

"Matron." A stout, red-haired fem approached with her head bowed. "I was captured when I was contemplating leaving my femtog to go into service. I couldn't bear a child and the elders had need of me. I am able to carry the mem. He will be safe with me."

Kia held her breath. If Moon was carried by another, he would be her responsibility. He would belong to her, unless he was courted and united with his own femtog. Her heart raced, but she didn't dare speak until she met with her sisters – until after their quest was complete.

Fem'ma rested on her elbow, still cradling Moon in her lap. Finally, she spoke. "What is your name and where is your village?"

"I am called Fawn. I lived where the White river falls from the plains into a green valley, five day's walk from here."

"You may hold the mem off the ground as demanded by respect and the law. I will train you as a proper matron and elderfem, but the mem will remain my responsibility. You will not call him by name."

Kia stole a glance at Moon's large brown eyes and smiling, full lips as Fem'ma passed the sling to Fawn. "I need to check on the others." She climbed to her feet to see to the needs of the rest of her clan. Ch`e had recovered enough to pass out willa leaves from her medicine pack. Clara and Daylin sat together, grieving. Kia went to them.

"Did you lose your sister in the battle?"

Daylin sniffled. "We lost her long before the battle. She vowed to escape and return home. She didn't go with us."

"She snuck away with the other cowards." Clara almost hissed the words.

"I'm so sorry," Kia said, her voice cracking in sorrow. "None of you could have known, but at the last bonding time, our villages were attacked. Your home has been destroyed."

Daylin wailed.

Clara held her sister close. "We know. Bird just told us what your elder said. We grieve for our families as well as our sister."

"Clara, our elder is your blood mother. She loves you deeply."

"If she ever cared for me, she would not have sinned. She would not have left me alone!"

"Enough of that, Clara. Fems, adult fems, do not carry hatred in their hearts. Your mother's greatest sin was her undying love and inability to put you in danger. She had no choice by to leave and enter the service of elders with her son."

"I was told my brother died. Are you saying that your Loresinger is my brother?"

"He is far more precious than just as a spiritual leader. He was born to lead the nation of Terians."

"I don't believe you." Clara collapsed, heaving with sobs.

"Please," Daylin said. "Leave us to grieve. I'm too tired to think about this. None of us have rested after our work in the jewel fields."

"I will. But first, can you tell me about Ch`e. We found her only a few days after the attack. My sisters and I love her and have asked her to bond with us, but she carries a painful burden which she cannot share."

"She is cruel and vain."

"That much I know," Kia said smiling. "But she is beautiful and the most skilled healer I've ever known."

"Her hearth mothers are, um, were the village healers, but her blood mother would never allow them to treat anyone without payment." Daylin wiped the tears from her eyes and continued. "The story is that her mother refused the attention of her father because she hated having a child."

"But," Clara added through jerky breaths, "her blood mother always dressed her in the finest furs and white leathers, and paraded her around the village like a prize. Then when they were in their hut, her mother would take her dresses away and make her wear cast-off infant cloaks. If Ch`e learned about healing, it's because she watched her other hearth mothers."

Daylin hung her head. "Ch`e did come to visit me. My mother is our village leader and my syr is our chief elder. But Ch`e demanded that I obey her…"

"I see," said Kia. "Ch`e is with fems who love her and need her very much. No one needs to fear her temper. I think it's part of what makes her beautiful. And she has saved many lives. I will love her until I die."

Song returned loaded with tubers and onions. "Misa is behind me, coming with water."

Misa carried two giant snail shells and several fems gathered for a drink. "The mem drinks first, and our elders," she said. "Then the rest of you. The water is cold and good."

Rok walked into the clearing and sat in the grass near Ch`e. "We found a good sized den, but it's filled with newborn swamp wolf cubs, and when the mother looked at us, curled around her babes and only whined, none of us had the heart to kill them for the shelter. But we brought red berries." She opened the pouch made by holding up the hem of her borrowed dress.

Song spoke. "There is an overhang near the stream. It's not very big, but I think we will all be safe there. In fact, we met Stix and I sent her back to find it. They had a successful hunt."

Stix trotted up behind Song. "Sisters! We have meat. I left our friends at Song's shelter to begin cooking."

"You left them alone?" One of the sleeping forms roused.

"Are you called Willa?" Stix asked. "Zara sent a message. She said, 'Come to me quickly and safely. I am preparing your favorite food.' But we caught many different kinds of game. Which is your favorite?"

"That would be the honking water bird with her eggs baked inside." Willa pushed herself up from her resting place and brushed the dust from her dress.

"We caught one of them along with six tree dogs. Possibly enough fur to make foot coverings for all of you."

Zara pushed herself to her feet. "We should hurry before none of us can move out of our sleep. Nella, Rose, wake yourselves. We have berries, water, and meat waiting at a safe shelter."

"Siena," Kia called up to the watcher. "Do you see danger?"

"Only one flyer still circles the Zid camp. The others have landed, I think. Can I come down and drink some water?"

Stix led the way back to the overhang. "Follow behind me in single file. It's not far. Try to step in my footprints. We are going to follow the stream a short distance. The Zid won't be able to follow our scent through the water."

Soon the aroma of roasting meat set Kia's mouth to watering, and everyone picked up speed, splashing though the creek and finally passing Stix.

"I can smell the cooking fire, but I can't see the smoke," Kia said.

Zara chuckled. "That's because we've learned how to cook meat without fire. We use these tools. Of course we never used this type as slaves, because they are also weapons. For some reason those beasts didn't trust us."

Kia almost felt like laughing, but the serious looks on the fems she'd rescued told her that none of this was funny. She remained silent.

The clan splashed out of the stream and flooded into the narrow shelter and hungry fems ripped pieces of meat from the roasted tree dogs. Willa fell into Zara's arms and Nella joined them before they tore into the fat waterbird cooking in a stone oven.

Before Warmsun reached her zenith, nothing was left of the meat, and soft snores echoed in the space. Kia never thought solid rock could be so comfortable. Her head drooped and she jerked upright again. She gazed over the sleeping bodies.

How can we survive this war? Please help us Veenah.

Moon sat propped up against Fem'ma's side and tucked safely in his sling. He whispered, "Sleep with your sisters, leader. I will stand watch."

Green the heart of anger
Which never felt the joy
Of comfort, love, and candor.
Left untended
Grace has ended
The gift it will destroy

32 Jealousy

Mountain songbirds echoed their music through the canyon before Warmsun's light showed in the sky. Ch`e shifted uncomfortably on the bare, rocky floor of the shelter and shivered in the cold. She edged closer to the fem she lay beside for a bit of warmth then awakened with surprise. She didn't know either of the fems next to her. She glanced around and saw Kia sleeping, leaning against the wall. Her heart fluttered with love all the way up to her throat. She shook her head and sat up.

Across the shelter, Rok and Stix lay with Song between them. The flutter filled her insides and she couldn't help but smile.

Why am I all the way over here instead of with the ones I love? We were all so tired. Did we sleep all day and all night?

Her pack gaped open and she remembered treating small wounds while she wolfed down her share of the meat. She hadn't even taken time to sample any of Song's tubers and onions which boiled in the giant snail shell.

Hmph, I was busy and no one offered me any. No, I was so busy I never asked.

Hunger, cold, and nature finally demanded that Ch`e move. She gathered her pack and tied her knife belt around her waist. Silently, she stepped over sleeping bodies. Near the ledge leading down to the stream, she found Fem'ma sitting up with Moon sleeping in her lap.

"Did you stand watch all night, Elder?"

"No. I had help." Fem'ma smiled.

Ch'e looked around the shelter. "Who? They were all sound asleep before they even finished eating."

"Moon took first watch."

"Oh, no. Did anyone see him?"

"I don't think so. He said he stayed in the sling – after he reached out and took the tree dog leg I'd been eating. I'm ashamed to say, I fell asleep. I'm surprised he didn't topple and hurt himself. He woke me at the proper time. The only thing he reported was some spotted does and their fawns coming to the water to drink."

"He is going to get us all in trouble."

"Child, he was so proud of himself for standing watch over these brave fems he almost cried."

Ch'e felt Kia's arms go around her and she leaned back into her sister, soaking up the warmth. "Happy morning to you, leader. Did you sleep okay, sitting on the hard ground?"

"I was so tired I never even noticed. But it sure is cold up here so close to the mountain. Maybe that's why it's forbidden."

"Please don't remind me. I was terrified to come here. I still may have to run away. Come with me to the stream. I'm hungry and I think there are fish in that little bend over there."

After relieving themselves, Ch'e led the way, her fingers entwined in Kia's.

"Be very quiet and don't show yourself over the water. Move as slow as you can. I'm going to wade in and try to flip them to you." She kicked off her foot coverings and used the long end of her knife belt to loop between her legs and hold up her dress, and then stepped into the clear water. "Ho! Perg's Fires! This water is cold!" she whispered, almost breathless.

Dipping her hand deep into the stream, she moved toward the schooling fish. Their silvery sides glimmered in the early dawn light. Her hand moved like one of them until she reached under the nearest. With a lightning-fast move, she lifted the fish from the water and flipped it to the bank where Kia waited with a willa stick to string through its gills.

Kia held up the prize and admired the rose-colored stripe running down its sides. "My favorite," she whispered.

Ch`e flipped a second, then a third in quick succession. She held still while the school settled back down, then repeated the process. Soon Kia waved to her.

"We have enough for everyone," Kia whispered. "Leave some for another day."

Ch`e remained focused. A particularly large specimen had her attention. It would surely have eggs and her stomach growled in anticipation of the delicacy. *Yes!* She flipped the monster fish to the bank and climbed out of the stream.

"This one is mine," she said, smiling. "Look how fat she is! Eggs, the food of Veenah. And there's enough down there to feed two villages and more."

"Um, sister, we still have a problem," Kia said looking at three willa branches weaving through two tens of gills. "This is more than we can carry. I don't even know if the branches can hold their weight. I can't believe you caught them so fast."

"I love fish," Ch`e giggled. "I used to chase them when I was really small. One of the village hunters taught me how to catch them instead of chase them, but I had to eat every one I caught." Her face clouded for just a moment. More seriously, she added. "I think I ate better than my hearth sisters."

Kia's arms went around her and they shared a tight embrace. "Healer, friend, and sister you will never suffer from want of food or love again. I'll see to that."

"Thank you." Ch`e pulled away. "Now we have to figure out how to take these to our army."

Stones slipped down the embankment in front of Stix and Rok. "I see we have fish, and fish, and fish!" Rok whooped. "I love my fishing sister!" She picked up one bunch and Stix lifted the other. Ch`e and Kia carried the third branch-full between them.

A few fems hurried to select their breakfasts even before they got back. The aroma of fish cooking with the heat of the Zid weapons quickly filled the air.

When they climbed to the shelter, Ch`e nearly dropped her end of the willa branch.

Clara, Daylin, and Willa, along with Zara and Nella knelt in front of Moon, who still sat in Fem'ma's lap. Willa held out the feathered skin of the water bird. "It's a shoulder cape to keep you warm when you sit at your hearth. When we are finished preparing the skin, we would like to present this to you as a gift."

Kia whispered, "I think they're courting him."

"Over my dead body!" Ch`e said between her teeth.

"Now is not the time, my love. Our bonding quest is only half way over. When Moonlight shows her full face again, we will ask him. Until then, we must trust his loyalty. Let's eat your wonderful fish. I want to see how you prepare the eggs."

Ch`e placed her catch on a flat stone and split open its belly with the tip of her knife. Growling under her breath, she said, "I trust no one."

As one we'll rise
Prepare to fight
Draw tight the bow
And hone the knife

33 Training

"Fems," Rok said, warming herself over a heated stone. "I am of a warrior class and I want to teach you some fighting skills. We don't have time for proper training, but we also cannot lose anymore of you. The death of our friends in the last battle I carry in my heart like a stone. If I had taught you better, they would still be with us."

"You don't even know us, Warrior." A thin, young fem called out. "You don't know where we come from or what skills we already possess. What makes you think you can teach us?"

"I have been trained since I was born. And I wasn't captured—"

"You were lucky. Everyone who roams the world gets captured and is either eaten or enslaved. We have been learning to work together for many seasons. Maybe we should teach you how those monsters think. Maybe we should teach you how to fight them."

Rok considered how to answer. "My sisters live in spite of many dangers. Your sisters fall with every battle, those who didn't run away." Her skin crawled as she thought up methods to strike down this sharp-tongued fem. But she had promised her leader to show patience, so she took a deep breath instead. "What name are you called, and what are your skills, fem?"

"I am called Rose." Her voice grew sharper. "You know the beautiful flower with the sharp thorns? I was a hunter for my village. If it hadn't been for me, all of us would have been captured. I led the attack party away from my village. And, I still live after four seasons in that

Perg-hole."

"Then you will be my second in command while we train our army. That way, we can learn from each other." Rok trembled at her own words. A breath before she had been willing to take down this fem in hand-to-hand combat. *Kia's compassion is wearing off on me.* "What say you? Do we work together, or keep losing our friends to the enemy?"

Rose laughed. "I say we start now. Everyone make a line down by the creek where the bank is wide and sandy." She took the hands of her two closest friends and led the way.

"Not me," Ch`e said. "I'm healer. I don't fight."

"Especially you, healer," Rose called out. "You have to protect yourself in war. And our elders should learn as well."

Rok heard Kia giggle, but before she could speak, her leader whooped.

"Yes, everyone *including* our beautiful healer. What is our first lesson?" Kia said as she faced Rose.

Rose grinned. "I don't know about anyone else, but I want to know how to do that dive and roll when you go from one hiding place to the next."

Moon struggled to push his head farther out of his sling. "I believe the old songs tell of the second in command. Her title is lewtentent. What skill may I learn?"

Silence claimed the company. Some shifted uneasily, most bowed their heads. Fem'ma eased her tunic up to re-cover her charge.

Rok said, "Our Loresinger will learn everyone's name and those who have passed on to Veenah. He will record each conflict for history. And in time he will display his true value to all of Terah." She waited while murmurs and whispers of approval traveled down the line of fems. "Now, the lesson is 'falling'. Every fighter will fall. The skill is to fall without getting broken." She demonstrated, then coached while each fem practiced.

"This time, when you fall and roll, you will fasten your sight on one place and keep that place in focus while you roll three times. You will spin your head to keep your eyes on that place. Everyone look at me, and roll forward. Fawn, you will practice with this basket of bird eggs I found. If we are attacked while you carry our Loresinger, you will need to protect him. To break an egg is to injure our most valuable member."

In spite of groans and complaints, the training continued and before Warmsun reached her zenith, Rok was satisfied with the move. But still she pushed, adding spear and rock throwing to the skill. She didn't allow the use of the Zid weapons, but made the fems practice with sticks as if they were firing the blasters.

Pride burned in the young warrior, not just for her own sisters, but also for the others, and for her new lewtentent. Only once did her voice raise beyond teaching. An ache rose in her stomach, remembering her own training.

What do I teach them next? Aga would not only teach but beat. Under her breath, she said, "I will never again strike in anger, but only in battle with the enemy."

"I didn't hear you," Stix stumbled toward her, panting. "Was that another command? I think we should rest and find food."

"Ha, sister. Do you think the enemy is planning to give you rest? I think you just said that it's time for you to teach our army your long-spear tactic." Rok laughed while her beloved sister groaned.

The drills carried the company up the flank of a tree-covered hill. Half of her warriors lay hidden in the brush with their long-spears, the other half carried crudely made grass shields in front of them, charging toward the hidden traps. At exactly the right moment, un-sharpened and un-deadly spears popped out of the grass to perforate the shields. Song lay at the heel of her long-spear, laughing. Her 'victim', Zara, rolled to the ground, panting.

"I don't know what's so funny about this," she hiccupped, "except that I never knew it could be so easy to do something so horrible. But can we rest now? I'm so hungry I could eat a targus beast all by myself!"

"I agree," Zara said. She pulled a handful of tart red berries from a low bush.

"I should say no," Rok said, wiping the sweat from her face. "But I can't deny you. And I suppose we can't fight if we faint from hunger. We should be able to find game this far away from villages."

Quickly the entire army was foraging for the nourishing berries.

"But hopefully we won't find any Zid." Kia plunked down beside Rok and Song. "Fem'ma and Bird haven't seen anything all day. I wonder what those creatures are planning."

"No doubt, another attack. Only one thing we know; this time they won't be so careless as to fly over us."

"Rok, have you noticed how all these hills look like little piles of dirt from up here?" Song said through a mouthful of berries. "They don't look at all like the mountains and hills where we used to live. They remind me of the pretend huts I used to build out of mud when I was a child playing *village* with my hearth sisters. We'd pile handfuls of dirt and try to build the biggest hut."

"You're right," Kia said.

Zara sat up to study the hills. "Look at this hill closest to us. It's a pile of small huts!"

"How could a hut be piled? It would break apart."

"They can't be huts," Zara said. "They're hardly big enough for only a few fems to sit in. Made of the same kind of metal our village gathers to make cooking pots. I can tell by the way they are rotted, like the pots the mother's throw away."

"But these look like they are sitting on pots. Very strange pots sitting sideways. What are they?" Song said.

Rok could hear the fear growing in her sister's voice. "Whatever they are, sweet Song, I don't think they are a danger. Most of them are half buried and all of them look like they haven't moved in many seasons. Trees are growing up through a lot of them."

The rest of the small army had gathered around. "I know what these hills are," said Bird. "They look like the piles we had to dig through to find gems for the masters. This is where the Zid dump what's left after they dig. I always wondered where the old piles went."

"This is why the mountain is forbidden," Song whispered. "The tallest part of the mountain looks like it is made from three giant piles. It is like the waste piles outside our village, only we bury our waste."

"Yes, it is waste, and it is dangerous," said Rose. "The dirt and stones which come from deep in Terah can turn the water into poison. Especially when it is heated to remove the gold metal from it."

Rok held Kia and Song close to her and stared at the white-topped mountain, so close to them. *What secret message could Veenah have sent to this place? Or is it only death that awaits us?*

A scream rose up from the edge of the gathering. "Look out! They're coming again!"

From the mouth of death
There comes new life.
From the mouth of lies
Exudes a gift.
From bondage
Love finds freedom.
From the wild
We come home.

34 Love Knows No Pain

The smooth hill offered no cover other than a few scattered trees and thick brush.

"Run for the mountain!"

A deep ravine followed a path past the small hill-piles up to the side of the mountain. This place had struck fear in Kia's heart her whole life. Now she charged for it like her life depended on it. Revived by adrenaline, she pushed upward, praying the steep sides of the ravine would keep her company hidden.

The ravine ended at a rocky cliff displaying a ribbon of waterfall which sparkled in the light. A net of vines knitted towering trees tight to the cliff. Birds burst from the foliage as the fems ripped their way into the deep woods.

"Keep going!" Kia screamed. The vision of Fem'ma, Moon, and Song in the screen on Pop's blaster burned in her mind, but her breath wouldn't allow her to warn the others. They had no cover in this place. No way to defend themselves. The solid rock wall in front of them was fractured and split at the surface and fems at the head of the fleeing pack found toe and finger-holds to climb. Kia searched out Fem'ma, still struggling through the tangle of vines and ran to her.

"This way. I'll help you." She wedged her fingers into a fissure and prepared to climb after her elder.

"No," Fem'ma barked. "If I fall, you'll be crushed."

"Then don't fall!" Kia braced her hand under Fem'ma's foot, then pulled herself up the cliff.

As soon as the first climber reached the top, she turned and helped the next one, then they helped another. Kia heard the whir of a skimmer and hung on the rock-face with one hand, while she aimed her blaster toward the sound. She fired the instant a movement caught her eye through the twisted tops of the trees and was rewarded by a shower of flames and shards of the vehicle flying around her as it hit the cliff only a few arm lengths away. The shockwave nearly knocked her down, but she hugged the fissure to which she was anchored and tucked her face under her arm. She felt the weight of Fem'ma's foot on her shoulder and gripped tighter. Pain radiated from her fingers all the way to her back.

"Hang on! I've got you!" With her head, she pushed up under Fem'ma's other foot and powered them both to the next hand-hold. Blood ran down her arms and her vision blurred. In the next instant, the weight on her body lifted. Screams filled her ears and she wiped the blood from her eyes with the back of her hand.

My blaster!

She'd dropped the weapon!

Looking down at the chasm far below, illness overtook her. She swallowed hard to hold on to what was left of her breakfast. Her head swirled and she pressed her face to the rock. Another scream. Ch`e!

The healer hung by one foot from a gnarled, vine covered root that snaked down the cliff from a dead tree at the top. Ch`e twisted in her trap and grabbed for the vine, but missed. Her pack fell from her neck, but she caught it, and then tried to use it to again catch the vine. Kia became aware of the zing of the hand blasters firing over her head. She reached for another handhold which would carry her closer to Ch`e.

A massive blast dissolved the cliff face where Kia had just been – and opened a wide fracture all the way to the top. The hole smoldered and shards of broken rock rained down on her. She lost her grip and grabbed for a split in the rock as she fell. Her body slammed against the cliff, knocking the breath from her, but her tortured fingers held her in place.

She was the last one on the cliff. Except for Ch`e. *Please, Veenah, let them all be at the top.* Fatigue took hold of her arms and the last of her strength faded.

"KIA!"

"Climb, Kia!"

She heard the shouts from above. Hands reached for her, but were too far away. Struggling for a better grip and a foot hold, she glanced over to Ch`e. The healer no longer struggled, still hanging upside down from her foot. Kia felt the stab of grief in her heart. Her medicine bag! The pack which Ch`e guarded and kept with her day and night, still dangled from her hand.

She's not dead.

Renewed, Kia again reached for the tiny finger holds closer to the vine-wrapped root and her newest sister.

"Kia! No!" Rok screamed down at her. "You'll fall! They're coming back! Climb!"

Kia reached to the side again. The loosened rock face crumbled and she slid down nearly a full arm-length. Then she moved sideways another step.

A faint voice drifted to her. Ch`e could hardly make a sound, but she called out, "I'm so cold. Go back. You can't help me. My leg is broken."

"I'm coming to get you." She scrambled for another finger hold and eased along the rock face. "I won't leave you to hang there for the death-birds." She glanced toward Ch`e again and gasped. The medicine pack was gone! Ch`e's hand hung limp, blood dripping from her fingers.

"No!" Kia sobbed. She was only a couple arm-lengths away from the vine. Her own fingers were torn and going numb. She leaped for the vine. The screams of her sisters filled her ears.

Wood and rock splinters tore at her arms and legs as she slid. Her feet and hands clawed for a hold and her toes caught in a loop of the vine. For an instant she saw herself hanging the same way Ch`e hung, but her hand wrapped around a sturdy branch and she righted herself. Ch`e's body dangled far above her. She'd fallen nearly half-way back down the cliff.

And the Zid were back.

The sounds of blaster fire echoed off the canyon walls. Kia

hugged the root, helpless to defend herself or even move. Opening one eye, she saw Ch`e's pack resting on the tattered remains of a nightbird nest just below her. Despite the war going on around her, she lowered herself and looped the pack over her shoulder. Another explosion rocked her in the nest, then the air again was silent. She reached for the vine and climbed.

With tears streaming down her face, Kia touched Ch`e's hand, expecting the same cold, lifeless feel of the fems she'd help to bury. But the hand was warm, even hot. Kia pressed upward and held her ear to Ch`e's chest. A weak thump! *Life!* Kia braced herself in the strong loops of the vine and began to lift her sister.

Ch`e's bare foot was swollen and turning purple and when Kia lifted her upright, the bones of her leg made a sickening grind. The vine creaked against the ancient wood of the root. Kia used her knife to break the loop holding Ch`e. But now they were both stuck. Kia no longer had the strength to climb. All she could do was cry, silently, and hold them both in place.

Something tapped her on the back of the head and her heart nearly stopped. She ducked her head and held on tighter. The thing now tapped her back.

"Kia!" Rok and Stix both called down to her. "Kia! Grab the rope!"

The tapping thing was a Zid rope – tied into a giant loop. She wrapped it around herself and under Ch`e's arms, and then winced in pain as the rope tightened and dragged her upwards. Hands grabbed her and finally she lay on a wide ledge.

Ch`e moaned beside her. "You came for me."

"Of course."

"But why? You could have died. Why did you risk your life for me?"

"You know why."

Ch`e smiled through her sudden tears and hugged Kia tight. "Because we are sisters."

Disguised with perfection
The tumor will grow
Polished and perfect
Death soon will follow

35 The Forbidden Place

Kia cradled the injured healer in her lap while Song found the Zid gel in Ch`e's medicine bag.

"Don't you let go of me, Kia." Ch`e's voice quavered in fear. "I think this is going to hurt worse than hanging on that vine."

"I've got you and everyone is here. Song, you know how to use that Zid goo. As soon as it touches her injury, she'll be screaming and kicking." Kia stroked Ch`e's hair and held her close, while Stix sat cross-legged and held her hand.

"I can tell you how bad it hurts, just put that stuff on thick and really fast," Stix said.

Rok paced back and forth. "Yes, hurry," she growled. "Those monsters will be back any time and I can't figure what they're going to try next."

Zara and Bird leaned in to watch. Zara whispered, "We never saw this medicine before the healer used it on us. The masters never used it to help us. They just let us die."

Song plopped a finger-full of the gel on the great purple bulge enveloping Ch`e's leg and foot, then spread it around before Ch`e could kick loose from the fems who held her.

Ch`e groaned through her teeth, then squealed and cried out. "Ooohhh! That hurts, that hurts, that hurts!" She buried her face in Kia's chest and sobbed. But after only a few breaths she lay quietly, shaking as if she was freezing.

"Come on!" Rok urged. "We need to get under cover before those things come back. Pick her up and carry her. Let's get out of here."

"And where are we going, warrior?" One of the fems grumbled. "We also need to find game. At least we need to feed the Loresinger and his matron."

"I don't think we'll see anything after that battle," Stix offered. "But we can be on the lookout for treedogs and longears. We don't have time for anything bigger."

"We're going up," Kia said. "I think what we've all been looking for our whole lives, and our mothers' and their mothers' lives as well, waits for us up there."

A chorus of worried responses met her.

"No one has ever been even this far up a mountain before."

"And especially not this one."

"I'm more scared of this place than I am of the Zid."

"So am I."

"I couldn't even bear to look at it when I was a child."

Kia stopped and faced her clan. "Any of you who are too afraid to go with us can stay here and try to find a cave or something. No one will think less of you. What we search for is Veenah's Word. She sends messages to Terah in the night. We've all seen the flashes in the sky. And nearly of them come to this mountain. I'm frightened, too, but we are on our bonding quest, and I believe our answers are up here somewhere." Abruptly she turned and continued up the ever steeper slope.

Clara spoke loud enough for everyone to hear. "I, we, were on our bonding quest as well. But I would have never disobeyed tradition to come across the badlands and travel to this mountain. I don't like it."

"I don't really want to go up there either. But it's better to stay together. I'm following Kia." The young fem puffed from helping to carry Ch`e. "Can you walk yet? I think the heat has gone out of your leg and it's not purple anymore."

"I can try, but don't let go of my arms just yet. I think it still hurts. Is anyone else having trouble breathing? I feel like I've been running all day."

Mumbles of 'yes' traveled through the group.

"My ears hurt," Someone said.

"Hey, look at how all these trees have fallen straight downhill. I've never seen so many laying all the same way."

"They usually fall all directions and make a messed up pile. Here it's as if a giant hand pushed them all over at one time."

Kia inspected the strange sight. Although tingles of fear traveled through her, she stared.

A giant hand. Veenah? Why would you push over so many trees? Or is this something evil?

"Come on," Ch`e urged. "Let's go. This place scares me to death. I think it's cursed."

"Fan out," Kia shouted, "but stay with your partner. Keep in sight of each other, and watch the shadows." She trudged forward.

Rok caught up with Kia. "Are you okay? You should have let Song put medicine on your cuts. At least on your hands. It doesn't hurt so much on small wounds."

"I'm fine. We need that medicine for the bad wounds. We may not be able to find more of it." Kia flexed her fingers. "Ooh, but they are a little stiff."

"Still—"

"Still nothing," Kia cut her off. "You wanted to talk to me about something else I'm sure." She gasped to take in more air.

"Did you notice that the Zid didn't fly over us at the cliff and waterfall?"

"Not really, I was hanging out on the cliff. I suppose I was drawing their fire for your army up above me." She laughed a little, but shuddered inside.

"Oh, yeah. And their weapons were weaker."

"You must not have seen the hole that opened up beside me and split the cliff like an axe."

"I did. And I thought you were lost." Rok looped her arm around Kia's. "The rest of us crawled to the edge of the cliff and shot our weapons down at the Zid and we were able to hit some of them. But, their weapons didn't have much strength to reach us at the top. And, they didn't try to fly over us or even beside us, like they did in the battle at the badlands. It was almost like their flyers wouldn't go up the mountain."

Clara walked a little closer. "I told you. The mountain is forbidden even to them, and they know it. And that pile back there proves it. Look, there's more of those logs. They all point the same way. I say we go back down. Right now!"

Rok stopped and held her fist in the air; her sign for 'stand still and be alert'. "Kia, wait here. I'm going to scout ahead. Something is not right. Rose," she hollered back to the group, "you're with me. Bring one more."

Kia scrambled up a spindly cone tree to watch. The warriors crept through the brush and prodded the fallen trees with their knives and spears. Rok pointed to something ahead and Kia saw a mountainous pile of dead trees at the bottom of a long, narrow clearing. Terror gripped her and she nearly fell from the branches.

"Rok! Come back! It's cursed!" She screamed, but the three warriors moved forward until they stood in the clearing in front of the deadfall – looking straight up to the white head of the mountain. *They've been enchanted! They can't escape!* She scrambled then leaped to the ground, grief ripping through her for bringing her family to this horrid place. She grabbed the nearest fem by the shoulders. "Form a battle circle around the elders and prepare to defend them! I have to save Rok!"

Shading her eyes from the brilliant light reflecting from the white top of the mountain, she reached the clearing and tackled Rok. "Don't look at it! It's dangerous! That's the thing which has drawn me, but it kills whatever is close to it! Look what it has done to the trees! We have to leave!" She wrestled Rok to the ground and tried to drag her away.

Rose pulled her up by the back of her tunic, laughing hysterically. "What has possessed you, leader? Haven't you ever seen snow?"

"What are you talking about?"

"The white covering on the mountain. It's not a white head, it's frozen rain. We call it snow. Where I come from it falls in the cold season and the children play in it."

"But why does it look like a giant hand swept all the trees into a pile and killed them?"

"That part I don't know." Rose looked back at the snow-topped mountain and rubbed her chin. "I don't know, but I'm not sure I want to find out, now that you mention it."

Stix, Clara and a few of the others approached with weapons

drawn. "We heard shouting," Stix said. "Is everyone safe?"

Kia still gripped Rok's hand, but held her arm out for Stix. "I think we're okay, just a little scared. This clearing is a mystery and that pile of trees is a sign of danger, I think."

Clara studied the deadfall. "You're right. Trees piled up like that make perfect dens for bears and mountain wolves. Neither of which I want to meet out here. We need to go." She coughed and bend double. "We have to find shelter and rest. I can't breathe."

"I'm having trouble as well." Rok puffed and tried to take a deep breath of air. "That's it! Air! There's no air up here. Their flyers need air like we do. I know it. Somehow they are alive." She stopped and waved the others closer and the battle circle broke apart.

"Impossible."

"I killed one with an arrow."

"And you injured another," Kia said. She clamped her mouth shut when Rok glared at her. She didn't dare let out the secret of the searcher Zid who rode that injured flyer. "But what about the Zid? What if they can climb like we do?"

"Then we know how they'll attack next. On foot." She jumped to her feet, then grabbed her head. "I'm dizzy! Everyone be careful from here on. Whoever carries a blade, we must have more spears, long spears, with sharp points. Help me cut them. Stay in the trees and away from this clearing. And watch the shadows! The enemy comes on foot!"

Kia called out. "We need a lookout. Who can climb a tree?"

Stix suddenly stopped and pointed. "I know why Veenah created this clearing. It's food for the mountain creatures. Look up there, uphill from the trees. Is that a woolie?"

Ch`e shaded her eyes to study the creature. "I've seen lots of woolies in the mountains near my village, but this one is strange. Its horns are straight instead of curled."

"So is its hair," Fawn said. "A woolie's hair is curly. That's why we can weave cloaks and blankets with it."

"Well, it is game, and we are hungry. I'm going to hunt it. Who is with me?" Stix slung a small blaster over her shoulder and selected a sharp spear.

Stix and Zara crawled through the brush. The animal stomped a front foot, on high alert. Then the weak beam of a blaster fell short and the animal bounded away, higher into the rocky mountainside.

Kia's stomach growled. "Has anyone seen any birds or berries?" She chopped at a young, straight tree, hacking off the branches.

Stix and Zara had not yet returned from the hunt. Kia added another crude spear to the stack and glanced at the sky. Warmsun was almost out of sight behind the top of the mountain, but the sky was still brilliant. She shivered. Fem'ma sat resting against a tree. Her breath showed like a smoky fire and small puffs drifted from Moon's sling. Kia thought it odd. Such a thing was common in the cold season, but this was the hot season. Maybe Warmsun needed air to work just like Terians and the Zid flyers did.

Gathering the branches which she'd cut from the cone trees, she set about constructing a sleeping shelter. "I suggest we make ready to camp here. It's going to be cold and the wind could blow, so build your shelters well." She stopped short. Clara and Daylin knelt in front of Fem'ma. She moved closer so she could hear Clara speaking.

"...and we've made your shelter sturdy and safe. When we warm the stones inside, Loresinger will be comfortable."

"Ugh," Kia growled through her teeth. Anger burning inside her made the hair on her arms stand up. "I'm not fit to ask Moon to be our husband. I didn't even think about his comfort. This will be the first proper shelter he's had since this war began, and a stranger provided it." She threw the last of her branches over the crude shelter and stomped over to Fem'ma. "Elder, allow me to help you get up so you can inspect your shelter." She purposely kept her back to Clara and Daylin.

"Ho! The camp!"

Kia snapped her head around hearing Stix call out. "We're here, love."

"We have meat!" shouted Zara. "And a warm skin for—"

"My kill, my skin to give."

Kia had never seen Stix angry – *except when she became jealous over Rok.* Her insides twisted with worry. Soon everyone would be quarreling over rights to court the only mem left in the world.

In silence and dark
The symbol awaits
Lifted and shining
The world celebrates

36 The Enemy Flows Like A River

Song shivered under the dark sky. She'd volunteered to stand first watch since she'd fallen asleep when they stopped to rest. She breathed into her hands, then rubbed her arms thinking of all the ways she could weave grasses into a cover. But the grasses on this mountain were short and weak. Not even her cooking fire, made with the driest wood anyone could find, had been warm. The darkness nearly crushed her and the feeble light from the dying embers didn't help. A crackle in the brush nearly made her scream an alert.

"It's only me. Sienna. Remember? The climber?"

"Yes. You scared the life out of me. Why aren't you sleeping with your sisters?"

"They aren't my sisters. Actually none of us are, except for Daylin and Clara. I'm not sure any of them would bond if they had to, except maybe Nella, and Willa, but they are blood sisters."

"But you all work together so well."

"Only to survive as a slave. But to answer your question, I couldn't sleep and I knew you were cold out here, so I came to sit with you."

"Thank you. I wonder why the blasters stopped working." She pushed the button for light, but it only produced a dim glow.

"They must sit in Warmsun after they've been used. We used them all day and never gave them a rest. It's like Warmsun feeds them or something. All they need is a good meal of light."

Song snuggled closer to Sienna, sharing their warmth and watching the Great Ladle spin slowly through the sky.

"What do you think is going to happen tomorrow?" Sienna said.

"Kia will lead us and Rok will protect us. Beyond that, I can't guess and I am afraid to think."

"Do you really believe in the prophesy?"

Song sat up with a start. "Yes. I believe with all my heart. And tomorrow we will continue to search for the message Veenah has sent to this mountain."

"I didn't mean to offend you. Come on, let's wake the relief watch."

"It's okay, you just surprised me. Would you like to sleep with us in our shelter?" Song stretched and yawned, then stumbled through the darkness searching for her shelter. Finally, she found it and tapped Stix on the foot.

*****

The instant Warmsun peeked over the far horizon, the mountainside was bathed in brilliant light. The camp slowly came to life. Song rolled over to let the light warm her face. She remembered to set her weapon in the light as well, but she guarded it. Not everyone carried a weapon. In fact, she'd found this one in the grass after the battle and climb up the cliff the day before. Rok slid her arms around Song, smiling.

"Happy morning, little sister. You should have awakened me for the second watch."

"You need your rest and your strength, my warrior. You have to protect me today. And you need to set your blaster in the light. It seems they are as hungry for Warmsun as I am for meat. I'll watch them if you need to check on the others." Song sat up and placed Rok's weapon beside her own, then reached for Stix's. "It's too bad Kia lost her blaster in the battle."

A short time later, she watched Rok coach the new army in another move. Roll toward the enemy and thrust upward with a blade. A shudder ran down her spine and her stomach turned. It was the move Kia had performed to kill the old bull in the citadel. How close had she come to losing her leader – and another piece of her heart, while she, herself lay safe in the shelter of a fallen wall? She shivered and rubbed her arms,

218

suddenly noticing that she was completely without a scratch, while nearly everyone else was stained with the blood of cuts and scratches.

Song swallowed her fear and pushed to her feet when Kia called out, "Let's go, fems." With a pain in her stomach, not from hunger, she looked down the slope. *Where is your message great Veenah?*

A shriek split the quiet camp.

"Attack!"

She fell to the ground at the same instant the tree she'd been standing next to exploded in a shower of flame. *My sisters!* "Kia! Where are you?" Aiming in the direction from which the shots came, she fired three short blasts.

"Stay low! Grab your spears!" Rok rolled toward the stack of freshly made spears and tossed them to the closest fems. "Shoot and roll to the next hiding place!"

Kia scrambled to a line of long-spear fighters and covered herself with fragments of tree branches. Without a shooting weapon, she'd have to rely on spear and blade.

Orange streaks of blaster fire lit up the forest and trees exploded into kindling. Another scream. "Ch`e! Medicine! Hurry!"

Rok bellowed a war cry. "They're coming up the hill! Get ready."

The spear in Kia's hand almost shook from her trembling. Five fems lay to one side of her. Three on the other side. Each held a deadly spear. *Please, Veenah, protect my family.* The sound of a Zid voice sent chills down Kia's spine. It came from next to her and the only words she understood was 'here' 'kill' 'eat'. She drew her knife, but the words came from Bird.

"Be still," the elder whispered. "I just told them we are hiding in the bushes."

In another breath the ground shook from the pounding feet of giant lizards lumbering toward them at an unbelievable speed through the thick brush and trees. *Wait, wait, wait.* Kia struggled to contain herself. If she sprang up too quickly, she would be in their jaws. Too late and they would pass unharmed – if they didn't detect the hiding fems and simply eat them.

Dry branches crackled and the stench of Zid breath choked her.

"NOW!" She yanked the tip of her spear upwards, bracing its heel in the ground behind her. The Zid could only hiss as the weapon sank into the soft underside of its neck. Kia rolled free of the falling monster and foul blood.

Bird scrambled backward, just out of reach of massive snapping jaws. The Zid hung only a moment on her spear which pierced its belly, then crashed to the ground, clawing at its wound. Around her, six of the monsters lay dead, on broken spears. Stix and two other fems gouged at a bull, staying just out of reach of it teeth. Kia remembered the tail, which would sweep them off their feet. This Zid would not just leave them like Pop had done. She drew her knife and dove into the battle from the side. The bull never saw her as she rolled between its sharp-clawed feet and slashed her blade through its abdomen.

"Thanks, Kia," Stix cried out. "We were in a bit of trouble there."

"Any time, love. I've got your back. Grab that weapon it dropped!"

"Fall back!" Rok screamed. "Up the mountain!"

A smaller Zid bounded through the thick underbrush and leaped for Kia, but it lodged between the narrow forks of a cone tree. It struggled, but only wedged in tighter. Nella and Willa leaped to its back and crushed its skull with clubs.

A weapon fell from the creature's paw and Kia scooped it up. "Get their blasters!" she screamed. Finding two more beside their previous owners, Kia dodged between the trees to join Rok. Still the ground rumbled with the tromping of the Zid.

"There's so many of them!"

Kia grimaced as bile rose in her throat. The forest pulsed with the hideous gray-green creatures. One stood to scan the area with his blaster then fired three shots. A fem screamed. Kia braced on a tree and found the monster in the small, green screen of her weapon. She pressed the button. Its side opened and it fell with a roar. The next three blasts blew her tree to bits, but she was already gone.

"Nice shot, sister," Stix said as she fired and dragged Kia to a new tree.

"Form a line! Stay low!" Rok shouted. "Shoot only when you see one clearly! Save your weapons!"

Kia tossed her extra weapons to waiting hands. She couldn't see Fem'ma anywhere. A knot formed in her stomach. A huge Zid struggled in the brush and trees. Kia took careful aim and pressed the button. At the same time her orange beam struck the beast, two others hit. It fell in place, but the forest once again lit up with blaster fire. Kia aimed for the place a beam had come from and fired. A death shriek rewarded her.

Foggy, cold breath around her mouth and nose froze in crystals and the skin of her arms stung in the cold, but Kia still felt as if she was sweating. She fired again, then leaped for another tree as the terah around her blew into the air. *They are moving slower in the cold.* But she could hardly see them through the trees. The brush parted and she and Stix fired together. In her terror, she felt comfort fighting next to her beloved. *Where are the others?*

The clear resonant voice of Moon rang over the din of the battle. He sang his newest song reclaiming the promise that no evil could stand against the righteous.

Kia leaped with Stix to the next tree – but there were no more trees. A cold wind blasted down the mountain bringing the sting of blowing snow. Panic crawled up from Kia's stomach and choked her. Although the Zid now moved as slow as a babe's crawl, they still advanced. And now there was no place to hide.

Rok grabbed her arm.

"We stand and fight. Shoot, throw rocks, throw clubs, anything to keep their attention. A few at a time will race across the clearing to the caves and rocky places where Stix and Zara killed the woolie. Pass it on. The elders will go after the first fems."

Kia dove through the scarce brush to fighters near the clearing. "Get ready to dash across when Rok signals. Cover the elders when they come across, then fire on the Zid so Rok and I can cross." At the sound of Rok's war cry, Kia sent the first two over. She resisted the urge to shoot at the exposed heads of two Zid, but they were focused on Rok, not the crossing. She grabbed Bird and another fem. "Go!"

Moon's voice rang loud and clear as he sang, but Kia couldn't see where Fem'ma hid with him. Ch`e's scream ripped through the chaos and suddenly Song and Stix were beside her. Kia dove through the brush toward them.

Ch`e, bent over a body, dug frantically in her medicine bag.

"Fem'ma! Wake up!" Sobbing, she globbed the healing gel on what was left of the elder's arm and face. This time the gel barely fizzed. Fem'ma didn't move or respond to the painful treatment. No foggy breath rose from her lips. Kia felt the strength go out of her legs.

"Fem'ma! No! Where's Moon!" Kia raked the elder to her side, hoping she had covered Moon, but his song echoed through the forest. Ch'e pounded on the elder's chest, sobbing.

"She's gone, sister," Song cried. "She's gone and we have to find Moon. Save the medicine."

"No!" Ch'e screamed and collapsed on top of Fem'ma's body.

Kia followed the sound of the song to a mound of snow piled around a fallen tree. A blaster beam erupted from the snow which was followed by the death knell of a Zid. The snow moved and another blast came from it!

"Moon!" Kia and Stix with Song close behind dove for the fallen trees. The snow was nothing more than the white skin of the straight-haired mountain woolie. A pile of white feathers pushed up above the log and another beam shot out. Moon's song grew louder.

"Moon!" Kia rolled to the ground next to him. "What are you doing!"

"My beautiful Kia!" Moon sang at the top of his voice, then coughed. "Oh, sorry. I didn't mean to shout into your face. Look! I'm a warrior!" He tugged at the sling, which had been his protective cover for most of his life, now covered with the white skin so that it looked like snow. The feathered cape made from the waterbird covered his head and shoulders and when he crouched down beside the white fur, he became invisible.

"I even move every time I shoot, just like our warrior instructed. We will win this war."

"Kia, we have to get him out of here!" Song yelled. She reached for the sling, then stopped, wringing her hands. "Somebody lift him from the ground!"

"My beauty," Moon said, "You can lift me, or I can walk."

"But…its—"

The log they were hiding behind suddenly flew into the air and broke into pieces. Kia and Stix leaped to the side and returned fire. Song scooped Moon off the ground, leaving his sling behind, and dashed for the clearing. Kia took one more shot while Stix grabbed the white fur and sling, then followed her sister across to the rocks. Kia's chest burned and her head spun. She fell, gasping for air. More snow seemed to be falling, but the sky was clear except for a few clouds forming around the top of the mountain.

Zara, Clara, and Nella screamed to Rok. "We're all here! Run!"

Sienna found a tree sturdy enough to hold her weight and fired into the Zid-filled forest while Rok and Rose raced across the clearing and joined them. A line of blasts hit Sienna's tree. Her scream was cut short.

"Stay under cover," Rok shouted. "They're coming, but they are slow in the cold."

"There's too many of them," someone wailed. "We can't kill them all."

Kia watched in horror as the merciless reptiles marched into the clearing. It was like a river flowing with Zid instead of water – and flowing uphill – toward them. More and more and more. Enough to fill all the villages she knew. She tried to take aim from the rock she hid behind, but sentries walking on their hind feet saw her movement and her cover blew to bits under their fire. Another fem tried to shoot, but she stood too high. Kia turned away as her body disintegrated.

"We can't fight them out in the open!" Stix shouted. "We have to get them back into the trees."

"They are between us and the trees! We're trapped!"

"Fall back!" Rok screamed. The powerful Zid weapons hit all around them, but the shards of rock dealt as much damage as a direct hit. Ch'e raced to the aid of another wounded fem. Kia retreated with the rest of the clan.

One by one, the hiding places were reduced to rubble. A movement up the hill caught Kia's attention as she dodged around the jumble of rock. Snow trickled in a stream toward the clearing. Still shivering in the cold, she followed the trickle up to the white covering of the mountain with her eyes.

What are you showing me, Veenah?

She'd seen waves on the lakes when she was a child, and she'd seen waves on White River, but high above her a wave of snow seemed to be frozen in place, hovering dangerously over her head. And the vibrations of exploding stone seemed to be making the snow ripple. Another trickle streamed down. Kia's head snapped around and she saw the clearing with new eyes.

"The snow!" Kia shouted pointing to the mountain top. "Shoot the snow! Make it fall on them!" She aimed her blaster at the wave, but it fell short. Everyone who held a weapon fired at the snow-pack hitting the lowest ridges.

A loud crack split the air and suddenly the world was white. Terah rumbled and shook under Kia's feet, but when she gasped for air, her mouth filled with razor-sharp bits of snow and ice. She ran harder as the roar of falling snow covered all other sound. Then the snow was all around her. Then she couldn't even tell which way was up.

I'm I running? Or falling?

Return to the waters
The giver of life
The heart made of stone
Laid bare with the knife

Remember the promise
And drive out the thief
Reclaiming your birthright
No longer in grief

37 The Jewel Of The Prophecy

It was over as quickly as it had started. The mist of snow settled and the light sparkled off the new bed of snow on the forest. Nothing moved where the army of Zid had been. Moon's song rang over the sudden silence telling a story of rocks and mountains falling on the enemy, but it was a happy song.

Kia pushed herself away from the heaps of snow then pulled Stix out. "Let's go join the celebration, my love. From the sound of our mem's song, I think we won."

"Maybe we won, but now we have other problems. Look where our mem sits."

Moon sang from the top of a rounded boulder draped with the white fur. Kia breathed relief to see that the feathered cape still covered his shoulders – and hands. Song stood beside him on the ground. Rok and Ch`e stood hand in hand on the other side. What remained of their army gathered in small clusters, staring or hiding their eyes. Kia and Stix took their places beside Rok, next to Moon.

"Don't be afraid of me, dear brave fems. We live in a new world. I am no different from any other mem. These dangers, this war, has made me stronger just as you have been made stronger."

"But, Loresinger…Why doesn't someone carry you? How can you break tradition?"

"What else could I do? When Ma fell, I had to do something. I couldn't just let myself be killed with her. She fought like a warrior, you know. And she protected me well. But the enemy can see through anything with their weapons and I believe they were trying to kill me in order to stop all of you. For every shot they fired at you, they fired many more at Fem'ma. It took five bolts at the same time to stop her and she still was able to push me to safety. I had to protect myself, or her death would be for nothing."

Clara spoke from the center of the cluster. "But you sit on the ground. You sit alone without help. How can you do this?"

"For the same reason you had the strength to survive. For the same reason all of us here survive. Look to your hearts, fems, and consider what you know to be truth. Search the promise of Veenah and find yourselves."

Kia remembered when Moon challenged her family with these same words and wondered what these frightened fems so recently liberated might be thinking.

Someone spoke in a muffled and trembling voice. "He's talking about the prophecy."

"I stopped believing in that lie the day my family died under the hand of those beasts and forced me into slavery."

"I don't know what to believe anymore. Everything we've ever been taught seems to be coming undone."

Mumbles continued through the group.

Bird stepped away from the others. "I was so young when they took me I hardly remember any of this." She glanced around at the fems she'd escaped with. "And none of the other captives ever said anything about prophecy or promises. But somehow I always had hope. I have nothing to believe in, and the only truth I know is that I was a slave and now I'm free."

Daylin took Clara's hand. "We have been slaves only a short time and we know all about this prophecy. My sisters and I were captured on our way home from our bonding quest. I don't think we even considered searching for some sort of jewel. But since we have been in that Perg-hole, we have seen more jewels than anyone could hope for, enough to cover an entire village and more. There is no power in a jewel. And that is the truth."

Kia shook all over as murmurs of agreement ran through the little group.

Angled away from the others, Fawn bowed her head. "I studied the prophecy with my husband before I was trapped and brought here. Imprisoned behind the stone walls, we all prayed for a strong hand to rescue us. I don't understand much about promises and prophecies, but in my heart I have always felt this call, even throughout the many seasons I was a slave."

Clara leaned heavily on her bond sister, tears flowing. "I have held hate in my heart from the time my mother was cast out. And even more hate when the monsters attacked my precious femtog and put me in that horrible camp. I had a chance to mend a little bit of what was broken, but I wouldn't give up my anger. And now it's too late. If the elder was truly my blood mother. I have lost her twice. I don't think that can be healed." She sobbed in Daylin's tight embrace. "But if by believing I might be able to once again join with her, then I will follow the teachings and prophecy of Veenah for the rest of my life."

"We all should have just let ourselves be killed," Willa hissed. "Just like my hearth sister, and likely my entire village."

Kia's gut wrenched when she noticed that Nella didn't stand among the survivors.

"I'm going to try and find my village," Willa said. "Who's with me?"

The group shifted uneasily. Kia's knees went weak. Suddenly, Song stepped in front of the boulder where Moon sat.

"I am the prophecy. I am the innocent and I have discovered the jewel. The true Jewel of Veenah. The one most valuable thing we all have and could ever have."

The group again shifted among gasps and whispers.

Rok stepped forward and took Song's hand. "I am the prophecy. I am the one who drinks strength from the white breast for the battle. I am the one who leads the Terians to victory."

Stix shook her hand loose from Kia and took Rok's hand. "I am the prophecy. I am the hunter who sits in the dark."

Ch`e was next. "I am the prophecy. You already know that for a fact. I am the healer. I've known it from my birth, but no one would listen to me. No one, that is, except my beloved Kia and my bond sisters." She stretched her battle-worn hand toward Kia in an invitation to join them.

"I am the one who was torn from her home, but here I am, back to life after what should have been death."

A tremor shook the ground sending the clan ducking for cover. Song yanked Moon from the boulder and crouched over him. Kia lay over both of them as rocks and debris fell around them.

"I think it's over," someone shouted.

"I'm sure Veenah would never bring us this far and then let us be buried under her mountain, my sweet Song," Moon said with a chuckle. "But I find that I am quite comfortable in your embrace."

"Oh! Forgive me!" Song jumped up, throwing Kia to the side.

"Well, is someone going to lift me back to my seat? Or shall I try it myself? I think I can do it." He wiggled to his side to stand up.

"Wait." Song brushed the dirt from her tunic, then shook the white fur clean.

"Is everyone okay?" Kia yelled.

"Call out!" Rok commanded.

"Kia."

"Song."

"Willa."

"Rose."

"Stix."

"Eve! Eve is here!" A weak voice sounded out across the snow-field.

"Who's Eve?"

Kia shaded her eyes against the white field to see the elder hobbling toward them, leaning on a stick. Her arm was missing and she had very little hair on one side of her head, but she was walking! "Fem'ma?"

"Ma! Is it you?" Moon wobbled toward the voice.

"Fem'ma!" Ch'e rushed to her side.

"It's a spirit! I saw her die!" Several fems backed away.

"No, I didn't die. I thought I was about to. It hurt, I fell, and then I woke up with that Zid foam coming out of my arm. That's when I thought I was dying. I hated putting Loresinger on the ground. And why is he on the ground now? Where is Fawn?"

"Here, matron." Fawn rushed. "What do I do?"

"I'm no longer matron. I cannot lift my charge. You are matron, now. I am Eve.

Moon wobbled to turn his back to the new elder. "Only lift me to my high seat. Use care," he said with a chuckle. "This should be good."

Fawn yelped with most of the other fems. "He stands!" Fawn cried out, backing away. "He stands and moves! What is this?"

"Mind your tone in the presence of a mem, young elder!" Eve said. "No mem is as helpless as some of you think. Every mem is capable if only we encourage them instead of doing everything for them. Now lift him to his seat. You have much to learn from this Loresinger. All of you!" Eve waggled the stump of her arm in the air toward the clan.

Moon cleared his throat, once again on his fur covered perch. "Sit and be comfortable, fems. I have seen prophecy fulfilled over and over since the attack which put me into the wilderness. This is another. Veenah is close to us this day and wants you to receive her gift and her message, though I still do not know what that message is. Now listen to the words of the prophecy.

> From the mouth of death
> There comes new life.
> From the mouth of lies
> Exudes a gift.
> From bondage
> Love finds freedom.
> From the wild
> We come home.

"Loresinger," Clara said, her voice quivering. "Please teach us. We have seen life come from death. We have found freedom because of the love of Kia's femtog. We are in the wild and I hope we can find our homes again. But what lie gives us a gift?"

"A day ago I could not answer that. But look at what happened today. What name have you always called this mountain?"

"Forbidden." The answer was a chorus from several fems.

"But I think you can see that this place is not forbidden. That was the lie. And what gift did this mountain give you today?"

Whispers ran through the group and heads waggled, but no answer came. Kia stared at the mountain, and the gash where snow once sat.

"The mountain won our battle. It gave us victory," Kia said softly. "And look, far up the side. That's the face of a fem! Does she have horns on her head? They look green. And she is so very big. How can anyone carve such a large face? And why put so many horns on her head?"

"I think that's a crown," Matron Fawn said. "During ceremonies in my village, the elders sometimes wear them."

Moon sang a short melody, then smiled. "She is the watcher who stands upon the tower and guards a precious treasure. The message of Veenah is up there!"

Kia still gripped Rok's and Stix's hands, but she took a step toward the dark scar above her.

"Wait for us!" Song grabbed Ch`e's hand and joined Rok.

"I've never been so frightened in my life," Ch`e whispered.

"We're all frightened."

"Fem'ma, I mean, Eve!" Kia said nearly losing her footing. "What are you doing?"

"I'm going with you. I know the prophecy better than any fem alive. You need me. And I need to see this."

They climbed over loose dirt and huge structures. The climb grew steeper the further they went.

"These rocks must have been made by the Zid," Kia said. "They're huge, and so flat."

Eve slowly shook her head. "Or they were made by Terians long ago. Before the Zid. These things are too big for the Zid to have use for, and why would they throw them away? This is what Moon always talked about."

"Nothing could have lived in this one. It looks like a giant tree with flat sides."

"Chopped down by our enemy and thrown up here to rot."

Kia looked down at the group they'd just left. Moon still sat on his white fur on the boulder. "They look as small as bugs from up here. We should rest a bit, and catch our breath."

Rok stared up at the giant face, half buried near the peak of the mountain. "I sure hope Terah doesn't shake again and cause her to fall on us. From here, she looks angry."

"She has been waiting for a long, long time." Eve whispered and sank to her knees. "She is not angry, this is the face of a mother filled with love, patience, and hope for the future. She will never fall on us. Moon was right. All these years he believed…"

Kia shuddered. Song leaned into her, shaking.

"Hey look!" Ch`e said pointing up the slope. "River clams! Even bigger than the giant watercat! Is everything bigger on this side of the badlands?"

"They're beautiful," Rok whispered, running her fingers over the shells of her necklace.

Eve clasped her hands to her face. "And they are exactly where The Mother's face is pointing. She's looking at them, like she's showing us where they are."

"They're so big. It would only take one of those to feed all of us, if it was alive," Stix said.

"Oh, don't remind me," Ch`e sighed. "We've had no real food since yesterday. Berries don't fill the belly for very long."

"I know we're supposed to be going straight up to the top," Kia said, "but, I want to go look at them."

"Careful," Rok said. "The dirt is loose here. This is where most of the landslide came from."

As they crept closer, Kia saw the outlines of many more giant clams buried in the dirt. "There must be tens and tens and tens of these up here."

Ch`e huffed. "I love to dig for river clams, and sometimes I find a whole bed of them. They look a little like this. But I would never take the entire bunch. This looks like those monsters just scraped the bottom clean and then dumped them here. Why did they do that?"

"They don't value life," Song whispered. She reached for the lip of a clam. "It's rough on the outside, but the inside is so smooth. It's not quite closed, but it doesn't have much dirt in it. Look how pretty it is."

Everyone gathered to admire and touch the iridescent inner shell. Kia reached for the next one while Rok scrambled up the loose dirt to inspect still another. Stix, Song, and Ch`e spread out, moving among the clamshells.

"This one is packed tight with dirt," Rok said, disappointed.

Kia reached for a specimen, mostly buried, looking like it was yearning for Warmsun. It was closed except for a tiny slit. She peered inside and a glimmer of shimmering white reflected the light of Warmsun. A shock like a bolt of lightning ran through her body and her heart skipped a beat.

The streaks of light come here.

"The message!" Kia shouted. "It's here in the heart of the stone, just like the prophecy says! The message of Veenah!" She tried to push her fingers through the narrow opening. "Help me get it! Look! It's exactly like the streaks of light we see in the night. It's even shaped the same."

Kia unsheathed her knife and dug away at the dirt. "Hurry, get it loose!" They dug and pried and tugged at the shell.

"Ugh," Ch`e groaned. "This thing is heavier than a targus beast."

Suddenly the shell fell away from its prison in the mountain. It started to slide down, gaining speed, and more rocks and dirt.

"Move!" Rok shouted. "The whole mountain is going to slide again!"

The shell came to rest on the stone tree below them, and the loose dirt settled. It sat on its spine, facing upward.

"It's smiling at Warmsun," Song said. "I think it's happy to be free."

"Is the message still inside?"

"Kia peered through the slit. "Yes, it's there."

"How are we going to get it out?"

"With our knives." Kia slipped the tip of her blade into the opening. Her blade was joined by Stix's, then Rok's. The shell creaked, then cracked, then shifted the tiniest bit. "It's no use, it won't go any wider." She tried to squeeze her hand inside.

"Let me try," Song said. "My hand is smaller."

Rok sniffled "Could this be it?" she said with jerky breaths. "Have we solved the mystery of the prophecy?"

Kia was surprised to see tears in the warrior's eyes.

"It might be, if we know what the message means," Ch`e said.

Song pushed her arm deeper into the shell while Stix and Kia tugged at the mouth, trying to open it further.

Eve rocked gently, hugging her one good arm around her middle. She turned her head away, but Song saw the glimmer of a tear slide down her face.

"I always knew," the elder said, her voice quivering. "I always knew the prophecy would be fulfilled in my lifetime. I knew it when I was a small child and I almost lost my faith when it didn't turn out to be me."

"I've got it," Song said. "And I think I know the message." She pulled and twisted and finally eased the pearl free of its prison. "Moon has been singing it over and over. Terah's heart holds tight the sign. Lifeless are the tears divine. Brilliant light now lies confined high above the timberline. Remember he said he couldn't figure out what 'timberline' meant? Look at the trees. They make a line all around the mountain. They can't grow any higher, probably because of the cold."

"Or they have trouble breathing the air, too."

"Well, we are high above the timberline, and this," she held up the pearl, "is not shaped like the streaks of light we see at night. It is shaped like a tear. It is the tears of Terah. We had to work together to free it from deep in the heart of stone. The message is, we," Song waved her hand toward the group waiting below. "We all have to work together to free Terah from the Zid who destroy her."

A cheer drifted up to them from the small crowd below along with a chant, growing louder and louder.

"Jewel! Jewel! Jewel!"

Song lifted the pearl over her head. Kia ran her fingers over the creamy-smooth surface. Her touch was joined by Stix, then Rok, and Ch`e. Eve's weathered hand rested over all of them as the cheers below raised to a crescendo of joy.

Kia sighed. "We must raise a larger army. We may have won this battle, but I fear the war is only beginning." She cast a worried look in the direction of the Zid citadel.

A low rumble sounded from Rok's chest. "We only woke them up and made them angry. They *will* be coming soon."

About Connie Peck

Before this book, it was always about the horses. After? Well, that's anyone's guess. Connie Peck started writing stories – strongly motivated by her father – at the tender age of eleven. Eventually her father submitted some of the stories to a few magazines. So....it was also at a very early age that she learned how to buck-up and keep trying after receiving a rejection letter. She did finally get a couple of articles published, which was a boon to her confidence. While writing off and on during the child-rearing years, she started writing in earnest after retiring. Always the DIYer, she started her own publishing company, and does it herself.

Connie grew up traveling the USA in the 1960s and 70s, from the deep south to the Pacific Northwest, the Southwestern deserts, and even up the eastern seaboard. Every mile, every town, mountain, river, valley, and lake, every smile, frown, and tear along the way has impacted and influenced her as a writer and as a human.

As an adult, she settled in Texas to raise her children, along with horses, dogs, and chickens. She has a tendency to do things a bit backwards, so when the kids were all in school, she decided to go back herself. She attended Central Texas College, then graduated with a teaching degree from Tarleton State University.

She taught science and reading first in Killeen, then Houston, and finally in Alaska before moving back to Texas. Now, semi-retired, Connie writes, rides, plays outdoors – and with her grandchildren, and lives in the back of a cow pasture with her husband, a dog, a horse, and a flock of racing pigeons.

Watch for the sequel to the Jewel of Veenah, Battle for the Jewel, and one day in the future, the trilogy will be complete with Freedom for the Jewel.

To read more of Connie Peck's books, look on Amazon and Kindle for:

The Black Pony
Midnight and the Racehorse
Legend of the Superstition Gold
Pony Stories
Belt Buckles and Tiaras
The Black Pony Adventures, Activity Book
Driving into the Son, a Devotional for Drivers

Do you want to make an author smile, laugh, and dance for joy? Write a review on Amazon, Goodreads, or where ever you find good books.

Want to expand a child's horizons? Give them a book.

www.ingramcontent.com/pod-product-compliance
Lightning Source LLC
Chambersburg PA
CBHW022112240626
47153CB00007B/2332